A LITTLE LEARNING

*A Selection of Recent Titles by J. M. Gregson from
Severn House*

Lambert and Hook Mysteries

AN ACADEMIC DEATH
GIRL GONE MISSING
AN UNSUITABLE DEATH

Detective Inspector Peach Mysteries

THE LANCASHIRE LEOPARD
MISSING, PRESUMED DEAD
TO KILL A WIFE
A TURBULENT PRIEST
WHO SAW HIM DIE?

A LITTLE
LEARNING

J. M. Gregson

This first world edition published in Great Britain 2002 by
SEVERN HOUSE PUBLISHERS LTD of
9–15 High Street, Sutton, Surrey SM1 1DF.
This first world edition published in the USA 2002 by
SEVERN HOUSE PUBLISHERS INC of
595 Madison Avenue, New York, N.Y. 10022.

British Library Cataloguing in Publication Data

Gregson, J. M. (James Michael)
    A little learning
    1. Peach, Detective Inspector (Fictitious character) – Fiction
    2. Police – England – Lancashire – Fiction
    3. Detective and mystery stories
    I. Title
    823.9'14 [F]

ISBN 0-7278-5763-0

Typeset by Palimpsest Book Production Ltd.,
Polmont, Stirlingshire, Scotland.
Printed and bound in Great Britain by
MPG Books Ltd., Bodmin, Cornwall.

One

There were four of them when the suggestion was first made.

It was just past midnight, the Friday night disco had finished, and they were sitting in the student bar of the University of East Lancashire. Last orders had been called some time earlier, and the exhausted staff had now managed to bring down the grille across the front of the bar counter.

They had been a much larger group earlier in the evening, but the others had their own agendas for the night; they had drifted away when the dancing finished. Lust was usually in the air at that heady hour on a Friday night: as the crashing rhythms of the music ceased, activated hormones began to throb even more insistently than the regular beat of the rock groups. Most of the students departed in pairs towards the dim lights of the residential hostels.

But four of them remained, obstinately ignoring the requests for their glasses as the bar gradually emptied. They were three boys and one girl; they regarded each other as 'mates', being second-year students in the Faculty of Humanities. They had been through a few crises together and felt that they knew each other well. They had all been drinking during the evening, and the effects of that coloured the discussion which followed. None of them was incapable, or even inarticulate. Rather were they at that pleasant stage of mild inebriation when ordinary conversation seems incisive and any mildly original idea seems quite brilliant.

Their security with each other made them feel thoroughly

relaxed. The evening had inured them for the moment against the injustices of student life, such as insensitive parents, unfair assessors and incompetent tutors. They did not want the joy of the evening to end, and yet were not certain how they might prolong it.

When Gary Pilkington said, 'It can't be all that difficult, you know, the perfect crime!' it fell among them like a diamond of originality.

Three pairs of eyes looked at him. It was a full three seconds before Darren Briggs said with what was meant to be a crushing put-down, 'Really? Why don't you hear of them being pulled off, then?'

He was aware as he said it that there was a flaw in his reasoning somewhere, but it wasn't until the other three smiled that his befuddled brain worked out what it was.

It was the one girl, Tessa Jones, who said, 'We wouldn't bloody know, would we, Darren, you wanker?' and set all four of them laughing together.

Darren, working hard at being a good sport, was a little more drunk than the others. He subsided into a sheepish grin, waited until the conversation picked up again, then ran his hand speculatively down Tessa's spine and inserted it into the top of her jeans, searching for the cleft at the top of her bottom with an abstracted air.

The girl removed his hand carefully, placed it between two beer mats on the table, and jammed down an empty pint glass hard upon the top of it, increasing the pressure with both hands until Darren squealed his anguish.

Tessa raised the glass, surveyed the white splayed fingers beneath it for a moment with her head on one side, nodded her satisfaction, and resumed the dialogue. 'I wonder how many successful murderers there are in this country, sitting smugly at home and knowing they've got away with it. We'll never know, will we?'

There was a pause. Then the fourth member of the group, Paul Barnes, spoke for the first time. 'There's a play about it, you know. *Rope*, it's called. It's about two blokes of about our age – students, I think – who plot a murder and carry it out. Good play it is, too. Lots of tension, as you gradually realize they're serious, see the killing happen, and then wonder whether they'll get away with it.' Paul was a drama student. He was willing, even eager, to enlarge upon the function of dialogue in creating dramatic tension to these laymen, if they proved a deserving audience.

He did not get the chance. Gary Pilkington said immediately, 'And did they? Get away with it, I mean.'

'I – I don't think so. I can't remember the denouement.' Paul produced the word with a flourish, as if he hoped it might restore his credibility. 'Usually people don't get away with it in the end, you know, in plays and novels. It's part of what we call the general moral satisfaction.' He produced his own grandiose phrase with heavyweight emphasis, hoping they would accept it as a piece of technical drama jargon. 'It's this appeasement of the collective psyche which puts things like murder into an acceptable context. The idea is to send an audience away challenged, satisfied, but not too disturbed, you see.'

'Right load of bullshit, that! But beautifully delivered, I'll grant you!' This trenchant opinion was delivered brusquely over the heads of the group by a member of the bar staff with a full tray of empty glasses. 'You guys got homes to go to, or are you bedding down here for the night?'

The four looked round at what was now an empty bar and stood up chastened, their chairs scraping noisily on the tiled floor.

Outside the bar, the drink insulated them against the sudden cold of the November night. They strolled rather unsteadily across the deserted, dimly lit paths back to the hostels. Darren Briggs, conscious now that he had drunk a little more than the others, put his arm uncertainly around the waist of Tessa Jones. She allowed him eventually to bear her away through the darkness. Though all four of them were aware that the pair were destined for separate beds, there was a vague and grudging admiration for Darren's hopeless persistence.

The other two men walked in amiable silence through the sharp night air, looking up at a million stars in a navy sky. They had reached their hostel and said their goodnights before Gary Pilkington, taking a last look at the remote beauty above them, produced the thought which hung for a moment in the night air – and hung in their brains for much longer than that. 'I bet *we* could murder someone without getting caught, if we planned it properly.'

Two

The campus was quiet at the weekends. Many of the students had cars, of varying ages and reliability, which carried them and their washing back to their homes and the girl- or boyfriends they had left behind. Two of those who didn't leave the site were Gary Pilkington and Paul Barnes.

Saturday was a dull November day, with damp in the air but no real rain. The two had not arranged to meet. Indeed, they did different things during the day, each trying to catch up on some work, without a great deal of success. Gary worked in his own room, staring hard at the history tomes in front of him but finding his attention straying to the drifting leaves outside his window as they thickened the golden carpet of autumn upon the ground beneath the hostel wall. Paul chose the library, and was for a time more successful in retaining his concentration for the task in hand. But there were other students there, who persuaded him without much resistance to go for a coffee in the student cafeteria, where of course he stayed longer than he intended.

It was all very predictable. It had all happened before. At this time of year, when the days shortened and most of the academic year still stretched ahead of you, it was difficult to summon the urgency occasioned by fear of the end-of-the-year exams or assignments which had to be in the next day. All the tutors emphasized that you had to pace the work, that a steady accumulation of knowledge and ideas would always prevail over late-year panics. And almost all of the students nodded their acceptance of this

5

commonsense advice, and then found it impossible to follow.

Paul Barnes found his way back to the library, eventually. But in another forty minutes it was time to go for lunch, and again he stayed away from work for longer than he intended to. He met a second-year student who had appeared in a play with him, and they went for a swift half of bitter in the union bar. One became two, and the swiftness stretched to an hour. It was a quarter to three when Paul got back to the library, and he found it even more difficult than in the morning to complete his notes for an essay on 'The Importance of Ibsen in the Development of European Drama'.

At four o'clock, he found himself dozing over those notes. At quarter past four, he went across the library to the drama section and found a copy of *Rope*.

You couldn't work on a Saturday night, no matter how hard you tried. Throughout adolescence, long before you came to university, when you had been under the baleful parental eye, Saturday nights had been for enjoyment. It was a habit which you were not easily able to drop, however hard you attempted it. Most students had given up trying.

The problem at the University of East Lancashire was that there weren't enough students around to make it worth organizing any formal social activities. The hearties who played rugby and soccer tended to take over the student bar with visiting teams for an hour or two in the early evening, but on this particular November day they must have been mostly playing away, for there were no sounds of the raucous merriment which often rent those hours.

As if by some prearranged signal, Gary Pilkington and Paul Barnes found themselves together in the television room in the basement of their hostel at eight o'clock on that evening. Half an hour later, they were the only two there, and neither had his attention on the television set in the corner as it winked its Saturday night banalities. It was another two hours until *Match of the Day*.

At nine o'clock, they went up to Paul Barnes's room on the second floor. He wasn't quite sure why, but he checked that there was no one in any of the other rooms on his corridor.

An hour later, the two had smoked a couple of spliffs and were feeling pleasantly relaxed. Except that an idea was nagging away at the back of both these undisciplined but lively young minds.

It took the second, smaller spliff to bring it out in words. Gary had settled his considerable bulk into a comfortable sprawl in the single armchair. Paul was lying on his bed, gazing at the ceiling through a faint haze of cannabis, when he said, 'I had a look at that play we were talking about when I was in the library today. *Rope*, I mean.'

'Hmmm.' Gary Pilkington, perfectly relaxed in his chair, didn't feel the need for any words.

'These two young American lads in that play. They got away with it because they were so cool about the way they planned it.'

Gary watched the smoke from the pot curling round his nose, then hanging in the air above his face, a small blue cloud of contentment, protecting him against the harshness of the world outside, giving him the confidence he pretended all day but didn't really feel within himself. He breathed out slowly and smiled. Then he said the single word, 'Fiction!'

'Pardon?'

'Fiction. That's all it is. Not real life. No relevance to us.'

Paul Barnes frowned. 'I think it was based on a real case in America, but I'm not sure of that. But that doesn't matter. Good drama is always relevant to real life.' He mouthed one of the slogans of the Drama and Performing Arts Department, finding that the words were for the first time important to him.

Gary smiled, feeling too lazy, too comfortable to argue the point. 'So tell me about it, you luvvy, you!'

7

Paul tried hard to concentrate upon marshalling an argument. 'Well, these two lads in the play were very like us, really. Looking for kicks. Wanting to show they could take the establishment on and make it look silly.' The introduction to *Rope*, which he had read earlier in the day, talked about how the pair who planned murder were totally amoral as well, and how much this helped them in their amazing deceptions, but this seemed scarcely the moment to introduce ethical considerations. Instead, he paused for a moment, allowing a delicious thought to run through his mind. 'We could do that, you know. Baffle the establishment.'

Gary turned his head and looked at his friend curiously, trying to decide if Paul was serious. His voice sounded in his own ears curiously like his father's as he said, 'It's not as easy as you might think to do that, you know.'

Paul finished his spliff, smiled at the ceiling, and took a decision. He rolled off his bed and into an upright position, in what he hoped was a single athletic movement. 'Come outside with me and I'll show you what I mean.'

There were neither the moon nor the bright stars of the previous night. It was mild and still, with a thin mist hanging over the quiet campus. They seemed to be the only people abroad at that hour; indeed, it was only the scattering of dim lights in hostel windows which showed them that some students were still on the site on Saturday night. The only faint sounds were of sporadic laughter from the student bar, and that was muted and low behind the closed doors. They did not step within a hundred yards of the place.

The administrative centre of the new university was a three-storeyed early Victorian mansion. The two young men were quite close to the building before they could discern the single light in the basement where the night porter had his office. They stood for a moment on the main drive, staring up at the neo-Gothic outlines of the stately home which had once been the focus of this three hundred acre estate, where a cotton magnate had built himself a palace which he felt would properly reflect the fortune he had made from his mills three miles away. He had naturally chosen the highest point of the gently undulating site for his residence.

To the only human figures who seemed to be abroad in the low cloud of this Saturday night, the stone turrets looked higher and more menacing than they did by day, when the stature of the old mansion was reduced by the plethora of new university buildings around it. They stood in silence for a moment, looking at the ominous outline, recalling a score of horror films for which it might have provided the setting.

Then Paul Barnes led Gary Pilkington past the old house and away beneath a pair of massive cedars to a minor paved road. Scarcely wide enough for the wheels of a car, it wound away from the taller buildings of the site, beneath oaks which still retained most of their autumn leaves, though there was a carpet of amber and brown on the ground around them. These colours were soon invisible, as they walked a hundred yards through a darkness which seemed to wrap itself conspiratorially around them, arriving eventually at a single small lamp upon a slender standard.

Here a drive swung right into the night. The white light above them was not much more than a token illumination in the darkness, but their eyes, accustomed now to the night, could just read a sign five yards to the right of the standard which carried the words 'Director's Residence: Strictly Private'.

Gary turned his face interrogatively towards his companion, and caught the excitement on his face in the pale white light of the lamp. Paul whispered close to his ear, 'There's no one there. They're away for the weekend. Come on, I'll show you!' He set off up the invisible drive towards the dim silhouette of a modern house.

Gary glanced nervously over his shoulder. There had been no need to whisper, here. And yet it seemed the natural way to converse in this deserted place. He followed the retreating shadow that was Paul Barnes, less because he wanted to share the thrill of trespassing on the Director's grounds than because he feared being alone in such an eerie place.

Paul was right. There was no sign of anyone in the rectangular mass of modern house. They went round the side of the double garage, passing through a patch of darkness so dense that they had to hold their hands in front of them to find whether the path was clear. The rear of the house was as quiet as the front. They passed the wide patio doors of what was obviously a lounge, then three other windows, before an extractor fan on a fourth told them that this long room at the furthest corner of the house was a kitchen.

Gary Pilkington found his voice at last, though it came in no more than a hoarse, urgent whisper to his companion's back. 'Let's get out of here, before someone comes and finds us! I don't know why you wanted to come round the back like this.'

But Paul Barnes had plunged on into the darkness, as if it was important to him to complete the circuit of the house rather than turn back the way they had come. He threw a chuckle back over his shoulder at his tardy comrade. 'Just casing the joint, that's all! Making ready for the perfect crime!'

Sunday. A short and not very sweet day, with drizzle in the morning and clearing skies as the temperature dropped sharply in the afternoon. On the site of the new University of East Lancashire, another quiet, almost dead day. Apart, that is, from two students with mischief on their minds.

Gary Pilkington was secretly hoping that the actions of the previous night had all been a hypothesis, a drug-induced fantasy which would be dismissed in the cold light of an autumn day. He was wrong. He did not go down to breakfast and stayed in his room for the whole of the morning. But when there was a quiet knock on his door at a quarter to twelve, he knew before he opened it exactly who his visitor was.

Paul Barnes studied his friend's face for any symptoms

of withdrawal, gave him a quick smile, and shut the door behind himself as he came into the room. 'Good recce we did last night, wasn't it? Time to start planning!' He handed Gary a small package in a polythene bag and planted himself in the single armchair.

'What's this?'

'A videotape. More research, if you like. So that we can continue the planning of the perfect crime.'

Gary sat down heavily on the edge of the bed he had recently tidied, positioning himself no more than four feet from his friend, so that Paul could appreciate how seriously he meant what he had to say. 'We can't go committing crimes, Paul. Not just like that. Not for no reason.'

Paul Barnes smiled into the earnest face confronting him. 'Not for no reason, no. For our own satisfaction, to prove that we can do it. To outwit the establishment, and bewilder the fuzz. And to embarrass that pompous twit Carter, who calls himself our Director.'

His face shone with the bright excitement of the enterprise. He reminded Gary Pilkington of the Jehovah's Witnesses who used to call at the door of his suburban home, shining with a certainty he could never feel and proof against all rebuffs. Of his old great-aunt, with the red, shiny face within her Salvation Army bonnet, luminous with a certainty about the Lord which the rest of the family had never caught.

Gary had always felt a respect for those people, so full of a faith he envied although he could never share it. But Paul Barnes had no such justification for his zeal. It was time to stop him. Gary was wondering what was the best method of doing that, without losing his friend. He said, 'We can't go committing crimes just for the sake of it, Paul. Apart from anything else, we'd get slung out of here on our ears, if we got caught. And no doubt we'd collect a criminal record as—'

'But we wouldn't get caught! That's the beauty of it, Gary. We'd be the only ones who knew exactly what had

11

happened, laughing up our sleeves whilst the campus buzzed like a beehive!'

'But someone always suffers, when there's a crime. We can't go—'

'Only that overblown idiot of a Director! And he deserves it. You must surely agree with that. And if we go about it carefully, some deserving charity might even benefit from our Perfect Crime.'

Gary wished he wouldn't keep using that phrase. It had acquired capital letters now, with Paul's repetitions. It was becoming like a political slogan, and as a student of history you always distrusted those. He said reluctantly, 'This play, *Rope*, which seems to have set you off on this idea. You said the two men in that killed a bloke. You're surely not suggesting that we should—'

Paul's laughter rang loud in that small box of a room. 'Kill Claptrap Carter! Bloody hell, Gary, you've let your imagination run away with you! How much pot did you smoke last night, for God's sake?'

Gary grinned sheepishly. 'Well, no, I don't suppose I ever thought you were proposing to kill off old Claptrap. But what else, then?'

'A burglary. Swift, efficient, successful. Away with the booty, leaving a baffled police force and a furious Director.' He beamed his confidence like a sun lamp upon his dubious colleague.

'But – but what do we pinch? And how do we get into the place? And how can you be so sure that we won't get caught in the act?' Gary was obscurely aware as he mounted this battery of questions that he had abandoned his stance of blank refusal. He wasn't quite sure how that had come about.

Paul Barnes grinned at him and triumphantly unwrapped his package. 'Play this videotape, and all will be revealed, my friend.'

Gary looked for a moment in puzzlement at the videocassette, then went to the other side of the room and slid it into the video recorder on top of his portable television set. Within thirty seconds, all was indeed revealed – or to be strictly accurate, the situation became a little clearer.

It was a recording of a television interview conducted some eighteen months earlier by Granada, for its north-west news magazine programme. The Director of the new University of East Lancashire had then just been appointed. With his high forehead, his receding hair, his slightly too well-fleshed appearance and his air of satisfaction, Dr Carter looked like one of those archbishops in the early Shakespeare history plays whom you were not meant to trust.

When he spoke, it became obvious why his new students had delightedly nicknamed him Claptrap Carter. He delivered a series of orotund educational clichés earnestly at the camera, as if they were new-minted personal discoveries. His mission, in life and in his new post, was to make sure that the underdog got a fair educational chance (i.e., being at the bottom of the educational pile, his new institution wasn't going to attract the best A-level grades, so better make the best of it). He had every confidence in the quality of the teaching and administrative staff of his new university, and proposed to give them a free hand (i.e., don't expect Dr Carter to be much in evidence about the place, and don't expect him to take responsibility for the cock-ups which will inevitably occur in the early years). The new university was not to be an ivory tower, and the already excellent relationships with the local populace would be a matter of great importance to him (i.e., don't blame us for the drugs and the graffiti, they were here before we came).

There was much more in the same vein. It was not so much what Carter said but the manner of its saying which caused him to be sent up mercilessly by students who had never even spoken to him. Claptrap Carter combined an oily delivery with a smile which would have caused revulsion in a home for the blind. The interview was conducted in his new home, the house which Paul and Gary had circumnavigated on the previous night. It ended with an obviously prearranged question from the interviewer about the contents of the bookcase against which Carter had carefully set himself.

Claptrap waved his hand airily towards the shelves of books behind him. 'Tools of the trade, you know! Just a selection of the books gathered over the years of a busy academic life.' He gave his interviewer his most oleaginous smile and leaned forward. 'But there is something I would like to say here. When our great new enterprise begins, we shall have some students who have been brought up in an environment where books were not taken for granted, like this. It is those students whom I wish to rescue from a Philistine world! It is those students whom I wish to make our academic bread and butter, in what I am sure will soon come to be known far and wide as the UEL!'

Perhaps because he was tiring of the word 'academic', which had been mentioned at least eight times in seven minutes, the interviewer sought to end on a more intimate note, by asking Dr Carter if any of the books had a personal significance for the new Director of the UEL.

Claptrap, delighted to have the initials he had suggested returned to him so promptly, adopted his humble but saintly mode, produced another excruciating smile, and extracted Thomas à Kempis's *The Imitation of Christ* and a copy of the New Testament from the drawer of the desk where he had placed them in readiness. 'I don't have many quiet moments, but when I have, I try to reinforce myself with some of the eternal verities.'

Carter then shut his eyes briefly and gave a little sigh. 'And in my more venial moments, I indulge myself by collecting books. These, I think, are probably the pride of my collection.' He then displayed leather-bound versions of each of Jane Austen's six major novels and tried desperately and unsuccessfully to connect the immortal Jane with the mills of industrial Lancashire. The interview ended abruptly.

Gary Pilkington had joined with Paul Barnes in giggling

derision during the more risible moments of it. His hilarity was abruptly dissipated by Paul's triumphant assertion as he stopped the videotape: 'There's our booty! Never could stand Jane Bloody Austen myself, but she must be worth a bob or two in her first editions!'

'But we can't just pinch them!'

'Not for ourselves we can't, no. But here's what we do. We hide them for a while. Then, when everyone is assuming that they've been lost for ever, we send them to be sold for a children's charity. At the same time, we make it public where they came from – an anonymous phone call, or something like that. Then old Claptrap Carter will be faced with the dilemma of either helping the deprived children he bleats about or getting his books back!'

Gary smiled. The Director's unctuous performance on the videotape was still fresh in his mind. 'Nice one! Where do we hide them, though? There'll be pigs running about everywhere, once the news of the burglary breaks.'

Paul Barnes knew he had won the argument now. 'That's easy. In the theatre store. There's a big area underneath the stage which no one uses, full of old flats that no one has pulled out for years. I'll put the books right at the back of there.'

Gary Pilkington took a deep breath. It was on, the Perfect Crime, in spite of all his reservations. He said, 'What if old Claptrap and his missus come back, while we're still in there?'

'We get out quick when we hear the car on the drive. We're going in at the back of the house anyway. But they won't come back. They always drive in early on Monday morning, when they go off for the weekend. I've seen them.'

Gary wondered for the first time just how long Paul had been planning this thing. He seemed to have done a lot of preliminary research on the subject. Probably, though, that was all to the good, now that they were committed.

Thorough preparation must be part of the recipe for the Perfect Crime.

Three

Twelve hours later, Gary Pilkington stood beneath the massive cedar beside the old mansion at the centre of the campus. He looked up nervously at the moon and willed his companion to return swiftly.

For the skies which had cleared in the afternoon had remained clear, and there was not a cloud visible now in the night sky. The stars shone diamond-bright and the moon was nearly full; in Gary's heightened imagination, the man in the moon seemed to be regarding these actions so far below him with a knowing smile. Everything was far too clear and bright, for those bent on a burglary. A bomber's moon, he had heard it called, from those nights sixty years ago when men like his grandfather had flown those creaking old planes over Europe to deliver their destruction.

There was a frost tonight, the first of the winter. It would be a sharp one. The grass was already beginning to sparkle, and Gary caught the flash of white on it as a belated car drove past the place where he waited beneath the tree and turned into the student car park. He stamped his feet on the ground, cautiously, trying to make no noise, and thought inconsequentially that it was not very long now to Christmas and its welter of tinsel.

Gary almost leapt into the air as he sensed rather than saw a presence behind him, in the deep shadow of the cedar. Paul Barnes's whisper came out of the darkness, 'Easy! It's only me. Who were you expecting?' Even on the attempted joke, he caught the tension in his own voice.

'I wasn't expecting you to come from that side.' Gary peered out nervously from his pool of darkness beneath the canopy of the great cedar. 'It's too light, with this moon. Maybe we should leave this for another time, when it's darker – like it was last night.'

Paul noted the need to put some courage into his companion. It was surprising that a big hulking bloke like Gary should be so edgy. He himself felt only the taut excitement of the moment, making each of his senses more alert, more effective, making his own being seem more alive. It was like that necessary nervousness you felt before going on stage. Except that this was better. This was for real.

He pulled the miniature of whisky from his pocket and unscrewed the top carefully, six inches below Gary's face, to show his companion how steady his hands were. Gary didn't wait to be invited. He snatched the little bottle and took a strong pull from it, then stood very still, feeling the spirit coursing hot as molten lead down his throat and outwards into his chest. He smothered the cough the neat spirit induced into a question. 'Is the coast clear at the house?'

'Absolutely clear! Not a soul around. I knew there wouldn't be. I told you, there'll be no sign of Claptrap Carter until tomorrow morning.'

Gary took a deep breath, knowing he must move whilst the effect of the whisky was still strong within him. 'Better get on with it, then!'

'Steady on, old lad. Remember the plan. We wait for the night porter to be off on his rounds before we move in.'

For two minutes, which seemed to Gary like ten, they stood motionless beneath the cedar. A car came up the drive, its headlights seeming to move unnaturally slowly as it came nearer and nearer. It came to within thirty yards of them, until it seemed that it must be the Director, returning after all to his house tonight rather than in the morning. Then it turned off towards one of the hostel blocks and disappeared. Paul Barnes, letting out his own breath slowly, caught the gasp of relief from the heavy shape beside him.

At that moment, the clock on top of the old stables behind the mansion tolled the chimes of midnight. That was a familiar phrase, thought Paul, as he counted them out. Falstaff, wasn't it, to Justice Shallow? 'We have heard the chimes at midnight.' Well, those old rogues would thoroughly approve of this present enterprise. No time for pomposity, old Falstaff hadn't. He'd have made mincemeat of old Claptrap Carter.

A moment later, they had what they had been waiting for. Each of them shrank back instinctively against the massive trunk of the old cedar as the night porter emerged into the darkness from his cave of warmth in the basement of the house. He stamped on the butt of his cigarette, flapped his arms across his chest a couple of times, and for some reason appeared to look straight at the tree which hid them. Then he switched on his rubber torch and set off towards the library, the first building on his hourly security round.

Paul, keeping a restraining hand upon the arm of his friend, did not move until the porter was three hundred yards away and out of sight. Then they moved cautiously along the path towards the single pale white light in front of the Director's Residence, and up the drive they had reconnoitred on the previous night.

As Paul had forecast, the light of the moon, dropping into the clearing among the trees which marked the Director's garden at the back of the house, made visible much more detail than they had been able to see on the previous night. There was a bird table, a garden fork left sticking in the ground, and a small pond, gleaming still as a mirror in the pale white light of the moon. Gary hadn't thought about how they were going to get into the place; somehow he had always assumed that Paul Barnes would know how to take care of that.

He was right. Paul now produced a large old car tyre lever

from beneath his anorak. Gary supposed that it must have been there all the time; certainly he hadn't been aware of it until now. He wanted to say, even at this stage, that this was a bad idea after all, that they should call it off. But he knew that he wouldn't be successful; knew also that he couldn't lose face in front of his friend. How many foolish actions are driven on by that small and ridiculous human reluctance!

Paul whispered, 'There's a small window in the utility room on the far side of the house, the only one in the place which isn't double-glazed. I'm sure the wood's rotten at the bottom of it!'

Gary caught the excitement in his voice. He wondered just how long Paul had been planning this venture, which for him had grown out of nothing in the last two days. He watched his friend working his improvised jemmy into the damp wood, started in fear as the wood splintered like gunfire in the still, freezing night.

'We're in!' The triumphant whisper came to Gary like a death knell from the wiry figure on his right.

There was no alarm system. Perhaps the position of the house on a normally populous college site had made the occupants careless of security. Perhaps the Carters had relied on their cocker spaniel, which had died a month earlier, to raise the alarm. Paul Barnes removed frame and glass carefully to leave a square hole of darkness, then slid his slender body through it and into the utility room of the big house. A moment later, he eased open the glass-panelled back door and admitted a reluctant Gary Pilkington into the residence of the Director.

Gary looked round at the rows of cupboards in the large modern kitchen, at the beakers left to drain upon the sink, feeling so tense that he feared that he would freeze into inactivity. He had never been in anyone's house without permission like this before. It already felt like a violation. 'What now?' he said hoarsely.

'Don't touch anything. We mustn't leave anything of

ourselves around for the police. We get those books, and then we go!' Paul was filled with an icy calm: the need to quiet the turmoil in his companion seemed to have stilled his own nerves.

'Where will they be, though? We couldn't see much in that video, you know. Just Claptrap Carter and the bookcase behind him.'

'Then it's his study, isn't it? That or just possibly one end of his sitting room.' Paul was suddenly tired of his lumbering, apprehensive companion. Better not let the fuzz get anywhere near him, when this was over. 'Look, you stay here and keep watch. I'll find what we want. No need for two of us to go blundering about.'

Gary was only too happy to go no further into the house. He glanced longingly at the kitchen door where he had entered, then set his gaze resolutely on the garden with its pool reflecting the moon. 'All right. If anyone appears out there, I'll let you know. Be as quick as you can, for God's sake!'

Paul moved deliberately slowly, enjoying his companion's apprehension, relishing his own coolness. He went and relocked the door through which he had let Gary into the house. In the unlikely event of the night porter varying his route around the campus, you didn't want him trying that and finding it open. The man was unlikely to notice the small window he had forced, which was in the deep shadow round the corner of the house.

He went into the hall before he switched on the small torch he had brought with him. Once he had got his bearings, he switched it off again: a light in a darkened house would be a dead giveaway to any unexpected late-night pedestrians outside. He had left the kitchen door open, so that there was just enough light coming into the hall for him to pick out the dark gleam of the brass handles on the various doors of this central hall. He opened them in turn, finding a large sitting room, with two sofas as well as a three-piece suite, but no bookcases; a dining room, with eight chairs arranged evenly around a long table, whose polished wood gleamed softly in the moonlight; another, smaller, sitting room, with a television set and a hi-fi stack, which an estate agent would no doubt have called a family room.

Paul moved back to the sitting room on silent feet. He called softly to Gary. 'Study must be upstairs. I'm going up there now. We've still a good quarter of an hour before the night porter is due.'

Gary did not turn round from the window. 'For God's sake be quick about it! I can't stand much more of this!'

He couldn't, either, thought Paul, as he went softly up the wide modern staircase. Not a man to take into the jungle with you, Gary Pilkington, for all his physical strength. You learned a lot about people in situations like this.

The first door he tried at the top of the stairs was a bathroom. Good thing he'd insisted on them wearing gloves, with all these brass handles to turn. It wouldn't take him more than a minute to try all of these doors, if he needed to. And once he found that elusive study, the books themselves would surely be easy to spot in their old leather bindings.

Then he noticed that one of the doors to the rooms at the back of the house was slightly ajar. Might as well try that first.

The moonlight was very strong in this room, falling in shafts through the twin windows across the coverlet of a kingsize bed, picking out the door of an en suite bathroom. The main bedroom, obviously. He was about to go on in search of the study when he saw something sticking out beyond the foot of the bed. The moonlight glistened softly on a leather toecap.

A pair of shoes, pointing up at the ceiling. And in them, feet. And above the feet, legs. As he moved his reluctant limbs across the room, Paul Barnes knew suddenly what he was about to find. A torso, and a head, in the shadow of the big bed. Wide, sightless eyes, staring unseeing as glass into his face.

Paul Barnes forced his unwilling, suddenly trembling hands into life and switched on his torch. There was a red, unmoving pool beside the dead face of Dr Claptrap Carter, now the late Director of the University of East Lancashire. Half the dead face, to be strictly accurate: the rest had been blown away.

Someone had been more serious than him about the Perfect Crime.

Four

'Detective Inspector Peach will see you now.' The female detective sergeant with the lustrous red-brown hair called Paul Barnes into the Bursar's office, which had been temporarily cleared of university clerical staff and handed over to the CID.

Bit of all right she was, thought Paul, as he followed her appreciatively into the office. Not much more than mid-twenties, he judged, and voluptuous with it. Not at all what he had expected of the police. He wouldn't mind giving her one, that DS Blake, when this was all—

'Right kettle of fish you've dropped yourself in here, lad! Stinking fish, too! Can't see either of you coming out of it smelling too sweet!'

The man who had so rudely shattered Paul's bedroom visions was stocky and powerful, with a shining bald head fringed with jet-black hair and a matching black moustache beneath very dark eyes. He had delivered his series of opening observations with mounting vehemence and increasing satisfaction.

Peach sat behind the Bursar's huge, leather-topped desk as if he had occupied the chair for years, not minutes, and gave Paul the impression that he devoured students for breakfast each day. His black eyebrows lowered themselves over the charcoal eyes, whose pupils seemed to bore like gimlets into Paul's inner thoughts. Peach managed the difficult feat of frowning with his forehead and smiling with the bottom half of his face.

Paul did not find it a pleasant smile. He said, 'We found him for you. Without Gary and me, he might have been lying there yet.'

Peach's smile broadened. 'True, that is, isn't it? We should be grateful to you, shouldn't we, at that rate? And yet when I look at you, my lad, gratitude isn't the first emotion that leaps into my mind.'

Paul steadied himself, trying hard to feel wronged. He hadn't expected this aggression, especially when his first contact with the fuzz had been that delectable female presence now sitting quietly on the Inspector's right. He tried to summon a sense of dignity. It wasn't a thing you needed often as a student, but it might be useful now. And he was a drama student, after all: these simulations were supposed to come easily to him.

He repeated loftily, 'If it wasn't for us, Claptr— Dr Carter might still be lying undiscovered in his house.'

Peach held his smile for a moment longer, like a headlamp on full beam. Then he rapped, 'What time did you report the discovery of a body, lad?'

Paul licked his lips. 'I couldn't be certain of the time. Time was the last thing on our minds when—'

'I'll tell you, then. Twenty to three in the morning. 0241 hours, as we say in the police service, to be precise. Unless you're now saying that you want to dispute that, of course. That's the time our station sergeant recorded for the phone call from your campus night porter.'

'No! I mean no, I don't wish to dispute that. If that's when you say our night porter rang you with the news, then that will be correct.'

'So that's when you found the corpse of your Director. Or five minutes before that, shall we say, to be strictly accurate?'

Paul Barnes didn't like the way this was going. He had expected to be interviewed with Gary Pilkington, so that he could act as spokesman for the two. But the first thing this man had done was to separate the two of them, treating them almost as though they had something to hide rather than as citizens doing their duty and being of assistance to the fuzz in exposing a crime for them. God knows what Gary would end up saying, if this man got at him.

Paul said, 'Well, yes, it must have been some time just before Percy rang you. We might have taken a few minutes to collect ourselves, before we went across to the porter's office and got him to ring through. It was the first time either of us had seen a dead body, you know. It might have thrown us a little off balance.'

'Oh, I'm sure it did! Often does, doesn't it, DS Blake? Makes people go quite weak at the knees, sometimes.' Peach whirled his attention back from the smiling features of Lucy Blake to the man on the other side of the big desk. 'But the usual reaction is to scream for help. To run to the nearest phone as quickly as your little feet will carry you and yell for the police!'

And that's exactly what Panicky Pilkington had wanted to do, thought Paul. Rush off and spill the beans about their plan for the Perfect Crime. Land them in hot water right up to their necks – the scalding kettle of fish this man Peach claimed they were in now, come to think of it. It had taken Paul a good two hours to calm Gary down, to work out the best tale they could tell and rehearse it. It wasn't a good tale, but it was the best he had been able to do, in those dire circumstances, with old Claptrap Carter lying dead and Gary Pilkington screaming in his ear.

He repeated that story now, carefully and doggedly. 'We'd been drinking and talking, on into the night, until we'd lost all track of the time. Students do that. It was Gary who suddenly realized that it was two o'clock in the morning. And yet neither of us felt like going to bed. So I suggested that we went out for a stroll around the site, because it was a beautiful moonlit night, cold and clear, and we thought the air would clear our heads.'

Paul, who had concentrated on the leather of the big desk as he strove to deliver the tale as they had agreed it, looked up nervously at Peach, wanting to be interrupted, feeling that the long silence from the other side of the desk made his words all the time less convincing. He received only another kind of smile from Peach, with the mouth slightly open and an inspectorial tongue caressing the startlingly white teeth. DI Peach looked like a Dobermann awaiting permission to attack a bone.

Paul dragged his eyes away from that round, expectant face and resumed his account. 'We were walking past the Director's Residence when we thought we saw a light inside – almost as if someone was moving about in there, with a torch. I think now that it must have been a trick of the moonlight reflecting on the double glazing. But at the time we thought we'd better investigate.'

DS Blake said quietly, 'You didn't think of going and raising the alarm at that stage, Mr Barnes?'

Bloody hell, thought Paul. He'd enough dealing with the Dobermann, without the female joining in with her questions. And raising the alarm is exactly what Panicky Pilkington would have done, of course, if they had really seen a light in the place. He said stubbornly, 'Maybe we should have done that. But our first thought was that we might catch someone in there.'

Peach beamed delightedly. 'Brave lads these, aren't they, DS Blake? The type that made Britain great, hidden away on our doorstep in our local university! Bloody stupid too, of course.'

Paul tried hard to ignore him, to complete the story they had agreed. 'We couldn't get in at the front of the house, but when we went round the back, we found that a window had been forced. So I climbed through and let Gary in by the back door. You – well, I think you know the rest. We didn't find anyone inside there, but we did find the body of Dr Carter.'

'And that's it?'

'Yes. I've told your officers all of it before.'

Peach shook his head sadly. 'Yes. Indeed you have. I just wanted to check that that was still it, you see. Because I don't think it sounds very convincing. What do you think, DS Blake?'

'About as convincing as a student pantomime, I'd say, sir. Bit better rehearsed, perhaps.'

She was training up nicely, was Lucy Blake, thought Percy Peach. He couldn't believe he'd resisted the move when that fool of a superintendent, Tommy Bloody Tucker, had allocated her to him as his DS.

Paul Barnes glared his disappointment at this vision of loveliness he had been relying upon for sympathy. He hadn't reckoned on Beauty siding with the Beast. Obviously, what people said was right: you couldn't trust the police, however beguiling the guise in which they came to you. He said sullenly, 'Well, that's how it was.'

Peach shook his head slowly, seemingly more in sorrow than in anger. He stood up. 'If you say so, sunshine. Better have a word with your partner in crime now, hadn't we? Perhaps the history student will recall the recent past more effectively than the drama student.' As the slight figure with the sharp, handsome features shuffled out, he called after him, 'We shall need your fingerprints, Mr Barnes. And send in your partner in crime, please.'

Gary Pilkington's nerve had not been improved by his wait outside the Bursar's office. He had spent the time going over and over the story that he and Paul – well mostly Paul, if he was honest – had put together to conceal the true purpose of their visit to the Director's Residence on the previous night. Repetition had not made the story more convincing in his fevered brain, but they were stuck with it now, so he'd better get it right.

He was not reassured by the sight of a thoroughly discomfited Paul Barnes coming out of the office. He had no time to speak to him, because that friendly woman detective came out and ushered him straight into the office and the smiling face of Detective Inspector Peach. The DI waved an arm expansively at the chair in front of the big desk and waited for Lucy Blake to resume her place beside him on the business side.

Peach studied the unsuccessful efforts of the big body opposite him to stay still for a moment before he said, 'History student, I believe, Mr Pilkington?'

'Yes.'

'Good memories, history experts had, when I was at school. Good recall of past events. Let's see how you are about last night.'

Gary struggled to rid himself of an obstinate frog in his throat. 'What – what exactly is it you want to know? We told one of your constables all about it this morning, and I thought—'

'I know. Dreary for you, isn't it, this repetition? But indulge me, please. Just take us through the whole thing again, will you, Mr Pilkington? Give you the chance to put right any mistakes you might have made, and DS Blake and I the chance to ask any intelligent questions we can think of. We'd like that.'

Paul didn't like it, not one little bit. But his brain refused to work when he bid it to work at its fastest. It would take him all his resources to remember and deliver the story as he had agreed it with Paul. He dared not look at those observant faces across the huge expanse of green leather on top of the desk as he began: 'Well, we'd been drinking and talking way into the night, the way students do. Then I suddenly realized that it was two o'clock in the morning. And yet neither of us felt like going to bed. So Paul suggested that we should go for a walk round the site. It was a beautiful moonlit night, cold and clear, and we thought the air would clear our heads. We were walking past the Director's Residence when we thought we saw a light inside.'

Paul stopped and swallowed, trying to get the next bit

straight in his mind. For the first time since he had begun, he looked up at the CID officers – and found them both regarding him with considerable amusement. 'What – what is it that's wrong?'

Peach stopped smiling for a moment to purse his lips. 'Your delivery, I'd say, principally. You've got the script off pretty well, but your delivery is very wooden. Needs more expression and variation, I'd say, wouldn't you, DS Blake?'

'Definitely more light and shade, I'd say. Mr Barnes could probably help you with that, being a drama student.' The smile sat more winningly on Lucy Blake's cheerful, light-skinned face, but that didn't make Gary Pilkington feel any better about it. He tried to speak, but found he couldn't.

Peach turned the screw. 'Dried, have we, Mr Pilkington? I'm sure we could help you with a prompt. Tell him how it goes on, DS Blake.'

Lucy Blake flicked back unhurriedly to a page in her shorthand notes. '. . . We saw a light inside. Almost as if someone was moving about in there, with a torch. We thought we'd better investigate. We couldn't get in at the front of the house, but when we went round the back, we found that a window had been forced . . .' She stopped, smiled, and allowed the pause to stretch on for seconds, which seemed like minutes for the agonized young man on the other side of the desk.

Peach eventually took pity upon him. 'You see our point, Mr Pilkington? It does rather smack of a prepared statement, doesn't it? Or a prepared fiction, if you're an old cynic like me.'

Gary forced his brain into action: it felt as if the gears had jammed. 'We did – did put our heads together, to make sure we told the same story. Every one says you have to be careful, in case the police twist—'

'You've told the same story, all right. The trouble is that

it stinks! You should have paid more attention to the tale you were rehearsing so carefully, if you wanted us to believe you. The matter of the tale is even less convincing than the manner in which you parrotted it off.'

'I suppose it may not sound very convincing, but—'

'It sounds like a pack of lies, lad. An attempt to deceive the police in what may shortly become a murder inquiry.' Peach's voice was suddenly harsh and impatient. 'I suggest you go and sit on the landing outside for a few minutes and consider your options, whilst I see whether Mr Barnes has begun to see sense.'

Gary did not look at Paul as he shambled past him in the doorway of the Bursar's office. He slumped onto the chair waiting for him outside, feeling like a wet cloth that had been wrung out between two strong hands and put out to dry.

Paul Barnes tried to speak to the distressed Pilkington as they passed each other, to find out just what it was that had so upset him. He needed to know for his own sake where they stood, whether his friend had been able to maintain his ground in there. Instead, he found himself back in the Bursar's office still uncertain of his ground, feeling the initiative slip from him to that bouncy little bald-headed Inspector who regarded him so balefully as he re-entered the room.

Peach leaned forward, put his elbows on the big desk, and spoke in an unexpectedly low voice. 'It seems to me, Mr Barnes, that what you have given DS Blake and myself so far is no more than a right load of old boots. I don't know about her, but my patience is wearing very thin indeed. We are in the early stages of what might well prove to be a murder inquiry. I would advise you to start telling us the truth about what happened last night. Immediately.'

Paul gulped. He didn't trust the police. These were in fact the first dealings he had had with them in his life, but everyone said you shouldn't trust them. Fascists, and unscrupulous bastards to boot, they were: that was the student view. But

30

he had to admit to himself that what this squat, loathsome man said made sense. You couldn't go pussyfooting about, not with dead bodies lying around. Paul licked his lips, looked for support to the female face with its nimbus of red hair, and said, 'You won't believe it, when I tell you.'

Lucy Blake gave him a small smile of encouragement. He watched her slim fingers tighten around the gold ball-pen as she prepared to record his amended version of events. Then Peach, resuming his most aggressive mode, rapped out, 'Try us with the truth, sunshine. Then we'll discuss why you chose to tell us a pack of lies previously.'

Paul wondered if he should tell them half of the truth, concoct some version of events which got round the fact that he and Gary had undoubtedly been guilty of breaking and entering into the house of the Director of their university. But his brain would not work properly under the baleful glare of those dark eyes. And it wasn't an easy thing to improvise any new version of events which would get them off the hook. And if he did, that wimp in bear's clothing Gary Pilkington would never back him up and carry it through. Paul Barnes had begun the process of transferring his resentment to his unwilling partner in crime.

He swallowed hard and said abruptly, 'It was earlier in the night.'

'What was?'

'The time when we found the body of Dr Carter. Just after midnight, if you must know.'

'Oh, we must. Don't be in any doubt about that. Just as we must have a proper account of the circumstances of that discovery.'

Paul nodded, then said with a last hint of defiance, 'You aren't going to like it, when you hear it.'

'Probably not. I haven't liked many of the things you've said, so far. But try me.'

'Gary and I had this scheme – well, it wasn't so much a scheme as an experiment, really, to test out a theory.'

'Fascinating. The workings of the student mind. Listen carefully, DS Blake: this will very likely enlarge your experience.'

The sergeant's smile on that soft face seemed suddenly almost as unnerving as her inspector's aggression. Paul tore his eyes away from both and cast them determinedly on the table. If he was to complete this bizarre tale and make it even moderately convincing, he would have to concentrate fiercely. 'We'd been discussing it for a few days. The Perfect Crime. Whether it was possible, I mean. Whether it was feasible to commit any sort of crime and get away with it completely.'

Despite his resolution to concentrate, he found himself looking up for a reaction. He found only mockery in those unblinking black pupils. Peach was secretly amused by the earnestness of this slim figure, now that he was admitting the truth. Did he seriously think this was an original concept? Did he think policemen themselves were not fascinated by the same idea? Did he not realize that they had to contemplate each year an increasing number of crimes which were quietly pigeonholed as unsolved, while the fiction was maintained to the public that the files were never closed?

Peach said eventually, 'And who was the mastermind behind this great enterprise? Who was going to be the Professor Moriarty of the campus?'

Paul was tempted to put the onus on Gary Pilkington, to play an apologetic Judas. A whole range of rationalizations with Gary, not himself, at the centre of operations suggested themselves to a mind suddenly agile again with the possibilities. Then he caught Peach's all-seeing eyes and abandoned the idea. 'It wasn't like that. We were both involved in the planning. It was all a bit of a joke, really.'

'A joke which landed you with a high-profile corpse and a whole welter of suspicion. Not to mention contaminating the scene of a murder. Quite a long way from the Perfect Crime, wouldn't you say?'

'Yes, I suppose so. But we didn't know we'd find a dead body, did we?'

'What you knew and what you didn't know remain to be established, thanks to the rubbish you furbished us with at our first meeting. Get on with this new story, please.'

Paul didn't like that use of the word story. They could twist anything, these buggers. He'd better do his utmost to tell this exactly as it happened. The trouble was, in the cold light of day, without the benefit of drink or pot to set things in context, the truth seemed more unlikely than fiction. How could they possibly have been so stupid?

He swallowed hard. 'Well, we tried to think of a fairly harmless exploit to test out our theory about the Perfect Crime. More of a student prank, really.' He grinned feebly, caught Peach's expression, and went on hastily, 'We knew the Director was going to be away for the weekend, and we were pretty certain that he wouldn't be back until Monday morning. So on Saturday night, we looked round the place to see how we might get inside.'

Peach glanced sideways at Lucy Blake. 'Listen to this carefully, DS Blake, and record everything. This might be important for that article you were planning on the criminal psyche.'

Paul tried to ignore him, to cast his mind back to what had actually happened. 'It was dark and misty on Saturday night, and there aren't many students on the campus at that time. We had a look round the back of the house, found that it wasn't overlooked by anyone, and that there was a small window there where we might get in. And we knew the route the night porter takes on his rounds, and the times when he would be well away from the Director's Residence.'

'Fascinating! Research and development, you call this, in universities, don't you? We're more inclined to call it casing the joint, and arrest people for suspicious conduct.'

Paul Barnes seemed to remember using a similar phrase himself, when he was setting up the enterprise with Gary. He tried to shut out Peach's commentary. 'Well, it all seemed pretty simple, at the time. So we went back last night. At just after midnight. I know the time, because the clock on the old stables chimed when we were waiting to do it.'

'Do what, exactly? Spray graffiti on the Director's walls? Steal his teabags? Or dispatch him from this world for ever?'

Paul realized that he hadn't said what they proposed to pinch. It all seemed very bizarre now. And certainly very difficult to explain away to this officer of the Inquisition. 'Sorry. I forgot to tell you that. We were going to take some books. It was more of a joke than a theft, really.'

Paul saw Peach's black eyebrows climbing towards the bald pate, so high that the face beneath them seemed suddenly longer, like an inquisitive owl's. He wished he could play the videotape of Claptrap Carter to these two, show them what a pompous twit the Director had been, show how the man had set himself up for this theft with his portentous moralizing about deprived students and the importance of books. Instead, Paul said limply, 'He had a collection of first editions of Jane Austen. We were going to remove those.'

Peach breathed out a long sigh of satisfaction as his eyebrows slowly returned to earth. 'That's breaking and entering and burglary admitted so far, DS Blake. The best is still to come, I expect.' He was sure now that this wiry lad with the sharp, intelligent features had been the motivating force behind both this crazy enterprise and the feeble attempt to deceive them with a different story. He deserved to squirm a bit – and when it came to squirm-inducement, Percy Peach was your man. You might even say he took a modest pride in it.

Realizing he hadn't allowed himself a smile since this account began, Peach now visited one of his most dazzling ones upon his unhappy victim. 'Right. So you're planning to break in through a back window and nick some priceless books. So who's your fence? Someone who plans as carefully as you must have lined up a fence to dispose of hot gear.'

Horror coursed through the veins of Paul Barnes. They were being treated like real criminals! How was he ever going to make it clear that it had all been a bit of student fun? It had, hadn't it? God, he wasn't even sure himself, now. And that shambling hulk of guilt he'd left outside was going to be no help, for sure. He said dully, 'It wasn't like that. We never thought of it as a real burglary!'

Seeing those Peach eyebrows rising inexorably again, Paul went on desperately, 'We didn't plan to make any profit out of it. Not for ourselves. We just wanted to see the pigs – sorry, the police – baffled and the crime unsolved. Then, after a decent interval, when no one had been arrested and it was clear that this was the Perfect Crime, we were going to send the books to be auctioned for charity and at the same time let Claptr— let Dr Carter know where they were. The idea was that if he claimed them back, he'd have to deprive needy children of the sum that would have been raised at auction.'

It had come out all of a rush, at the end, as the increasingly grotesque nature of the logic became apparent and Paul became ever more fearful of interruption by the appalling voice of reason that was DI Peach. He ended breathless, and Peach let his gasps resonate through the quiet room for a moment before he said, 'Well, well, well! Oh dear, oh dear, oh dear! I thought I was well versed in the workings of the criminal mind by now, DS Blake, but there is always something new for us to learn. Breaking and entering for charity, now! Risking the end of promising student careers and long stints of porridge, just for the sake of hiding away a few books, annoying the Director, and just possibly raising a few bob for children in need. Eventually. Oh, and for "the pleasure of seeing the pigs baffled", of course. We mustn't forget that. You made a note of that, did you?'

Lucy Blake made a pretence of studying her notes whilst she fought back a smile. 'Yes, sir. Got the very words here.'

'Sorry!' said Paul automatically, and then immediately decided from Peach's expression that apology was a mistake.

'So where are these trophies now, Mr Barnes? Where have you deposited the first editions of the immortal Jane?'

That was a literary reference, wasn't it? Surely the pigs weren't supposed to be able to make those? Paul said miserably. 'Still on the Director's bookshelves, I expect. We never got to them. I found Dr Carter's body and we got out.'

Peach's eyebrows lifted again, this time in delight. 'So there's no evidence to support this unlikely tale of philanthropy. Nothing to prove that you didn't break into the place with the express intention of killing Dr George Andrew Carter, the Director of the University of East Lancashire.' He rolled the full name and the title with relish off his tongue, as if it gave even greater weight to this sensational demise.

Paul was emotionally exhausted by now, too wrung out to be scared any more. He said, 'We didn't kill him. Didn't have any intention of killing him. It was a shock when we found him lying there.' He shuddered involuntarily at the recollection.

Peach studied him for a moment. 'Do you know, Mr Barnes, I'm inclined to think you might at last be telling us the truth. If only because if I were trying to deceive the law, I'm sure I could make up a much more convincing story than that.'

It took Paul a moment to work out that he might be off the hook, for the present. He said, 'Er, Gary and I have rather a lot at stake, haven't we? We might be thrown off our courses, for a start. Does – does all this have to come out in public, Inspector?' He gave the ogre his title for the first time, feeling as if he were trying to bribe the Dobermann with a bone.

'Oh, I should think it has to, wouldn't you? You'll almost certainly have to give evidence of finding the body, in the Coroner's Court, and perhaps later on in a Crown Court, depending on the cause of death. Possibly even in the

Central Criminal Court at the Old Bailey, if this business ends with a high-profile trial. I should think you could become quite a local celebrity – for a short time.' Peach beamed his satisfaction in that thought at the boy who had tried to deceive him.

Then he looked at the forlorn figure on the other side of the desk and said, 'Look, if you've now told us everything, and we find it tallies with what we find in that house, we'll do our best to keep you out of it. We can't prevent some crafty defence counsel from probing into exactly what you were about when you found that body, but he won't do that unless it helps his case, and at the moment I can't see how it would. I should think your university tutors are bound to find out about it, but you'll have to plead youth and stupidity – which shouldn't be difficult, for either of you daft sods – and throw yourselves on their mercy.'

He took Paul Barnes outside onto the landing, told an enormously relieved Gary Pilkington that he had no need to see him again, and sent the crestfallen pair upon their way. Not really a fair test of the Peach skills of interrogation, these students, he thought.

But it had filled in the time and made it clear what had happened last night. By now, the Scene of Crime team might have something to report from the house across the way. It was time to begin piecing together just what sort of a person this Dr George Andrew 'Claptrap' Carter had been.

Five

It was one of the best English autumn days. Peach stood on the steps of the high stone Victorian mansion, sniffed the air appreciatively, and surveyed the scene.

There were students streaming in various directions, concluding their morning lectures and making for the refectory or bars, bustling like ants about their business. The day was still, and a pale sun shone out of a muted blue sky, illuminating the amber and orange on the oaks and limes which had grown here for almost two centuries, making the eye aware of subtle shades which it would have missed on a duller day. This wasn't a bad place to be, especially when you had the delightful Lucy Blake at your side.

Peach looked at the masses of scurrying humanity and frowned. 'If this is murder, there are a thousand bloody suspects. Every bugger you can see out there had access to the Director's house!'

It was no more than the ritual protest of a professional about to embark upon a difficult task and DS Blake recognized it as such. She knew that she was merely responding in kind as she said, 'We'll prune the field down pretty quickly. You've already eliminated two of the students.'

They walked from the front of the house over to the massive canopy of the old cedar, then along the shaded path which Paul Barnes and Gary Pilkington had trodden during the darkness of the previous night. Even with the site busy with pedestrians moving in different directions, this was a quiet place, for the path led nowhere except to the Director's house, invisible beneath the trees until you reached the single lamp standard forty yards from its front elevation.

This was a very different building from the neo-Gothic stone mansion house at the centre of the estate, but impressive in its own way. The style owed something to the mock-Georgian fashion of the 1990s, but the size and the setting of the house, on a spacious plot among the trees, with no other building in view, gave it an elegance which was surprising in a brick building no more than ten years old.

The pale but steady November sun glinted on the rectangular windows and warmed the brick of the frontage to a surprisingly mellow hue. The police cars parked in front of the double garage were invisible from where the pair stood, and the isolated house seemed quiet, even deserted, as they gazed up at its broad frontage. Then, as they moved towards it, they caught a glimpse of figures moving behind the glass and were brought back abruptly to the real business of the day.

Jim Chadwick, the sergeant in charge of the mixture of police and civilians who made up the Scene of Crime team, greeted Peach with a professional pessimism which echoed that recently expressed by the inspector himself. 'Bloody great barracks of a place to search, this is!' he said gloomily. 'Some of us will be here for a couple of days, I should think, before we've got round this lot. Might help if we'd any idea what we're looking for!'

He didn't get any of Peach's normal acid in the reply. Percy had a lot of respect for Jim Chadwick, who had been a detective sergeant at the same time as him, a thief-taker with his eye just as firmly on the ball. Chadwick had been shot through the shoulder after a bank raid; could have taken a sick pension and retirement into some less demanding occupation; had opted instead to stay with the police service; had carved himself out this role as a scene-of-crime expert, when deprived of the more active career he would have preferred. He knew now that he would never progress beyond sergeant, but from all outward signs he bore no resentment of that fact.

Chadwick was a copper's man, not a PR merchant. He knew what coppers wanted from the place where crimes had taken place; he had a CID man's eye for details which might seem insignificant to others. It was Peach who had ensured that he was assigned to investigate the scenes of only the more serious crimes on the patch. That had never been stated, but both of them knew it.

Jim Chadwick looked carefully past them to make sure no higher rank was muscling in on what promised to be a high-profile crime. 'Jack the Lad didn't take kindly to being hauled out in the middle of the night. Binns the Blood has been this morning.'

'Jack the Lad' was the police surgeon, whom Chadwick, purely on the basis of his youth and bachelor status, suspected of being a local Lothario. It was not surprising if the young doctor was less than happy to be brought from a warm bed, whether his own or some anonymous lady's, to certify as dead a corpse which had plainly ceased to breathe at least twenty-four hours earlier, in which the first signs of rigor mortis were already apparent. But he knew as well as everyone else that this was one of the rituals which must be observed: the first essential was that the fact of death had to be established and confirmed by a doctor.

'Binns the Blood' was a different and far more important professional. Dr Mark Binns was the pathologist, who had visited the site whilst Peach was having his fun with the two students who had discovered the body. Binns had taken body temperature and anything else he thought significant at the house, and sanctioned the removal of the corpse for the more leisured and searching investigation of the post-mortem.

'The night porter saw bugger-all. Anything useful here?' said Peach. They spoke in shorthand, these two, the result of long years in the job.

'Binns confirmed it as murder,' said Chadwick gloomily. 'Lot of bloody use that is, as you'll see when you look at him.

40

Man would have had to be a contortionist to shoot himself from that angle.'

Peach saw what he meant as soon as they reached the main bedroom of the house. The corpse lay on its back, staring at the ceiling, but what was left of the head was slightly on one side, and they could see a ragged-edged but surprisingly regular bullet wound in the back of the it, just above the line of the collar, which had faint powder marks upon it. He said, as though completing the words of a ritual, 'No sign of the weapon, I suppose?'

'No. And sod-all else, so far.'

'Any ideas on how the bugger got in?' Automatically, Peach spoke of the killer as a man, because statistically it was overwhelmingly likely to be so. Their criminal would remain male, would continue in the argot of the service to be called words like 'chummy', until he had some more definite identity. It didn't mean that females wouldn't be considered as carefully as anyone else; it was simply a recognition of the statistical probabilities of the serious crime scene.

'There's a window forced at the back. Small one, in the utility room. Someone's prised away the frame where it was rotten at the bottom. Jemmy, or a big tyre lever, by the looks of it. It's the only window in the house that doesn't have modern double-glazing, as usual.' Chadwick's tone held in it his contempt for a public that was too often penny-pinching when it came to security.

Peach shook his head. 'That's the way those students got in. The ones who found the body.'

Chadwick brightened up a little. He didn't like students, thought most of them were a waste of public money, even if they didn't get grants any more. 'Don't suppose there's any chance those buggers did for him, is there? Resenting being slung off their courses, or getting lower grades than they should have? Or in a drug-crazed orgy of violence?'

Peach smiled. 'Afraid not, Jim. Dr Carter was cold and dead long before they found him, I think. It will be small

41

consolation to a fascist hyena like you, but the tale they told us at first was a right bucket of you-know-what. They found him a couple of hours before the time they claimed. And it wasn't because they saw any mysterious light in here. They were bent on a little petty pilfering. Well, not so petty, as a matter of fact. A set of valuable first editions. I think they got a hell of a shock when they found the late Dr Carter.'

He looked down at the corpse, with its single remaining eye like glass and the foot-wide pool beside the head, which had thickened until it looked more like crimson jelly than blood and brains. If those lads had really never seen a dead body before, it must have given them a hell of a shock when they came upon it in the darkness as they crept into the room. As a guardian of the law, he found that imagined picture very satisfying. That would teach the young Turks to go breaking and entering.

Chadwick nodded his agreement to a sentiment which had remained unvoiced. 'Did they say they found the window already forced when they got there?'

'No. They admitted to using a tyre lever on the bottom of the frame, where the wood was rotten.'

'In that case, your killer was probably known to the victim. There's no other sign of forced entry. Either he had a key or he was let in, probably by the deceased. Unless you think he came in whilst a door was open and simply waited a few hours for the chance to surprise the Director.'

The two men grinned at each other. They had the working policeman's contempt for such more unlikely possibilities, which they regarded as the material of crime fiction. Peach said, 'I expect that there are a lot of keys floating about, in a place like this. And probably a lot of people who might have had reason to be let into the house, as this is a college. Sorry, a university, as we must now call it!'

Another grin, in which the two old male sweats allowed Lucy Blake to join them. The locals had a scepticism about this grandiose label clapped on a college which even ten years ago had been 'Brunton Tech' and well down the academic hierarchy. Now it had this spacious greenfield site and undreamt-of new resources. And a rather smarmy new Director who appeared frequently on regional television news programmes; a Director who was now extremely dead.

Peach walked out on to the landing. Inured as he was to crime and death, he still found it a relief to be free of that sinister thing on the floor, with its accusation of violence as yet unpunished. He watched the photographer taking pictures of the stairs, noted the fingerprint girl industriously lifting prints from the grey powder on the banisters, and said tersely, 'Anything missing?'

Chadwick followed immediately the train of his thought. Had someone engaged in some form of burglary been surprised by the man who lay dead behind them? Someone who had killed him in panic? It was usually the first thing relatives thought of, perhaps as part of a reluctance to admit that the man they had known had any enemies among his intimates who hated him enough to kill him like this. He said, 'Nothing obviously missing. We shan't be sure until the wife gets back and goes round the place, of course. Where is she, by the way?'

'At her mother's. I've encouraged her to stay there for a couple of days, until you've gone through this place thoroughly. The porter's identification of the body will do for the moment; she can do the official one after the post-mortem, when he's been tidied up a bit. Her mother's place is up near Kendal; I'll go and see her up there, I think.' All three of them knew that spouses were always the first source of police interest in a sudden, violent death.

'Are there children?'

'Two. But they're eighteen and twenty. Old enough to be away at university themselves. I've told them not to come here. They're going to comfort their mother at their grandmother's house.'

Very soon now, as soon as Chadwick signified that his

body could be removed from the scene of crime, the mortal remains of George Andrew Carter would be placed in their fibreglass 'shell' and taken to the pathologist's laboratory in the 'meat van' which waited outside. Peach pushed open the door next to that of the bedroom where he lay.

This room was a small, neat study, its walls lined with bookshelves, its small desk without paper, pen or word-processor upon it. Over years of experience, CID men develop a 'feel' for empty rooms. Perhaps this one was used by some-one obsessively tidy, who insisted upon leaving everything neat. But DI Peach sensed that this was a room which had been little used.

He walked over to the single glass-fronted bookshelves, on the north side of the room, where the sun would never fall. He saw the gold-tooled titles of the Jane Austen novels which the students had been planning to appropriate. The rich leather spines of *Emma* and *Persuasion* and *Pride and Prejudice* seemed to carry more than their normal significance, after this ill-starred youthful enterprise.

When they went out again onto the landing, the two constables who were going through the house on hands and knees with tweezers had reached the area outside the room where the corpse lay. It was a necessary but time-consuming business, this gathering of any fibres, hairs or tiny pieces of detritus which might be of later significance in proving that a suspect had been here. Chadwick said, 'The refuse collection is on Fridays, so there's nothing outside the house. Just our luck. We've bagged what little rubbish there is inside. I haven't had the chance to look at it in detail yet, but I'm not hopeful.'

It was DS Lucy Blake, feeling herself a little shut out of this male colloquy, who said, 'I made a few discreet enquiries around the offices when I got here this morning. I gather Dr Carter wasn't at all popular with his academic staff.'

Six

B y two thirty on that November afternoon, when Percy Peach had forsaken the green pastures of the University of East Lancashire for the industrial centre of Brunton, the November sun had disappeared and the skies were full of low cloud.

An appropriate setting for a meeting with his chief, Superintendent Thomas Bulstrode Tucker, thought Peach, as he glanced up at the sky before disappearing through the portals of Brunton Police Station. He didn't like the man he called Tommy Bloody Tucker, who in his view was a pompous windbag, a hypocrite, an idle sod and a craven wimp. Apart from those things, Percy conceded, Tucker might be no more than dislikeable.

As the superintendent responsible for the CID section, Tucker was in charge of all murder investigations. It was his habit to claim the credit for all successful cases and to blame the incompetence of his staff for any failures. He would not stir from his desk throughout this case. Percy didn't mind that: it was par for the course with the modern police hierarchy, and even what the system suggested they should do. What he didn't like was the total incompetence of Tucker, so that he got neither support nor direction from the man who should have been giving him both.

Denis Charles Scott Peach, universally known to his colleagues and a considerable number of people in the nation's prisons as Percy, compensated himself by enjoying a certain amount of fun at his superior's expense. In a service which was highly conscious of the respect due to rank, this had earned Percy an almost legendary reputation. Percy rode his luck and taunted Tucker mercilessly, because he knew two things.

The first was that he himself had no promotion aspirations: he was perfectly content with the role of inspector, which kept him working at the crime-face rather than in the office culture of the police top brass. The second was that he knew that Tucker was totally dependent upon him for the successes he claimed in his CID section, and could thus not afford to do without him. Threats of transfer had been raised from time to time, but never implemented. Tucker and Peach were metaphorically joined at the hip, Percy said, with as much in common as Karl Marx and Margaret Thatcher.

He went up to Tucker's office on the top floor to report on events at the University of East Lancashire as soon as he had eaten a belated sausage and chips in the police canteen. Tucker looked at him accusingly over the half-moon glasses he wore at his desk. 'Couldn't find you this morning. Had to send you a memo!' he said accusingly.

Percy wondered whether to string him along for a while. He always enjoyed Tucker's feeble attempts at bollocking, but he hadn't a lot of time to waste. He said, 'No, sir. Had to go to court first thing, to deliver a statement. Told you on Friday, if you remember.'

'Did you? Well, perhaps you did, I suppose, if you say so. Anyway, it was inconvenient. Serious crime occurring, and you nowhere to be seen. It was urgent. I had to type the note myself.'

'Yes, sir. I thought you might have.'

Tucker looked at him suspiciously over the gold-rimmed half-moons, then glanced at the word-processor on the side of his desk which was his gesture towards modern technology. It had taken him ten minutes before he could get the thing to print out the three-line missive he had laboriously typed. But Peach surely couldn't have known that. 'Anyway,

I'm glad you got yourself belatedly out to the campus at the UEL.'

'Yes, sir. I was puzzled at first, but I knew you must have something serious in mind. Trust your leader, I told myself, whatever he says; he never lets you down. So I grabbed a toilet roll and went out there.'

'Toilet roll?' Tucker's long-suffering face showed what Percy considered an agreeable degree of bewilderment.

'I suppose it's some new kind of code, sir, to keep things confidential where necessary. Well, it had me fooled, for one! I took it quite literally, when I read it.' Peach cackled uproariously at his own expense, a noise which made his long-suffering superintendent cringe in anticipation.

'Code?'

'You really must explain it to me, sir. My dull old brain hasn't got the hang of it at all, I'm afraid.'

Tucker said between teeth that were beginning to clench, 'I have no idea what you're talking about, Peach. Explain yourself, please.'

Peach's expressive countenance managed to look both puzzled and pained. Then, moving in slow motion, he produced the Superintendent's carefully preserved note from the pocket of his jacket and handed it across the desk. Tucker had typed in capitals to emphasize the importance of his command: 'DIRECTOR OF THE NEW UNIVERSITY OF EAST LANCASHIRE HAS SHIT HIMSELF. TAKE APPROPRIATE ACTION AND GET OUT THERE IMMEDIATELY.'

Tucker read his message three times before his eye caught the error. He sighed heavily. '*Shot* himself, Peach. Shot himself! The meaning would have been obvious to a six-year-old child!'

'Didn't have one available, sir, at the time. Course I realized that was probably what you meant, when I got to the UEL. Felt a bit of a fool, though, brandishing my toilet roll, with the Director lying dead. Still, I showed them your note and explained the misunderstanding. The Bursar's staff and I had quite a laugh about it, in the end, so that was all right.' Peach smiled his satisfaction at the memory of his public-relations triumph.

'Right, Peach! You've had your fun, if that's what you think it is. Let's have your damned report!'

Temper, Tucker, temper, thought Peach. But even Percy recognized that he could go too far, when he saw his superior bristling with fury. 'Yes, sir. Of course, sir. Well, the first thing is that when I'd realized your typing error and explained it to the Bursar, you were still wrong.'

'Wrong?'

'Wrong, sir. Not only had the Director not shit himself. He hadn't even shot himself. Foul play, sir.'

'Not suicide?' Tucker's face fell. A high-profile murder was the last thing he needed, with staff off sick and Christmas already looming in his mind. Barbara would give him hell if he couldn't take his usual long break between Christmas and New Year.

'Definitely not suicide, sir. Man would have to have been a contortionist to do it himself, Jack Chadwick says. Don't expect that was one of the requirements laid down for a university leader.'

'Murder?'

'Oh, I should think so, sir. Socking great hole in the back of his head. Big pool of blood and brains on the carpet beside—'

'Don't give me all the detail, Peach. Just tell me who the hell did it!'

'Don't know, sir. Not yet.' Peach refused to be thrown off balance by the colossal effrontery of the man. He leaned forward confidentially, as if about to impart information of great importance. 'Matter of fact, sir, between the two of us, I haven't a clue. George Andrew Carter had been dead for at least twenty-four hours before we got there, the pathologist says. Found by two students, he was. Eventually.'

'Ah! Leading suspects, then.'

Peach nodded, pretending to weigh the idea. Then he said decisively, 'Already eliminated them from the inquiry, sir.'

'Oh!' Tucker's face fell, then assumed an expression of immense craft as he said, 'Well, you'll check their home backgrounds before you rule them out completely, if you take my advice. And see if they've run up any debts.'

Peach wondered quite how killing off their Director might be expected to solve a student debt problem. But he didn't care to probe further into the labyrinthine depths of Tucker's reasoning when there was work to be done. 'We could do them for breaking and entering, if we'd a mind to. And they've contaminated the site of a murder, plodding around the place. But they didn't kill Claptrap Carter.'

'Claptrap Carter! Peach, this is an academic of considerable standing. A scholar and a gentleman. You will remember that during your investigation. Is that clear?'

'Yes, sir. Member of the Lodge, was he?'

'That has nothing to do with it! I've told you before that Freemasonry – mine or anyone else's – has nothing to do with police work.'

A Mason then, the Director, thought Percy. No relevance to his death, in all probability, but a fact to be stored up against the possibility of further fun with Tucker. 'You don't think he might have had rivals for Master of his Lodge, sir? People who might have cared enough to kill him, to remove a powerful contender from the field?'

'I do not, Peach. Your melodramatic ravings about motive sometimes make me worry whether you're the right man for the job or not! If it's not those students you have so readily dismissed, consider the family. Three-quarters of murders are committed by people within the family, you know.' Tucker delivered his well-worn and slightly out-of-date statistic with satisfaction, then sat back further in his chair. 'You would do well to remember that.'

'Really, sir? Well, you'll be happy to hear I'm off to see the wife and family now, sir.'

'Get about it, then! Don't waste your time here, Peach. I'll hold the fort for you here!'

'Very good of you, sir. Tower of strength as usual.' Before Tucker could move it from where he had set it down on the desk in front of him, Peach picked up the memo about the late Director of the UEL's bowel trouble. Might be useful during some pub gathering of the CID section, that, to add to the folklore of their leader's gaffes. 'I'll get off right away, then.'

He didn't see any need to tell him that the wife was sixty miles away to the north, well out of the Brunton ambit of Tommy Bloody Tucker.

Most people didn't consider a chaplain a key appointment when they thought about the staffing of a new university. And the UEL was so new that its leader still hadn't changed his title yet from Director, which he had been in the old college of higher education, to Vice-Chancellor, which he was entitled to call himself, now that the new institution had been confirmed as a university. Nevertheless, the UEL had a chaplain.

Thomas Matthews wasn't a chaplain with an established chapel, like those in the older and larger universities. He had been grudgingly allotted a terrapin building on the edge of the campus, with an old industrial oil heater which seemed to give off more fumes than heat. He held services here twice a week and gave Communion on Thursdays. In the ecumenical spirit of the new century, he had encouraged his Roman Catholic, Methodist and Islamic fellows to come and use the building and minister to their flocks, but there had so far been little enthusiasm from either clergymen or students. Well, it was early days, yet.

And Thomas Matthews himself, although an official appointment, was only a part-time chaplain. He had a parish of his own, two miles away on the edge of the industrial town of Brunton; his meagre stipend there was considerably supplemented by his salary for two days a week at the new university.

Tuesday and Thursday were his official days. But the Reverend Matthews spent most of the Monday after the death of the Director on the UEL campus. He saw the entrances of Paul Barnes and Gary Pilkington into the Bursar's office on the first floor of the old mansion, as well as their discomfited exits. He wanted to speak to them, to offer them spiritual support, and to find just what they had been up to that they were of such interest to the police.

But neither of them was a regular attender at the distant wooden building with the distressingly small sign announcing 'University Chaplaincy' on its wall. And neither of them, despite their distress, showed any signs of seeking spiritual consolation when their ordeals had finished. The Reverend Matthews, DD, despite his anxiety to know just what was going on, had more sense than to invite a rebuff by approaching them.

Sometimes he envied the Romans their sacrament of confession.

In the afternoon, he secured himself a seat by a west-facing window on the first floor of the library. He could just see the garage of the Director's house from here, though the house itself was hidden in the trees. He watched the grey polystyrene 'shell' being taken from the police van and then returned with its grim contents, to be driven slowly away and off the site. He watched the various comings and goings of the Scene of Crime team, saw little groups of students collect around the path to the house, then melt away, as they realized they were going to discover nothing of the action within it.

At four o'clock, as the first rain began to fall from the now cloudy skies and the early November dusk moved towards darkness, the chaplain emerged from the library, turned up his collar, and strolled quickly along the path beneath the trees and past the Director's house. There were still two police cars in front of the double garage, and plastic tape on an improvised fence, cutting off access to the house itself and the area around it.

The Reverend Matthews took this in, but he did not stop, despite the cloak of near-darkness. He walked on, to his deserted wooden chaplaincy at the edge of the site. He climbed into his car and drove slowly home to his small modern vicarage, beside the tall, blackened stone church which was now much too big for its congregation.

He felt safe once he had shut the door of the vicarage behind him, here in his small, modern, private world. He went into his study and picked up the phone there. He exchanged terse greetings, then said, 'The police are still in there. There's every sign they'll be back tomorrow. I'm sure they won't find anything. But the best thing you can do is to keep well away.'

Seven

Peach enjoyed the drive to Kendal. The M6 north of Preston becomes ever more attractive as it runs towards Scotland. Most of the heavy traffic has turned off for Manchester, Liverpool and the numerous smaller industrial towns of north-west England: the horrendous reputation of the M6 for roadworks and traffic hold-ups is confined to the area between Birmingham and Preston.

Except for weekends, when holiday traffic pours towards the Lake District, the section which runs past Lancaster and towards the southern end of the Lakes is a pleasant drive. And all the more pleasant with Lucy Blake at your side, thought Percy contentedly. He wondered how long it would be before Tommy Bloody Tucker tumbled to what the rest of the station already knew: that Percy and Lucy were 'an item'. Probably the silly old sod wouldn't even have met the term yet, thought Percy Peach with satisfaction.

He eased the Scorpio up to eighty, the speed at which he reckoned he was safe from exciting the interest of the motorway traffic police, and slid his hand over Lucy's. A moment later, he gave her thigh an affectionate squeeze. 'Don't handle the goods in transit, please,' said Lucy. 'Keep both your hands on the wheel and both your brain cells on the matter in hand!'

Percy thought of saying that he would have concentrated completely on the matter in hand, if only she had allowed that hand free range. Instead, he sighed and said, 'Sound upset, did she, our Mrs Director?'

'I didn't speak to her. I spoke to her mother when I arranged our visit. *She* sounded very upset.'

Mothers-in-law weren't supposed to be upset by the death of their daughter's spouse, thought Percy. He was sure that the mother of the woman he had divorced seven years ago would greet his own death with unabashed glee. They drove past the turnings to Blackpool and then Morecambe, Lancashire holiday towns where the seaside-postcard legend of the mother-in-law, which was now so politically incorrect, had been fostered.

Percy favoured most things which were politically incorrect. But he liked Lucy's mum, a sprightly, cricket-loving lady of sixty-seven, the only woman he had ever met who had recognized that the man the police service universally knew as 'Percy' had actually been named after the late, great Denis Charles Scott Compton, the laughing cavalier of cricket. He almost missed his motorway exit through wondering if the feisty Agnes Blake might eventually become his mother-in-law: very dangerous ground, that.

The house they wanted was to the north of the pleasant old town of Kendal, almost in the Lake District National Park. They caught the impressive outline of the Langdale Pikes and the southern fells of Lakeland as the road climbed a knoll before dropping into a village in the shelter of the hill. The house was detached, not large but solid and foursquare, built of grey-blue Lakeland stone at the turn of the nineteenth century. The orange berries of pyracantha blazed bright against the wall by the front door.

They had rather expected the owner of the house to admit them, but the woman who opened the door before they could even touch the bell was no older than her mid-forties. She was tall and erect, with neatly cut ash-blonde hair and a turquoise lambswool sweater above a well-cut grey skirt. She held out a hand to each of them in turn, waved aside their identification cards, and said, 'I'm Ruth Carter. You want to see me, I believe. Please come inside.'

Lucy Blake caught a glimpse of an older woman, smiling wanly at them from beneath dishevelled hair from the doorway of a kitchen at the end of the hall, but Mrs Carter took them into a sitting room at the front of the house without introducing them to anyone else. She said by way of information, 'My mother now lives here on her own – my father died six years ago, only a year after they'd retired here from Manchester.'

Lucy said, 'I spoke to her on the phone. She sounded quite upset by what has happened. Not unnaturally.'

Ruth Carter nodded. 'George's death has hit her hard. She was very fond of him.' She paused, then added almost reluctantly, 'He was very good to her, in his own way, was George. It's natural she should be upset, as you say. I'd prefer it if you didn't speak to her, unless it's absolutely necessary.'

Peach said, 'I don't see why we should bother your mother. Not at this stage, anyway.' It implied a lot of things, that last phrase, to the attentive listener. Principal among them was the thought that if Ruth Carter cooperated as fully as she should, her mother could be left alone. 'This is just routine, Mrs Carter. As we didn't know your husband, we have to build up a picture of him for ourselves from those who lived their lives around him. Speed is important: that is why we have to intrude upon your grief so quickly. I apologize for that.'

'There is no need. I appreciate what you have to do. I wouldn't want to impede your work in any way.'

'That's very understanding of you. We shall be as brief as we can.'

He's less at his ease with middle-class women than with yobs most people would run a mile from, thought Lucy with amusement. If this wife had resisted, had given him something to bite on, he'd have been at her with his usual aggression, but he was fencing for an opening here, wondering how to get her on the back foot before he began the routine questions.

Or perhaps she was being a little too harsh on Percy: he could be surprisingly tender-hearted when he met real suffering, though he would never have admitted it. Perhaps he was treading carefully over a widow's pain. Except that to Lucy, Ruth Carter did not seem to be tortured with grief. Her oval face was white and strained, as you might have expected, with little or no make-up beneath the rather attractive waves of soft blonde hair. But she seemed perfectly composed as she invited them to sit on the sofa and then sat down opposite them in a heavy armchair; she was even calm enough to be watchful about her actions and her words, in Lucy's view. But even though she was only twenty-seven, Lucy had already seen enough to know that grief took many forms, that those who displayed it most obviously were not always those who felt it most deeply.

Ruth Carter said, 'You mentioned that you were part of a large team when you rang, DS Blake. Am I to assume that this is now a murder inquiry?'

It was Peach who answered her. 'Officially we must wait for the verdict of the Coroner's Court on that, Mrs Carter. But we believe it was murder, and we are proceeding on that assumption.'

'How did he die?'

She must surely have known. It had been included in the radio bulletins. And she would certainly have asked the WPC who came here to break the news at eight o'clock this morning for the details. 'He was shot through the back of the head at close range.'

'It couldn't have been suicide?'

'No. The angle of the shot rules that out, in my opinion and that of the doctors who examined him.' He was carefully neutral. Most people found suicide a worse fact than murder in someone close to them, but there were no absolutes in the awful stresses brought by a sudden death. 'I shall be able to tell you more about the type of firearm involved in a few days.'

'It wouldn't mean much to me. I know nothing about guns.'

'Your husband didn't possess one?'

'Not as far as I know.'

It was an answer which revealed rather more than she intended when she made it. If she genuinely didn't know whether or not her husband possessed a firearm, it meant at the very least that the two had some secrets from each other. Ruth Carter appeared to be careful in her replies, anxious not to give away more than she had to. But she might of course be merely numbed with shock by the suddenness of this death, feeling the first resentment at the stripping away of the layers of privacy which was now inevitable.

'Had he any interest or expertise in firearms?'

'None whatsoever.'

'And when did you last see him, Mrs Carter?'

The blue eyes narrowed a little, making the small lines around them more noticeable. But if she realized the question registered her as a suspect in this death, she gave no sign of it. 'When I left the house on Friday afternoon to drive up here. About two thirty, that would have been. Because George wasn't coming with me, I was able to get away early, so as to drive here in daylight and get ahead of the weekenders. The M6 north is always busy on a Friday evening with the second-homers. Even in November.'

Peach nodded. 'Would your husband normally have come with you?'

There was the faintest of hesitations before she replied, 'Yes, more often than not he would. He liked my mother, and she him.'

'And why didn't he come with you on this occasion?' She looked at him sharply, and he said evenly, 'We have to piece together what happened in the last hours of his life if we are to discover exactly how he was killed; you must see that.'

'He said he had too much work to do this weekend to get away.'

'And you believed him?'

'Yes.'

'Have you any idea what it was that detained him?'

'No. The UEL has only been operating for fifteen months. There is a constant accumulation of small problems. Many of them are minor administrative details. But they take time.'

She spoke as though repeating a formula, and they knew that she had used those words before, perhaps many times.

'How long were you married to him, Mrs Carter?'

'Twenty-three years. We met when we were students, married when I was twenty-two. He was two years older than me.'

'Please understand that I have to ask this, in the case of a violent death. How happy was your marriage at the time of his death?'

She had been picking off the routine questions swiftly and efficiently, as though ticking them off on a list of what she had expected. Now she looked angry for a moment, though she raised no objection to the question. There was an obvious effort of will as she said, 'It was as happy as most marriages, I suppose. We had our ups and downs, like everyone else.' It was the first cliché she had allowed herself, and a quick, unexpected flash of contempt burst into her sallow face, either at the thought itself or the lameness of her language.

Peach said, 'You can do better than that, I hope. Was there any serious trouble between you in these last few months? Did you have a quarrel before you left him on Friday?'

'No!' This time the denial came too quickly and too vehemently. Then Ruth Carter eased herself back a little into the armchair, forcing herself to take time. She looked like a woman who hated to display emotion, but whether this was habitual or a piece of caution applied to this particular situation they could not tell. She crossed her long legs for the first time, and Lucy Blake was surprised to see that they looked like those of a much younger woman.

Then she folded her arms, so that they could see the slim

wedding and engagement rings on the finger of her left hand, and said, 'Look, I understand why you have to ask these questions, but I can't be of much help. I can't compare our marriage with others, give it some sort of rating, because you don't know how other people are getting on unless they choose to tell you. We had been together twenty-three years, raised two children, and there was no question of a divorce. That should tell you something. We got on reasonably well – perhaps better than that.'

And perhaps much worse, thought Percy Peach. But you're not for telling us that. He said, 'Did your husband seem at all disturbed when you left him?'

'No. Perfectly normal. He went out of the house and back into college at two o'clock, saying that he'd see me on Monday. Things were exactly as usual, as far as I can recall.'

'Thank you. Now, another unwelcome question, probably. But obviously a necessary one, in these circumstances. We need to know of any enemies your husband may have had.'

She smiled, with a touch of real amusement. 'My husband had made his way through the academic rat race to a post many people would covet. You make enemies along the way, inevitably.'

'Serious enemies?'

'More serious than the people who think we live in ivory towers would ever credit, Inspector. People who think they have a grievance can be both extremely petty and extremely vicious, at times. But I don't know of anyone who might have nurtured enough resentment to shoot George through the head.'

Peach nodded. 'I may need to speak to you again, in due course. When we know rather more about the circumstances of this death.' He tried to make it sound a little like a threat, but he was no more successful than previously in breaking through the defences of this composed, rather impressive woman.

Lucy Blake looked up from the notes she had been taking and said quietly, 'You say you met as students.'

'Yes. We really got together when I was in my last year and George was doing an MA.'

'So you probably had an academic career of your own.'

It looked for a moment as if she would reject this line of enquiry. Then, perhaps accepting the question because it came from a woman, Ruth Carter said, 'I did, for a few years, yes. I had a better degree than George, as a matter of fact. Then I gave up serious academic work to raise my children. Most people still did that, you know, twenty years ago.' There was an edge of contempt, and perhaps too of regret for the years gone and the opportunities missed, as she looked at this serious-faced girl with the greenish eyes and the lustrous chestnut hair who was pursuing a career of her own.

The reaction didn't prevent DS Blake from persisting. 'So you haven't been teaching anywhere, these last few years?'

'I've done a couple of evenings of history teaching for the WEA for several years, now. I enjoy that. Adults who are keen to learn and stuff that's worth teaching!' Her sudden animation made them wonder how she estimated her husband's work and the steps he had taken to secure his elevated post. 'As a matter of fact, I've been wondering whether to go back into a full-time post in higher education.'

'Thank you. It may seem to be of no relevance to you at this stage, but we need the fullest possible picture of the household where a murder victim existed.'

Peach stood up. 'As I said, we shall probably need to see you again. If you think of anything which may help our investigation, however trivial, please get in touch with me immediately at Brunton CID section.'

'When can I return home, Inspector?'

He hesitated. 'It would be best if you could leave it until Wednesday morning, if that's possible. And – well, if you can arrange it, you should have someone with you when you go back there, I think.'

She gave them that small, composed smile which they now knew well. 'Thank you for thinking of that. I shall make appropriate arrangements.'

Peach would have given quite a lot to know what they might be.

As she took them out through the hall, the woman they had seen briefly in the doorway of the kitchen as they came into the house was waiting for them. Her face was stained with tears, her flying grey hair a contrast to her daughter's neatly arranged ash-blonde waves as she said, 'He was very good to me, was George. Good as my own son. Make sure you get whoever did this to him, won't you?'

Ruth Carter, a good half a foot taller than her mother, quickly put her arm round the trembling shoulders and led her firmly away. But the picture of that distraught elderly woman stayed in both their minds as they drove back to the motorway.

It was the only instance of raw, painful grief for the dead man they had seen so far.

Eight

The death of the Director of the UEL had surprisingly little immediate effect on the activities of the university. The sensational event was a source of intense speculation among the academic and other staff, but only a few found that their working day was much changed.

The students were affected even less by the passing of a figurehead who was necessarily quite remote from their everyday life and concerns. The teaching timetable went ahead as usual on the Monday when the news of the death broke. Despite a lively interest in the comings and goings of the police, only a few of their immediate contemporaries were even aware of the part that Paul Barnes and Gary Pilkington had played in the discovery of the corpse of Dr Claptrap Carter, their sometime Director.

There were many theories of how the great man had died, and some lurid rumours which were quite without foundation were circulating on the campus by the time that the day's teaching finished in late afternoon. But the death did not otherwise affect the lives of the students, who had their own concerns of lectures, tutorials, lab sessions and assignments to occupy them. It was difficult to feel much grief for a man you had never known apart from his rather risible public performances.

And when you are nineteen, there are more personal and pressing concerns. For Peter Tiler, these were principally concerned with his ongoing campaign to get a girl into bed. By half-past nine on the evening of the day when Carter's body was discovered, Peter was oblivious to every other concern.

It was supposed to be very easy, no more than par for the course for a university student. Girls were sexually liberated now, at ease with their hormones and as anxious to explore sexual experience as their male counterparts. Peter had heard about it, had even read about it, and could remember it quite clearly in print. He was a first-year maths student who had read a lot of print, and was still young enough to believe that all printed material carried the stamp of truth.

But none of the print had told him that acne did not disappear obediently with university entrance; nor that boys would outnumber girls by six to one in the Maths Department; nor that all the first-year girls would be appropriated by the second-year students in the first week, while he was still finding his feet as a fresher in the university. There were plenty of girls in other faculties, of course, but they all seemed to him articulate and highly sophisticated, with groups of friends who knew each other well. Peter Tiler was finding it difficult to break into the charmed circle of female companionship.

But he thought of himself as a logical man. So he considered his situation and worked out a plan. With the things he had stacked against him, the things the magazine and newspaper articles hadn't acknowledged, he needed some sort of artificial aid; something above and beyond his own personality. He tried a little pot, before he went to the disco on Friday night, to give him confidence. And it had worked: he'd found himself a girl.

Well, some people might have said that was putting it rather too strongly. But he'd found it much easier than previously to talk to girls, had been able to relax and chat with them as if he'd been doing it for years. And he'd eventually succeeded in detaching one from the group, a girl with bright eyes and dark hair who was studying medieval economic history. That was quite a mouthful, but Peter frankly didn't care what she was studying, so long as she took an interest in him.

And she appeared to do just that. She had agreed with only a little hesitation to see him again, this Monday night. Kathleen Stevens, she was called. Peter found that he repeated the name to himself constantly over the weekend. It had a pleasantly old-fashioned ring which for some reason he found reassuring. He was glad he had arranged to take her off the campus. He didn't fancy conducting the tentative moves towards copulation under the critical eyes of his peers.

He even had doubts about whether he should try for bed, on this first occasion. He wouldn't mind if it took several meetings, really: not if they got on well with each other. But if he didn't at least try, he'd probably be thought a wimp. Or even gay. The girl he'd been left with at the end of the Freshers' Reception, on his first day on the campus, had asked him if he was gay, presumably because he hadn't made any great physical moves towards her.

They were going to the cinema, in Brunton, to see *Billy Elliot*. Peter didn't know much about it, but Kathleen had said she'd like to see it, and he'd jumped at the chance to get her to himself and away from the campus.

Now, as he made himself ready to go, he found his confidence ebbing away. His red spots on his forehead looked worse than ever when he inspected them in the mirror over his washbasin. After he had shaved and showered, he put on liberal applications of deodorant and after-shave, but you couldn't disguise what people could see for themselves. It had been all right on Friday, in the darkness of the disco, but tonight Kathleen Stevens would see him as he really was. He wished they could be transported without sight of each other into the darkness of the cinema. But all he could do was pull the baseball cap he was planning to wear a little further down at the front.

At half-past six, he smoked a small joint of the pot he had found so helpful on Friday, then slipped the remaining spliffs of it with the tablets of Ecstasy into the pocket of his anorak. No going back now, he told himself. Over the top. Wasn't that what soldiers said, when they walked towards death? Silly expression, then. He grinned at himself as the pot surged through his veins. No going back now!

Kathleen Stevens wasn't quite as beautiful as his imagination had made her over a fevered weekend. Her face was a little larger and her eyes a little smaller than he had thought: the subdued lighting of the disco was kind to other people as well as to him.

But she smiled at him, and her face lit up from the anxiety it had shown when she thought he might not be there. She was very pretty when she smiled, he thought. And curiously, he found that he was pleased that she was not quite the stunning beauty he had envisaged. It made her easier to talk to. Perhaps, if all went well with the evening, easier to seduce.

They travelled together on the college bus that ran every half-hour into Brunton, and Peter realized that Kathleen was almost as shy as he was. She insisted on paying for herself at the cinema, pointing out that both of them were students. The film was good, but there were parts of it he hardly saw, because he was so preoccupied with his tactics towards the girl next to him. It was a pity it was so funny, because it was difficult to make progress with a girl who kept bursting into delighted laughter with the rest of the audience.

But he had his arm round her by the end of the film and she seemed quite contented, even submissive, as they walked hand in hand to the pub he had chosen afterwards. It was an old-fashioned pub, Edwardian he thought, and while it had been expensively modernized in recent years, the brewery had retained some of the original alcoves with single small tables down one of the walls. Peter installed Kathleen in one of these and bought her the glass of white wine she requested.

He lit up a thin joint as they sat with the drinks and offered it to Kathleen. She looked startled, took a single short puff and blew the smoke out quickly. She refused any further offers and watched Peter puffing enthusiastically, trying to encourage her by his nonchalant air. Eventually, she said quietly, 'I don't think you should do that, Peter.'

He stubbed the joint out in the ashtray: it was almost finished anyway. 'Your wish is my command!' he said, emboldened as he had hoped by the little intake of pot. He went without consulting Kathleen to get more drinks. While he was at the bar, he put the ground Ecstasy tablet into her second glass of white wine, keeping his body carefully between the bar and Kathleen, so that she would not see what he was about. It refused to dissolve, remaining fairly obviously a powder at the bottom of the glass.

Peter seized a cocktail stick from the bar and stirred the wine furiously. It would have been better if he could have got some of this new drug Rohypnol he had read about, which dissolved instantly and was undetectable, the one they used in date-rape cases. But he'd had no chance of getting that, had been lucky to get the six tablets of Ecstasy which the man had called Silver Dollars. And everyone said Ecstasy worked, that it got the girls going and removed all inhibitions. He gave the glass a last, furious stir, summoned his most confident smile, and turned back to the table with his half of bitter and the glass of white wine.

He had been so preoccupied with his plans and with keeping his movements secret from Kathleen Stevens that he had forgotten the need for any other sort of concealment. He had been completely unconscious of the man in nondescript blue jeans and sweater who watched him with interest from his position five yards to his left at the bar.

Even when he followed Peter across to the alcove with the drinks, it was Kathleen who noticed him first. Peter Tiler had still not registered his presence when the man said quietly to Kathleen, 'Don't drink any of that, love. There's no knowing what it might do to you.'

Peter turned in startled indignation, to find himself staring into cool brown eyes, above a thin line of a mouth and a stubbled chin. The mouth said calmly, 'I am arresting you on suspicion of possession of a Class A drug. You do not have to say anything, but it may harm your defence if you do not mention when questioned something which you later rely on in court. Anything you do say will be recorded and may be given in evidence.'

The mattress in the cell was thin, the bed beneath it hard as concrete. It was not at all the kind of night Peter Tiler had planned for himself.

The Scene of Crime team took a long time to search the site residence of Dr George Andrew Carter, and ended with an extensive collection of bagged and labelled articles from the five-bedroomed house of the Director. When you do not know what you are searching for, and almost anything may later prove significant, you have to take note of a huge range of items.

And the death of a high-ranking academic, like that of a high-ranking businessman, means that the place where he conducted his work is almost equally likely to provide clues to his demise. DI Percy Peach descended upon the Director's personal secretary 'like the wrath of God', as she later resentfully described it to her eagerly listening colleagues.

Peach, sizing up a woman whom he immediately saw as the Dragon at the Gate, was in no mood to be driven off: he drew his sword and charged. 'I need immediate access to all your files, all correspondence, and the diary you and Dr Carter kept of his weekly appointments,' he said.

Ms Angela Burns, forty-five, iron-grey of hair, eyes and manner, donned the mien which had terrified students and sent many a tutor retreating in confusion. 'I'm afraid that will not be possible. There is much material in the files which is highly confidential. There may be meetings noted in Dr Carter's letters and diary which are completely private matters and—'

'Good! It is the confidential and private material which is of most interest to us. So if you can assist us in pinpointing the key areas, you will be helping the police in the course of their enquiries – which of course you are only too anxious to do.' Peach's eyebrows arched interrogatively above his terrier smile.

'You really must understand, Inspector, that I can't—'

'No, Ms Burns, it is you who must understand. You must understand that you can't get in the way of a murder inquiry. We are given wide-ranging powers to go where we want and to see whom and what we think is appropriate.'

She folded her arms, trying desperately to summon a defence against this assault from a quarter she had never had to deal with before. She said icily, 'Do you have a search warrant, Inspector Peach?'

Percy beamed delightedly. 'I don't need one, Ms Burns. Not to search the Director's room; not to go through his files; not to read his correspondence; not to demand and receive the fullest cooperation from Dr Carter's personal secretary. Not a pleasant thing, murder, but it gets rid of a lot of red tape.'

Ms Burns's forehead furrowed like the ridges of a thunder cloud beneath the tightly disciplined grey hair. She wouldn't retreat. She wouldn't put up the white flag. She would never openly acknowledge that this bouncy little man from a world she had never encountered before had a victory. But she was an intelligent woman, and she sensed that further resistance would only lead to greater embarrassment. Defer with dignity, if you have to, was always her counsel to more junior members of the administrative staff.

She didn't often have to practise it herself, but this seemed like one of those rare occasions. She said stiffly, 'I shall of course give you whatever help I can, Inspector. I am as anxious as you are that whoever did this dreadful thing should be brought to justice.'

One of Peach's virtues was to be generous in victory. He rarely rubbed an opponent's nose in the dust, especially a nose as worthy as that of the admirably loyal Angela Burns. 'Thank you. I'm sure you are. And my detective constables know what to look for. They will cause you some inconvenience in going through the files, but no more than they have to. And they are strict respecters of confidentiality. Nothing we collect from here will become public knowledge, unless of course it has a bearing upon a later court case.' He ushered in the DCs, one male and one female, who had ten minutes before his arrival been brusquely dismissed by Ms Burns, and set them to work on the files with her as their knowledgeable assistant. Then he went through the outer office into the Director's room.

Claptrap Carter – Peach had already accepted his right to the epithet – had done himself well. This was a spacious room on the quiet side of the old mansion, with its 1840s stone-mullioned windows still intact. The view was over trees, with glimpses of clipped grass between and beyond them and not a building in sight. Oak and beech, still retaining most of their leaves, showed orange and yellow behind the more delicate tracery of silver birch; despite the frost of Sunday night, the leaves of two mature maples glowed brilliant crimson and amber within a few yards of the late Director's big curved desk.

There was nothing on the desk, and little of interest in its drawers, save for a large, red-backed appointments diary on which Peach spent most of his time. You could find out quite a lot about a man from a diary, even when it was merely a record of work scheduled and completed, rather than the more personal and intimate daily chronicle of feelings and reactions which police people always preferred. Even a record of meetings attended and interviews conducted could give a picture of a working existence, which for all they knew at this stage could be just as important as Carter's private life.

And there were odd snippets which were not concerned with the work of the UEL at all. Peach confirmed from the entry 'Lodge Ladies' Night' in Carter's neat, small hand that he was a Mason, and stored it away for future reference. He would have some fun with Tommy Bloody Tucker about his fellow Mason, with any luck. If they drew blanks elsewhere, they might even have to look into Claptrap's Masonic connections, eventually.

Peach made a note of those appointments which related to individual tutors rather than more general meetings of committees and working parties. He had picked up a list of staff from the Bursar's office, and he was able to identify the posts of various tutors on the list. Probably they all had some perfectly sound and perfectly innocent reason for seeing the late Director, but they would all have to be patiently checked out by members of his team.

The simple initials 'S.T.' occurred several times in the diary. Peach looked backwards over the year, as well as at the week ahead, and found no fewer than six recordings of these initials in the preceding three months, which included six weeks of the summer vacation. There was no one on his list of academic staff who matched the two initials.

He went back into the outer office, prepared to take his sword to the dragon once again, and found that the scaly fire-breather had become a pussy cat. Ms Burns was going through the correspondence file with the young woman DC at her side, explaining what the correspondence was about, searching hard for any mysterious elements in the letters Dr Carter had received and the replies she had typed. He smiled at the neat grey head and the younger, less disciplined brown one in such earnest conversation. Murder, the worst of crimes, had about it a charnel-house glamour; even people initially hostile to the inquiry often became quite excited by it, once they felt they had a part to play in unmasking a murderer.

Peach showed Ms Burns the diary, prepared for her to bridle at this interference with her late employer's personal working record. Instead, she asked if she could be of help with any queries. 'Can you tell me who "S.T." might be?' he asked. 'He or she occurs several times in here, but there doesn't seem to be any tutor or senior member of the administrative staff with those initials.'

She took the desk diary from him, flicked over the pages, scanning the entries he pointed out. She frowned a little, then her face cleared and she said, 'Of course! Those aren't a person's initials at all. "S.T." means Senior Tutor. The man you want is Walter Culpepper.'

Peach was deliberately noncommittal as he said casually, 'Friendly with Dr Carter, was he? They seem to have met each other fairly often.'

Ms Burns became suddenly very formal again. 'The Senior Tutor oversees all the student admissions to the university. It is inevitable that he and the Director will meet fairly frequently.'

Peach pretended to be more ignorant than he was, another tactic in which he was an expert. 'Important figure in the place, is he, the Senior Tutor?'

Angela Burns looked at the bland, questioning face suspiciously for a moment. 'The Senior Tutor is one of the key figures, especially in a new university like this, where we are not certain of the quality of intake we can expect in the different subject areas. He lives on the site and keeps a constant overview of the state of recruitment for the year ahead.'

'So he and Dr Carter saw quite a lot of each other.'

She picked her words as carefully as a politician. 'It was inevitable that in the course of their professional duties their paths would cross quite frequently. Essential, in fact, for the smooth running of the institution.'

Peach grinned. He was beginning to like the dragon, after all. He wished he had someone like her to look after his own interests back at the police station in Brunton. 'They didn't like each other, then.'

'I didn't say that.'

'You didn't have to. I somehow divined it. That's what comes of being a detective, I suppose. So Walter Culpepper and Dr Carter were at each other's throats most of the time, and lived on the site together. Makes you think, doesn't it, when you find one of them lying shot in his house?'

Ms Burns wasn't used to meeting men like this strange little inspector, who seemed to be so adept at spotting the things you had meant to conceal. He was teasing her now, as no one in the UEL would have had the temerity to do: she realized that, but she found to her surprise that she was rather enjoying it.

She found it hard to prevent the corners of her mouth from wrinkling upwards as she said, 'You'd better decide on that for yourself, Inspector. I'm sure you'll find Dr Culpepper more than a match for you.'

Nine

C armen Campbell stretched luxuriously in front of the full-length mirror, taking advantage of a facility she could never enjoy in her own tiny flat. She had bra and pants on now, after a leisurely shower. She ran a wide-toothed comb through her thick black hair and allowed herself to relish the beauty of her skin; it had that colour of rich milk chocolate which she revelled in and which men seemed to find so exciting.

She had not wasted her day off from the university: she would go back with her batteries refreshed, well prepared for the trials of the week to come. Strange how you could use such a lot of energy, could finish the afternoon exhausted, and yet feel regenerated. It depended on the activity, of course. A change is as good as a rest, they said in that part of Lancashire where she had now made her home. And this had certainly been a change: an afternoon in bed with your boyfriend was so very different from your normal working day that it was indeed as good as a holiday. An activity holiday, that would be.

Carmen enjoyed taking her time as she dressed; that was part of the luxury of the moment. She could hear the sounds of movement in the kitchen and sitting room downstairs. Keith was making her a meal. She thought fondly of his careful movements, of his face earnest with concentration as he studied the instructions on the packets and looked into the pans. Keith was as white as she was coffee-coloured, as English and careful as she was Caribbean and impulsive, and she liked that.

She liked the way his reserve broke down in bed, how he became wilder and louder than her, so that she and not he had eventually to control things. She smiled reminiscently as she sat on the edge of the bed and began to encase her long legs in jeans which would not obscure their shapeliness. She knew men found her exotic, though she felt herself quite ordinary, merely one high-spirited girl among many who had enjoyed the Barbadian beaches. Well, a little more intelligent than most of the others, she allowed. That was what had carried her across the seas and into a whole new range of challenges and problems.

She was almost dressed when Keith called urgently up the stairs, 'Come down quickly! There's going to be something about your place on the news.'

She slipped on her flat shoes, came lightly down the stairs, grinned at the vision of Keith in his pinafore, poised with wooden spoon in hand in front of the big television set in the corner of the room. He had called her when the news headlines were announced. They had to wait a few minutes for the item which had made him call so agitatedly up the stairs.

There were pictures of the UEL site from the air. After a generalized view of the campus, the camera zoomed in like a cinematic opening to an aerial view of the Director's Residence, tucked away in the sylvan privacy of this idyllic greenfield site, while the newsreader gave the bald facts that had so far been released about the sensational murder of the Director of the newly established University of East Lancashire.

Then there were more pictures from television cameras at ground level, showing the police cars around the house, following an unmarked van as it first entered the drive, then shortly afterwards drove away from the site, the unstated but strong implication being that it carried the murdered body of Dr George Andrew Carter inside it. Keith sat on the edge of his armchair and watched fascinated, whilst

Carmen Campbell stood motionless behind him, with her hands resting lightly on his shoulders.

They didn't say anything until they were sitting opposite each other at the table. Keith wanted to discuss this murder, feeling the excitement of the link, however indirect, between this vital girl who sat quietly eating his food and the sensational happenings forty miles away. He wondered how upset she was by this death. 'You knew him, didn't you?' he said tentatively.

'Not intimately I didn't, no.' She giggled a little at the *News of the World* meaning of that word, thinking of the tumbled sheets she had left upstairs when she had rushed down to see the television item. 'He appointed me, so I met him then. But he was far too exalted for me to have much contact after that. Bit of a charlatan, they say. Not much of an academic at all, but a great bullshitter. The students called him Claptrap Carter.'

'You don't usually get bumped off for being a bit pompous, though. A bullet through the head seems rather extreme, even for the most annoying bullshitter.' Keith worked in advertising and was something of an expert on bullshit.

'I expect there's more to it than that. There would be a lot more killings in educational institutions, if people took to shooting people for a bit of pretentious twittering.'

Keith wanted to speculate more about this particular death, but she stilled him when they had finished eating by a swift, valedictory smooch, and pointed out that she must catch her train back to Brunton. She rode the few miles to the small Cheshire station on the back of his motorbike, swaying expertly with every turn of the big Honda Fireblade, making him feel that even her necessary clutching of his waist was personal and sexy.

Carmen grinned at him as he took her helmet and stowed it in his pannier, bought herself an evening paper, leaned from the train window, and kissed him briefly but expertly, rolling her tongue around the inside of his teeth in a way which recalled past joys and promised future pleasures. She waved and smiled as the diesel pulled smoothly away, the bright glitter of her eyes still visible an instant after he had lost the movement of her dark hand. It was a moment which made Keith feel very special.

The Monday evening train was not crowded as it sped north; Carmen had a compartment to herself. She sat very still for a couple of minutes, reviewing the events of the last two days. Then she read the newspaper story of the murder of Claptrap Carter back in Lancashire. It added very little to the account they had watched on Keith's television set. It gave a few more details about the time of the discovery and carried one or two conventional reactions of shock from the staff and students of the institution. Everyone was baffled by this awful happening. No one had any clue as to a possible motive.

Carmen Campbell settled back into her seat and closed her eyes, swaying gently with the movement of the speeding train. She would be home within the hour. Her long weekend had been very satisfactory.

A steeply sloping roof, with just enough irregularity in the red tiles to suggest the age of the place. Clematis and climbing roses on either side of the front door, the last crimson roses still singing a brave November swansong against the mellow brick. A hedge of fuchsias behind the wall at the front of the house, flanking the wrought-iron gate. A building dating from the nineteenth century, when this place had been a stately home, with its own small village of workers on the estate. The Senior Tutor's cottage was a less impressive building than the Director's house, but it had a charm which that more modern building could never have aspired to.

Peach's first reaction to Walter Culpepper was that he was a perfect match for the building in which the accident of his career had placed him. He opened the door a fraction as they shut the gate behind them and his swift glance took in Peach from head to foot, then transferred itself to a slower and more appreciative survey of Lucy Blake. With his red face behind his thick glasses, his prominent ears, his receding hair, his mobile mouth, and the impish mischief in his watery blue eyes, he looked like a garden gnome upon whom you would not care to turn your back.

'You must be the fuzz.' He held out a bony hand to each of them in turn as Peach introduced them. 'Walter Culpepper. I prefer to get the name in early, in case people giggle. They do sometimes.' He threw a startling high-pitched laugh over his shoulder as he led them into a high-ceilinged sitting room and gestured towards an elegant chaise longue. 'The Culpeppers were big in the reign of Henry the Eighth. Too big, in certain areas. Thomas Culpepper was put to death in 1542 for bedding Catherine Howard, the fifth wife of Bluff King Hal. One "p" in those days, but then you didn't live long enough for the dreaded prostate, if you went about rogering queens.' He grinned a puckish grin, then glanced at his watch. 'You come most carefully upon your hour.'

Peach nodded. 'And something is almost certainly rotten in the state of Denmark, Dr Culpepper.'

The Senior Tutor's eyebrows lifted a fraction as his *Hamlet* allusion was returned to him. Flatfoots weren't supposed to be able to exchange literary references. That oaf Carter certainly hadn't been able to. This might be an opponent worthy of his steel. '"O cursed sprite, that ever I was born to set it right." Except that I'm not, am I, Inspector? That's your job.' He beamed his delight in the thought.

'That's true. With your able assistance, of course.'

'Of course! But not very able, I'm afraid. This is a new experience for me. Murder of roguish Director in the halls of academe at dead of night. Dorothy L. Sayers and all that. Not that the UEL has much in common with the ancient halls of Oxford, eh?' Again that unexpectedly high-pitched chuckle came across the room at them, emphasizing the preposterous nature of the comparison.

But rather than taking up the contrast, as Culpepper had hoped, Peach seized on a particular word. 'Roguish, Dr Culpepper? Am I to assume that you held a low opinion of your Director?'

The Senior Tutor looked to either side, as if checking that no one was eavesdropping in the empty house, then leaned forward confidentially. 'I had certainly no very high opinion of Carter. Claptrap Carter, the students called him, you know!' He clasped both hands across his thin knees for a moment, and laughed as heartily as any schoolboy at that welcome thought.

'You didn't like him.' Peach issued the words as a statement, not a question, but his eyes twinkled almost conspiratorially, encouraging this sixty-year-old juvenile towards further indiscretions.

'I thought he was a complete charlatan.' He turned his attention to Lucy Blake, who had begun to take notes with her small, gold-cased ball-pen. 'A wanker and a tosser, in police-speak.'

She smiled: the sprite's amusement was infectious. 'Charlatan will do, I think, for the moment.'

'I'm glad to hear it. This dumbing down which is everywhere around us hasn't spread to the CID, it seems. Unless you two aren't typical?'

It was an invitation to be indiscreet about their own environment, but he was disappointed. Peach said, 'You can probably help us a lot more than you think, Dr Culpepper. In Dr Carter, we have a murder victim we have never met; who can obviously not speak for himself about whatever enemies he may have had; who is yet dependent upon us to find his killers. We are dependent in turn upon the assistance of those who were closest to him as we try to build up a picture of the sort of man he was. People like you, who met him frequently in the course of their work.'

'In the course of my work, yes. Socially, no. I kept as

far away from Claptrap Carter as it was possible for a man to keep while still fulfilling the functions of a Senior Tutor.'

'Which are?'

Culpepper pursed his lips, looking for a succinct way to sum up his multiple functions. 'To oversee the intake of students. To arrange student interviews with a view to admission in the following October, as necessary. My role really dates from the days when we were a college of education – a teacher-training institution. It was then possible to maintain a clear picture of admissions in all areas, to see where we were short of students and where we had a superfluity, and could thus afford to be choosy. I have maintained that function in the new and enlarged institution. But it is now too big an area for one man to keep a detailed picture. The job will be divided and devolved among our new faculties, probably from next year.'

When he was serious, thought Peach, you got a glimpse of the fierce pride this man took in the efficiency with which he conducted his work, which Angela Burns had hinted at when he pressed her. The Senior Tutor slipped back into his mischievous mode as he said, 'I used to take the responsibility for maintaining certain academic standards among our student intake, but that function has passed, sadly. Now that every tinpot institution can call itself a university, it is obvious that the ones which find themselves at the bottom of the pile, like the UEL, will be scraping the bottom of the barrel, if you will allow such a profusion of metaphors.' His smooth, small red nose wrinkled in distaste, whether at the standard of student they admitted or at his own clumsy phrasing it was not clear.

'And you didn't always see eye to eye with your Director?'

The red face twisted again into a smile. 'You express it with a restraint I had not expected in a policeman. We hated each other's guts, to be frank. But we were locked together in our jobs, rather as people used to be trapped in unsuitable marriages. Divorce wasn't possible for us.'

'Surely one of you could have taken another job.'

'I suppose we could. You do right to remind me of the realities of the world outside this particular ivory tower, Inspector Peach. But we were the victims of our own success. Or rather of the expansion of higher education. I doubt whether I could have got another job with the same pay and stature. And I'm quite sure Claptrap Carter would have been laughed out of court if he'd tried for the vice-chancellorship of one of our existing universities. He was a little man, with a little mind, Inspector Peach.' He turned with a happy smile to the woman beside him with her notepad. 'You can record that, if you like.'

Peach was suddenly impatient with this intelligent elf who wished to dance his magic rings around them. He studied the animated, cheerful red face for a moment, then said quietly, 'It is the enemies of Dr Carter who are bound to be of interest to us at present, of course.'

Culpepper was delighted rather than abashed. 'Better to be an honest enemy than a hypocrite, Inspector Peach. I have already decided that neither of you is stupid. I deduce therefore that you have probably done a certain amount of research before you came here. In my view, you probably already know that there was no love lost between my late Director and me. So why dissimulate?'

Peach grinned back, his own face seeming for a moment to reflect the archness of this appealing imp with the quick and sinuous mind. 'I know that you were interviewed with Dr Carter for the directorship of the new university.'

Culpepper was careless of any personal danger in his delight that his surmise had been right. 'There you are, then! A motive leaps out at us. Academic jealousy: the defeated candidate bides his time, watches the movements of the hated victor from his privileged position on the site, then kills him when the opportunity arises. The superior candidate driven beyond endurance by his rejection! Because I was superior, Inspector. If you'd known Claptrap Carter, you'd appreciate that that isn't an extravagant claim!'

Peach was not smiling now. He said quietly, 'Why was he chosen, Dr Culpepper?'

It seemed for a moment as if the Senior Tutor would go off into some farrago of obscure complaint about the academic pygmy who had been Carter. But perhaps he caught some of Peach's sober realism, for he eventually said softly, 'He was appointed by well-meaning local councillors, in the main. It was before we had university status that he got the post. We were merging three institutions into a college of higher education. Carter was the head of what was numerically the biggest one – what had been no more than the local college of further education a few years earlier. I had taught in universities and was running our degree programme in what was then a teacher-training institution. Probably neither of us would have got the job in open competition against outsiders. Carter certainly wouldn't.'

Peach nodded. It fitted the facts he knew. Carter was a political appointment by councillors who knew him and had never had to arbitrate on matters of academic distinction. He was a small man who had been in the right place at the right time, and who had been carried upwards with the institution. He said, 'You're telling me that he was a Philistine appointed by Philistines.'

Culpepper was delighted with the phrase. 'Yes. They were out of their depth, and it wasn't all their fault. They should never have been called upon to make the appointment. But then I don't suppose many people foresaw this place being a university at the time they made it.'

Peach wondered how he could go on working for an institution which he obviously held in such contempt. But then he went on working for Tommy Bloody Tucker, didn't he? You kept your own bit of the sty as clean as you could, brought your own integrity to what you were doing. He fancied Walter

Culpepper might well be an able and conscientious tutor for the students he dealt with. He wouldn't have minded being taught by this appealing, quick-witted sprite of a man.

But if he cared so much for what he did and his old-fashioned notion of academic excellence, he might also be the man who had dealt with the leader he held in such contempt. Peach said, 'Had your recent disagreements with Dr Carter been more vehement than usual?'

Culpepper smiled, leaned forward. Peach was astounded to see that he regarded him as a sympathetic audience. 'You may well ask. We had a major row last week: it was over academic standards, as usual. He wanted to take students with the very minimum qualifications, in the areas where we were short: mainly the sciences and the social sciences, as usual. He wanted them to have unconditional acceptances, on the strength of two Es at A-level and without interview. I wanted us to be a little more selective, at least until later in the year, when we would have a clearer idea what our recruitment figures were. He gave his orders. I refused to take them. Said it would be over my dead body – you had to use a cliché, if you wanted Claptrap Carter to understand you. But in the end it was he who provided the dead body, wasn't it?' The Senior Tutor's high-pitched giggle showed that he thought that a highly satisfactory outcome.

Peach did not smile. 'He would have won, in the end, wouldn't he?'

Culpepper's mirth died abruptly. 'I suppose he would. "Standards" is a dirty word, in a world of blood and iron.'

'Dr Carter hardly strikes me as a Bismarck, but I agree.' Percy found he was absurdly pleased to have picked up the reference again, to be able to bandy words with this frolicsome Feste. If his father had not died suddenly when he was about to go to university, he might have had the benefit of minds like this. English or history, it would have been. He had long since ceased to regret the omission, but moments like this brought shafts of regret. He pulled himself roughly back to the matter in hand. 'Where were you on Saturday evening, Dr Culpepper?'

'That's when he died, then, is it? Well, I'm afraid I have the requisite alibi. I was up at my son's house, in Settle. It was my wife's birthday, you see, and they put on a little party for her.' He glanced automatically towards the baby grand piano at the side of the room, and they followed his gaze to a photograph in a silver frame, of a younger Culpepper with a surprisingly pretty wife smiling at his side, and four children between about eight and fourteen in front of them in a family group. As if he found such contemplation an indulgence, he said sharply. 'You can check it out with all of the parties concerned, if you like. I'm sure they'll bear me out.'

Peach smiled. 'I'm sure they will. What time did you return to the campus?'

The brow above the elfin face furrowed, for almost the first time in their exchanges. 'About half-past eleven, I think, or maybe a little earlier. It takes about an hour to drive back from Settle.'

'All right. Now, whatever your feelings about Dr Carter, I want you to treat this question seriously. Can you think of anyone who had reason to dislike him seriously?'

The smile was back on the elf. 'I like that, Inspector. I fear most people nowadays would have said "to seriously dislike him". Split the infinitive, you see. You didn't. And no, I can't think of anyone who might have killed young Claptrap. Not at this moment. But I assure you, I'll give it serious thought. However I felt about the fellow, I don't think people should be allowed to go bumping people off like that. Just as if we were in America.'

'Please do go on thinking. You live on the site and probably have a clearer idea than we do of who had access to the Director's house at that time.'

'Almost anyone, I'm afraid, in the darkness of a Saturday night. You'd be surprised how quiet the campus is then.'

Percy and Lucy were silent as they drove away. They were

easy enough with each other now not to fill silences which were better devoted to thinking. They were off the university site and driving back towards Brunton before Percy said, 'Interesting chap, that. Not the sort we normally have to deal with.'

There was another silence before Lucy Blake said thoughtfully, 'I had ample time to study Dr Walter Culpepper, while you two were playing your word games. Very bright, but a bit unbalanced, I thought. I wonder if he's unbalanced enough to have murdered his esteemed Director.'

Ten

Mrs Ruth Carter did not return to the Director's house until Wednesday morning, as Peach had suggested. She insisted on Tuesday that her children go back to their studies in their different universities, assuring them that she would be fine, that going to the house where their father had died would upset them far more than it would her. She would let them know when the body was released for a funeral: the police had warned her that there was no immediate prospect of that.

For the young man of twenty and the young woman of eighteen, it was a difficult situation: a father dead and removed to the mortuary from that huge house which did not belong to them, which they had scarcely occupied enough to call a home. The Carters had only moved in eighteen months ago, with their father's appointment to the Directorship of the new UEL, and they had been away for much of that time. They looked at their mother, saw her restored amazingly quickly to that composed, well-organized figure they knew so well, and decided that it was best to leave her to deal with the situation in her own efficient way. Both of them were secretly relieved to be able to get back to their own friends and their own student concerns. What had happened at the UEL was a nightmare, but it still seemed slightly remote from them.

For her part, Ruth Carter found on Tuesday night that for the first time in her life she was glad to see the back of her children. Mark and Samantha had never been as close to George as to her, and his own ruthless ambition and their developing adolescent concerns had driven them further apart in the last few years. She saw that they were shocked by the manner and suddenness of this death, rather than devastated by grief, and she was relieved for them.

But she breathed a long sigh of release as she saw them depart from her mother's house near Kendal. Very soon now, she would be away from here herself, and the need for her to dissimulate would be over.

On Wednesday morning, Ruth drove slowly south down the M6 in her Fiesta, composing herself for the next stage in this extraordinary drama. She was surprised how calm she felt, even as she turned from the B-road onto the familiar UEL campus. She had felt during the days in Kendal that everyone would be watching her at this moment, that she would be the centre of student and staff attention as she returned to the scene of her husband's murder.

But it was not like that. No one took any particular note of the bright red little car as she drove up the drive towards the old mansion. Even when she turned abruptly beneath the high trees with their autumn canopy and drove the brief distance to the Director's house, she was conscious of no curious eyes marking her return.

She had been told that there would be a policewoman here to greet her at her house. She was not sure whether that was a public-relations measure or a wish to see how she reacted on her return; Ruth knew that the spouse of a murder victim was always a subject of police interest until cleared of suspicion. But she had been at her mother's for the whole of the weekend, hadn't she? Surely that was the blandest and most impeccable of alibis, respectable to the point of being dull. So she had no need to feel embarrassed now.

The bright girl with the striking red-brown hair who reintroduced herself as Detective Sergeant Blake certainly seemed to have no suspicions. Her bright eyes, blue in the daylight on the doorstep as she greeted the returning widow, almost green when they sat in the more subdued light of the kitchen, seemed to carry only concern and sympathy, not scepticism. Though she had seen the girl with Inspector Peach less than two days previously, Ruth had not immediately recognized her. Well, that was all to the good, she decided: it would show a fitting degree of disorientation in the face of tragedy.

Lucy Blake did not press her about the depth of her grief. She noted that although Ruth Carter had assured them on Sunday that she would bring someone with her for the ordeal of re-entering this familiar house, she had felt strong enough to come alone. Lucy told her, almost apologetically, that there was a counsellor waiting to offer her services in the sitting room. 'People are often much more disturbed than they realize, in situations like yours,' she said. 'Delayed shock can be the worst kind to deal with.'

'I'm all right. I don't need counselling.' Ruth was trying to conceal her resentment that these strangers should be here, that even now she should be prevented from locking her doors on the outside world and exulting quietly in this death, feeling the strength and the freedom of her new situation.

Lucy Blake didn't argue with her. She nodded slowly. 'Is there anything you would like to tell me, before I go?'

'No. I've nothing to add to what I told your Detective Inspector Peach on Monday.' She paused, looking round the familiar kitchen, watching the steam rise from the mug of tea which Lucy had made for her, resenting even that small incursion into her territory by strangers. 'There's one thing I'd like to do, though. I'd like to walk round the house. With you beside me, if you have the time.'

They both knew what she meant. She wanted to see the place where her husband had died. And Lucy Blake was glad to have the chance to accompany her, to observe her reaction as she stood on the spot for the first time since that violent death. If it was the first time, of course; Lucy made the inevitable CID reservation about a woman whose self-assurance had already given her a certain amount of mystery, in a case they seemed no nearer to solving.

Ruth Carter offered her nothing she could pin down, nothing which could establish the woman as either the conventional stricken widow or the cold-hearted accomplice in murder. They climbed the stairs deliberately, then moved slowly round each of the five bedrooms and two bathrooms on the upper storey of the big modern house.

She let Ruth Carter decide the order of this progress, and they came to the main bedroom, the one where George Andrew Carter had been shot through the head less than four days earlier, last. The widow hesitated for no more than a fraction of a second on the threshold, then stepped into the big bedroom with its two rectangular windows and its large, neatly made bed.

The photographers had been able to photograph the body from all angles at their leisure, so there was no chalk outline of the position in which the corpse had lain, that evocative image so beloved of crime fiction. And once forensic had taken all the samples they needed, the floor had been cleansed of blood. There was no more than a damp, slightly discoloured patch on the carpet beyond the bed. But even that was evocative enough in its own way, for the active imagination, and Lucy studied her charge for any evidence of faintness or distress.

There was none. Mrs Carter walked slowly to the far side of the bed, looked without flinching at the spot where her husband had fallen, then gave a brief nod of her head. Without either of them speaking, the pair descended the stairs and went on a brief tour of the ground-floor rooms, ending with the sitting room where the counsellor waited patiently to offer her services.

DS Blake introduced them, then said she must be on her way. Ruth Carter waited until she heard the front door of the house close behind her and then said, 'I don't need counselling.'

The woman was a motherly blonde, perhaps ten years older

than her. 'A lot of people feel that, love. But we don't always see our own needs very clearly, in a situation like this.'

'I see mine quite clearly. I want to be on my own. I shall come to terms with what has happened in my own way.'

'There is no shame in feeling the need for a little support. It is a dreadful thing which has happened to you, one which most people never have to deal with. I'm not saying we can solve any problems. Not really: you'll have to do that yourself, by coming to terms with what has happened, as you say. But we can be a support. I know you have your own children, that they have been with you in the days since this happened. And you will have your own friends here. We never try to interfere with any of that. But sometimes someone from outside the situation, someone with experience, who has seen awful things before, can be of use to you, can provide the kind of support which—'

'I don't want your help.' They were sitting opposite each other, and Ruth looked for the first time into the blue, concerned eyes. 'I appreciate that you can be of help to some. Perhaps of great help, for all I know. What I do know is that you can't do anything for me.'

The woman rose, sensing the moment when it was no longer sensible to press. 'I'll leave my card on the mantel-piece. If you should change your mind, if you should feel that we can be of help in any way at all, please don't hesitate to call me. There's no shame in allowing yourself to call on others for a little support, you know, Mrs Carter.'

Ruth Carter, recognizing a sentiment the woman had plainly uttered many times, smiled into the concerned face and offered her hand again. 'I promise I'll call, the minute I feel you can help me. It's just that at this moment, I feel a pressing need to be on my own.'

The counsellor nodded, put on her coat, turned as she went down the drive to give a small valedictory wave to the calm figure standing so still in the doorway of the big house. Grief took people in different ways. It was part of her role not to make moral pronouncements. When she took a last look back at the house in the trees, the front door was shut.

The counsellor hurried along the path under the trees, back towards the main car park where she had left her car. She had gone no more than thirty yards when she glimpsed a rather gangly man coming the other way, his coat collar turned up against the November cold. It was in truth very mild, but the man certainly looked cold, with his nose reddening in the damp air. She sensed as she looked at him that he had been standing around here for some time.

Waiting for that policewoman to drive away? Waiting for her to leave? Waiting his moment until the woman in the house should be left on her own? He was a well-dressed, rather diffident figure. He did not look as he came abreast of her to be at all dangerous. But the widow should be left alone with her grief, as she had requested: the counsellor was jealous enough of her own role to feel that if Ruth Carter did not require her company, she could benefit from no one else's. She said, 'Excuse me, but were you going to the Director's house?'

He looked for a moment as though he would deny it. Then he must have sensed that she would know he could be going nowhere else, along this path. He said, 'I was, yes.'

'I'm afraid I have to tell you that Mrs Carter doesn't wish to be disturbed. She's had a bereavement. A particularly distressing one, I'm afraid. She's expressly asked to be left alone.'

The man hesitated, until she thought for a moment that he would turn and walk back with her. Then he said, 'I know all about that. Perhaps I should introduce myself.' He tugged rather self-consciously at the top of his coat, pulling it away from his neck to reveal a thin line of white dog collar beneath. 'I'm Tom Matthews, the University Chaplain. I know what's happened. And I know Mrs Carter. I – er, I feel I must offer my support at this time.'

She should have felt a little jealousy at his presumption that he could succeed where a professional counsellor had failed. Instead, she was sorry for him, sorry for a poor clergyman who felt that his supposed contact with the Almighty could enable him to offer comfort where it was not wanted. She said, 'I'm a counsellor, and she's just rejected my services. I don't know if Mrs Carter is a Christian, but I can't see you having a much better hearing than I had.'

The Reverend Thomas Matthews smiled – a professional smile, she felt. 'I *am* the appointed University Chaplain. It is my duty to offer whatever comfort I can, at a time like this. And I do know Mrs Carter, a little. I feel she will probably see me. At least I must try.'

He raised the end of his cap to her, in an old-fashioned farewell she found curiously touching. A nice man, this, going forward with fortitude to his inevitable dismissal. She hoped Mrs Carter would rebuff him gently. She rejected the temptation to wait for him, to witness his doorstep dismissal and then commiserate as they went away together. It was unworthy; in the unlikely event of his comfort being accepted where hers had been rejected, she should be pleased, not miffed. In a way, they were part of the same service.

Tom Matthews looked round as he went up the drive to the house to make sure that he was not observed. Ruth Carter must have been watching through one of the front windows, for the door opened silently as he arrived, and he passed smoothly into the interior of the house.

For just an instant, they were awkward with each other. Then he said, 'I thought they'd never go. I was getting quite cold, stamping my feet underneath those trees.'

She said tersely, 'The policewoman was all right. But then I had to get rid of the counsellor they had arranged for me.'

He nodded. 'I saw her. She tried to stop me coming in. Said you wouldn't want to see me.'

They burst out laughing together at the absurdity of that thought. Then she was in his arms, feeling his hands pressing urgently on the small of her back, searching for his lips with hers, until they fastened upon each other, tenderly at first, then with the urgency that had been building up since the weekend.

Eleven

The pigeon stared down speculatively at Detective Inspector Peach as he parked his car against the wall of the police station car park. Percy looked round at the rotting sycamore leaves, up at the low grey clouds of the dismal sky, and caught the bright bead of the pigeon's eye. 'Morning, Charlie,' he said. The pigeon regarded him speculatively for a moment, then raised each foot in turn, delivered a non-committal coo, and defecated slowly on top of the wall.

'Exactly!' said Peach. He sighed and went into the station.

He climbed the stairs gloomily, rehearsing his report on the state of play for Superintendent Tommy Bloody Tucker. 'Thought I'd just put you in the picture about the Carter case, sir.'

'Made an arrest yet, have you?' said Tucker brightly.

That's all I need on a miserable Wednesday morning, thought Percy. Tucker in his martinet mood, trying hard to be brisk and unforgiving, like a proper superintendent. 'Bit of a puzzler, sir, this one is.'

'That's Peachspeak for no progress, isn't it? Oh, I've worked with you long enough to know you pretty well now, Percy,' said Tucker jovially, rather pleased with himself.

Use of first name: always a danger signal, Percy reminded himself. 'Wide range of acquaintances Claptrap Carter had, sir.'

'No excuse for backsliding. Lots of crime victims have a wide circle of acquaintances, you know. And I'd rather you didn't call the victim Claptrap. It might slip out in public.'

'Claptrap Carter, sir,' said Peach, ruminatively and unrepentantly. 'Everyone seems to have called him that. Freemason, you know, sir.' He announced the victim's membership of the brotherhood as if it immediately explained the nickname.

'Yes, I do. And I can't see how that it has anything to do with the case. You have a phobia about the Masons, Peach.'

'Yes, sir. No Masonic connections to be investigated, then. That will certainly cut down on the work for the team. It seems a bit sweeping, but if you're confident we can safely ignore all the Masons in the area, I'll announce it at tomorrow morning's briefing for the team. I dare say it will raise a few eyebrows, especially when it gets out to the press, but if those are your orders—'

'Those are *not* my orders, Peach! We have to keep an open mind on this. However unlikely it may seem, you should not rule all Masonic people out of suspicion. Though scarcely any Masons are in fact convicted of crimes, we must show that we—'

'Almost eight per cent, sir, last year, on our patch.' Peach produced the statistic while gazing sphinx-like at the ceiling. The day was improving already.

Tucker glared. Ineffectively. You couldn't get in a good glare on a man who was staring at the ceiling. 'What do you mean, eight per cent?'

'Eight per cent of male criminal offences in the Brunton area were committed by Masons, sir. Little bit of research of my own, that. I thought you might be interested.'

'But how can you know that when – when—'

'When it's a secret society, sir? Oh, but as you have told me so frequently, the secrecy is no longer important. And you're right, sir, in a way. As you always are. I found when I asked around I could soon find who the Masons were. Some of the hard men even seemed to think it would help them, to declare their Masonic connections. It didn't, of course.'

Tucker glared again, so fiercely that it hurt his eyes. It was worse than useless: that round moon face was now angled at forty-five degrees towards the ceiling. 'That is no doubt what the national proportion should be, considering the number of Freemasons in the country.'

He's fed me just the line I needed again; you couldn't have a better straight man than Thomas Bulstrode Tucker, thought Peach. He transferred his gaze from the ceiling to his chief's face and gave him the most dazzling of his smiles. 'Not so, sir, actually. At the latest count, the number of Masons in the country is well under two per cent. Which gives us an interesting local statistic. In the Brunton area at least, it seems that a man is four times more likely to commit a crime if he is a Mason.'

Tucker's jaw dropped. 'Four times more likely?'

'That's it, sir. Interesting, don't you think? I thought that when I can find the time I might produce a little monograph on the subject. Just like Sherlock Holmes used to do.'

'Sherlock Holmes?'

'Fictional detective, sir. Bit of an old junkie, too. We'd have him for it, nowadays.'

'I'm well aware who Sherlock Holmes was, thank you, Peach.'

'Yes, sir. Well, as I say, we'd have pulled him in for Class A drug possession, today.' He grinned conspiratorially as another delicious thought possessed him. 'I wonder if he'd have been a Mason, today, sir. He had a bit of a fascination with secret societies, and Dr Watson certainly strikes me as a potential member of the Brotherhood. It's—'

'Peach! Will you stop this nonsense and brief me about your progress!'

'Of course, sir. Well, as I say, I haven't actually begun to write the monograph about the local connections between Freemasonry and crime yet, but I've got the statistics all ready. And Alf Houldsworth says the *Evening Dispatch* would be interested, and possibly the nationals, and—'

'You will not release any such material!' The mention of Alf Houldsworth, the mischievous one-eyed crime reporter of the local daily, made Tucker tremble with apprehension and fury. 'You will come to me before you propagate any such nonsense. I shall check whether it is genuine.'

'Yes, sir. I'll make a note of that, and communicate it to the lads downstairs. All nonsense must be checked as genuine by Superintendent Tucker before general release. I've got that.' He stared at Tucker's desk, furrowed his brow, and nodded very seriously, as though each movement of his head was driving the announcement into his memory.

Tucker knew from experience that he should cut his losses and abandon this, before things got even more surreal. But he felt he must make at least a token defence of local Freemasonry. 'I expect you were including motoring offences in your statistics.'

'Yes, sir. And fraud.' He wasn't going to tell Tucker that a local accountant, convicted of eight offences, had upped his local Masonic count dramatically. 'And wife-beating. There was quite a bit of domestic violence, as far as I can remember.' Peach's round face brightened cherubically on that thought. A vision of Tucker's Brünnhilde of a wife with a whip floated beguilingly across his mind.

'Right. Back to business, Peach. Are you near to an arrest in the case of Dr Carter?'

'No, sir. Enquiries are proceeding apace. No prospect of an immediate arrest.'

'If you spent more time on real crime, and less on your fantasies about Freemasonry, we might have better results.'

'Claptrap Carter was a Mason, sir,' said Peach enigmatically. He was now staring hard at his favourite spot, which was precisely two inches above Tucker's head.

'Have you interviewed his wife?'

'Yes, sir. She doesn't seem stricken with grief. Doesn't

seem to have been particularly close to her husband, for someone married for over twenty years.'

Tucker's eyes lit up. 'Then in my view you should investigate her very closely. Three-quarters of killings are domestic, you know.' He produced the statistic which every policeman knew with a flourish, as he was wont to do, although he wavered between three-quarters and four-fifths as his chosen proportion.

'Yes, sir. The killing took place some time on Saturday night, as you will remember. Mrs Carter seems to have been safely ensconced at her mother's in Kendal for the whole of the weekend.' Peach stared obsessively at that spot on the wall behind his chief, inscrutable as a statue.

'I see. Well, just be certain she's not lying, that's all. Anyone else in the frame?'

'Senior Tutor at the UEL, sir. Chap by the name of Culpepper. His ancestor rogered Catherine Howard, he says. Fifth wife of Henry the Eighth, sir. Executed for it, apparently. Proper bit of lese-majesty, that.' Pity there wasn't more of that sort of thing in the police hierarchy, thought Percy. Be a brave man who rogered Barbara Tucker, though.

'Why suspect this fellow?'

'Didn't like Carter, sir. They were rivals for the Directorship, eighteen months ago, and he lost out. He certainly hadn't any high opinion of Claptrap Carter's intellectual capacity. And he admitted he hated his guts. That's a quotation, sir,' Peach said apologetically.

'Really. Well, he's certainly a candidate for your killer.'

'Yes, sir. He's not a Mason, though.' Peach said it dolefully, as if this considerably reduced the chances of Culpepper being their man.

'Peach, will you please rid yourself of this obsession with Freemasonry and get on with your work! You've wasted quite enough of my time.'

And you of mine, thought Peach as he went back down the stairs. He glanced through the window. There was a gleam of watery sun among the clouds now. The day was a little brighter than when he had climbed those stairs.

Peter Tiler had never spent such a miserable couple of days as the ones following his arrest after he had tried to dissolve Ecstasy in Kathleen Stevens's drink. A night in the cells, a harsh grilling, a grudging release, with the certain knowledge that he would hear the details of the court hearing on the charges of possession and attempted date-rape in due course.

When he got back to the site, his worst fears were realized. Kathleen had already been notified that she would be required as a witness in the eventual court case. He realized now, when it was too late, that she was as naïve and inexperienced about sex as he was. And consequently outraged by what he had attempted. And a practising and devout Roman Catholic, one of the few who did not seem to have rebelled against the moral straitjacket of the nuns. Just his luck.

Kathleen refused to listen to his explanations, forbade him ever to come near her again, and retired tearfully to her room with her rosary.

On Tuesday, Peter had endured an excruciating interview with his course tutor and been told that his academic future hung in the balance. Now, on Wednesday morning, just when it seemed that things could not get worse, he heard that there were two CID people on the campus again, talking to Kathleen Stevens.

At eleven forty-five, Peter Tiler was summoned to an interview with a Detective Inspector Peach.

Peter had never met anyone quite like DI Peach. Within two minutes, he had decided that he never wished to do so again. Peach for his part saw with his experienced eye a foolish young man, in whom there was no really vicious streak, who had strayed onto paths where he should never have trod. But Peach hadn't a lot of time to waste; it was only the fact that Tiler was a UEL student that had brought the affair to his notice, and he didn't want to spend many minutes on what might well lead only to a dead end, as far as his murder case was concerned.

'Date-rape, eh? Nasty business, that. Very politically incorrect. They'll throw the book at you for it, I shouldn't wonder.'

Tiler said wretchedly, 'It wasn't rape.'

'Only because an officer of the law prevented it. Nipped in before you could actually get your todger on the job, it seems. Drugs involved, too. Nasty business.' Peach repeated one of his favourite phrases and shook his head sadly.

'Only pot. And one tablet of Ecstasy. And I'd never have raped Kathleen Stevens,' said Peter, doggedly but hopelessly.

Lucy Blake, who had studied the wretched youth silently from her position beside Peach, said softly, 'Where did you get the drugs from, Peter?'

It was the first police voice Tiler had heard since his nightmare began which seemed even vaguely sympathetic. He knew he should be cautious, but his whole being wanted to respond to it. 'On the site. There's a bloke who comes to the student bar on Wednesday evenings.'

'A student?'

'No, I don't think so. I've never seen him any other time.'

Lucy leaned forward, waited for the hunted eyes to look up into her own ultramarine irises. 'Listen, Peter. You're in trouble, as DI Peach has told you. But it might not be as bad as it seems at this moment, if things go well for you. It appears that Kathleen Stevens is not anxious to pursue any charges against you. I'm not sure I'd feel so charitable, in her position, but it seems she just doesn't wish to drag the two of you through the courts. That still leaves the drugs. We don't do deals with people in your position. But if you cooperate, and we're able to arrest a supplier, it's possible you won't be charged with possession. No promises, mind:

that won't be my decision, or even DI Peach's. I'm simply advising you about the best course of action.'

She was serious, low-key, yet urgent. If her voice carried conviction, it was because her concern was genuine. Peter Tiler was immature and foolish, not vicious: she had no wish to see his whole life blighted by a criminal record for Class A drugs possession.

Tiler looked from the unrelenting face of Peach to this prettier and more sympathetic one, and then gave them everything he could. Description of the campus supplier, the range of drugs he offered, and the exact time when he dealt. Peter didn't know much, but by the time they left him to reel back to his room they had all of it.

It was all concluded swiftly and efficiently, the way Percy Peach liked it. He said as the CID pair lunched in a pub, 'You were good in there, kid. Putty in your hands, that lad was.'

Lucy Blake sank her strong, very white teeth into a ham roll and munched appreciatively. 'You'd set him up. The lad was at the end of his emotional tether. Ready to grasp at any comfort.'

Peach pulled at his pint of bitter, wiped his moustache carefully with his paper napkin. 'Maybe. I wish they were all as easy as that. But we're a good team, you and I. And Tommy Bloody Tucker still doesn't realize it. He thinks I resent you.' He slid his hand over hers for a moment to emphasize the absurdity of that delightful misapprehension.

'I didn't notice much resentment last night!'

Percy was silent for a moment, savouring the vision of the buxom Blake in the shortest nightie he had ever seen. 'You led me on, with that garment. Shouldn't be paraded before active male hormones without a health warning, nighties like that!'

She arched her eyebrows in surprise. 'Winceyette, that was. For winter warmth, the box said.'

Peach laughed. 'Can't provide much warmth when it's round your neck for most of the night.'

Lucy finished her roll, sipped at the pure orange juice which was all she allowed herself during the working day. 'Perhaps I should put the garment away. Perhaps it's dangerous to inflame the thinning blood of an older man.' Peach was ten years older than her twenty-six.

'Don't do that, love, please! I'll do press-ups, control my blood pressure, even go to the gym, if I must. But please don't withdraw the fanny pelmet from circulation!'

'We shall see,' she said contentedly. It was nice that a man who was so much in control in his work should be content to be so much under her spell away from it.

Twelve

C armen Campbell sat on the table at the front of the room, pushed her hands beneath her thighs, and said, 'So what do we make of all this?'

She had the complete attention of all twelve students in her tutorial group. She was an excellent teacher, well prepared, lively and with that enthusiasm for her subject which always communicated itself to an audience. She was also very supple and very curvaceous; she had extraordinarily long legs within her tight jeans; she had well-formed breasts which asserted themselves explicitly beneath her charcoal sweater; she had large brown eyes set above the high cheekbones of her smooth, chocolate-coloured face.

And nine of the students in this tutorial group were wide-eyed young males. Carmen Campbell could have talked in a monotone in Serbo-Croat and kept their attention.

Instead, she spoke in excellent English, with an attractive hint of Caribbean sun in the accent. Her subject was social psychology. She had just showed the group a videotape demonstrating how people's actions were conditioned by group expectations. A series of otherwise reasonable people who supported Manchester United had ignored a figure in distress at the roadside with a supposedly broken ankle when he wore a Liverpool shirt. Then they had offered instant assistance to the same man in the same situation when he wore a Manchester United shirt.

Students and tutor had a lively discussion about group pressures and inclinations, which were all the more sinister because they were unconscious, and Carmen invited the group to speculate about the implications of this for the situations they met in their own lives.

Some interesting exchanges ensued, with much hilarity as the students raised several group situations they met regularly on the campus of the UEL.

The time flew by, until Carmen experienced that most flattering thing for tutors, a look of disappointment on some faces when the time came for the session to end. The girls thanked her for the material; the boys gave her that special, guarded smile reserved for women who feature in their erotic fantasies in the small hours. Once they had gone, Carmen gathered her books and her tape and prepared to vacate the tutorial room.

She was approaching the door when it opened abruptly. A compact, dapper man stood before her, looking her up and down without any of the embarrassment she associated with males at a first meeting. He had a very bald head, a little startling above a face still in its thirties, a fringe of very black hair and an equally black moustache. He said, 'Miss Carmen Campbell? I'm Detective Inspector Peach and this is Detective Sergeant Blake.'

They came forward, showing her their identification cards. She had not seen the girl at first: she was as tall as her superior officer, with milk-white skin and striking hair, almost Titian as it caught the low November sun through the window. They did not offer to shake hands. Peach said, 'We need a few words with you, to clear up one or two loose ends.'

'That's all right. I've finished my teaching commitments for the day now.' She flashed him a smile from her wide mouth and her very white teeth. Her large brown eyes expressed a slight, unspoken surprise.

'It's in connection with the death of your Director, Dr Carter.'

They watched for her reaction, but she gave them nothing more than a polite, slightly surprised nod. Carmen had dealt with police before. They were the same the world over, in some respects: they would go for any sign of weakness, take up any strand of information you inadvertently offered them. It was best to let them make their own running, until you found out how much they knew.

When they got nothing from her, it was Lucy Blake who said softly, 'That doesn't surprise you, Miss Campbell?'

'Please feel free to call me Carmen. Even the students do that. And no, I don't suppose it does surprise me, really. Old Claptrap was murdered, wasn't he, poor guy? I expect you're questioning almost everyone on the campus. Among the academic staff anyway. Though I've no idea how these things work, of course.'

She gave them that wide smile, with a hint of mockery at its edges, and Peach acknowledged it with a grimmer smile of his own. 'We often have to talk to a lot of people in the days after a murder, yes, unless it's what we call a domestic. But we narrow it down pretty quickly, as a rule.'

Carmen did a swift calculation. Wednesday afternoon. Almost four days now, since the murder. Was she one of the many in the blanket early coverage, or one of the select few left after the field had been narrowed down? She said, 'I'm willing to offer any you any assistance I can, of course. But I can't really see how I can possibly be of any help to you.'

She hadn't asked them to sit down, preferring to imply that this exchange would be no more than a brief formality. But Peach now nodded to the single chair beside the overhead projector at the front of the lecture room, while he and Blake sat down on the chairs recently vacated by the two male students who had sat nearest to their coffee-coloured Aphrodite. 'We have been going through all the papers of Dr Carter. Things we gathered from both his house and his desk and files at work.'

Carmen hoped that the quickening of her pulse didn't show in anything external. Her work had made her something of an expert in the signs people gave in different group situations, but it was different when you were the person in the spotlight. And she had never been able to study people involved in a murder investigation. She said as nonchalantly as she could, 'And you came up with my name, somewhere among this mass of material?'

'Not exactly. We came up with the initials "C.C.". Several times. We thought it might be you.'

Her brain was working fast, very fast, but she felt refreshingly cool. However much they knew, they couldn't pin anything serious upon her. 'I suppose it could be me. But without knowing the context, I can't be sure, can I?'

Peach smiled. He would reveal that context in his own time, not hers. Keep them on the back foot whenever you could was his motto, whether they were GBH men with tattoos all over their arms or voluptuous academics with skins as smooth as milk chocolate. 'We found those initials in several places, Miss Campbell. In some instances, they had a time after them, which suggested meetings. Are you indeed the "C.C." we are seeking?'

She felt as though they were encircling her, quietly cutting off her means of escape. If they trapped her in a lie, things could only get worse. She smiled, lapsing into an American idiom which seemed more informal. 'I guess I might be. I did have some meetings with Claptrap Carter.'

Peach's eyes had not left her face for a full two minutes now. He nodded. 'Details, please.'

'Well, I saw him at my job interview, when he and others appointed me.'

'Of course. We've already discounted that. The Director's personal secretary, Miss Burns, helped us eliminate many such dates.'

So they'd had old Tindrawers Burns helping them. The thought shook Carmen a little. She should have expected it, but somehow she hadn't expected the icy front of Miss Burns to be scaled so easily, even by the police. She fenced for a little longer, trying to buy herself time to think. 'Yes. Well, it's difficult for me to remember what the others might be, when I don't have the dates.'

Peach nodded at Lucy Blake, who already had her notebook open. 'How about the eighth of July? Or the sixteenth of September? If it helps to jog your memory, both of those are Saturdays, Carmen.'

She noticed that the girl had taken up the invitation to use her first name, whereas Peach had ignored it. The old hard cop/soft cop routine. But it seemed to come naturally to this hard-as-nails little bundle of muscle and this well-formed, well-organized girl with the peaches-and-cream skin. Carmen wondered how much they already knew, how much they were trying to lead her into a string of lies she might regret. Honesty was definitely the best policy, until you were absolutely forced to lie. She sighed, gave them a quick, nervous smile of concession, and said, 'All right. I was hoping you wouldn't dig it out, but I suppose I should have expected it, once George was murdered. We had a thing going, the two of us. Oh, I know—'

'What kind of a thing, Miss Campbell? You will understand that it is necessary for us to be quite clear about this.' Peach's voice cut through her embarrassment like a knife.

She was shaken for a moment. Then she shrugged and said ruefully, 'I shouldn't have thought I could get away with it. It was a bit cheap, calling him Claptrap, wasn't it, when I knew him as George?' She gave them a sheepish smile, which Lucy Blake thought almost as winning as her welcoming one. 'The students and a lot of the staff called him that, and I suppose I thought I could distance myself from this, by calling him that.'

'Distance yourself from what, Miss Campbell?' Peach was unsmiling, insistent, observant. She was beginning to find his scrutiny unnerving.

'From – from all this.' She lifted her arms and held them wide apart, then let them drop back to her sides. 'From the murder investigation. From the murder itself, perhaps. It was pretty unnerving to find that a man I'd been to bed with had been killed like that.'

'I see. So you were planning to conceal your relationship with Dr Carter from us, to save yourself from being implicated.'

'No! To save myself from embarrassment. To save myself from having my private life paraded before staff and students! You can imagine how some of my colleagues would have enjoyed gossip like that!'

'So you decided that you would lie to the police investigating a violent death. Not the best way of avoiding embarrassment, as you may eventually discover. More important than that, it makes us wonder what else people might have been concealing when we find that they have lied to us.'

Those remarkable brown eyes seemed bigger and wider than ever as she glared indignantly at him. 'There was nothing else. Look, when you come from the kind of background I've had, your natural instinct is to distrust the police, to withhold whatever you can about yourself from them!'

Indignation sat well upon her, making her more striking, more than ever like some Inca goddess. Peach studied her silently for a moment, wondering exactly what was happening in the brain behind that smooth forehead. It was Lucy Blake who said, 'You'd better tell us a little about that background, hadn't you, Carmen?'

Carmen hadn't meant it to come to this. She had taken the deliberate decision to tell them things about herself and George Carter, to outline the nature of that relationship on her own terms, to reveal as much as she thought necessary. But the combination of Peach's unashamed confrontation and this Titian-haired girl's quiet insistence was prising more from her than she had intended. She paused for a moment, gathering her resources, trying to organize what she was going to say into some coherent account that would give no more away than was necessary. 'There isn't a lot to tell. I had what I suppose in this country you would call a wild youth. In

Barbados, it wasn't a lot more than par for the course. I got in with the wrong set.'

'Surprising how many offenders seem to have done that,' said Peach drily. 'Must be the same in Barbados as it is here. Makes you wonder who the ringleaders are. Modest people, criminals.' He dropped the word like a stone into a smooth pool, and watched for its effect upon Carmen Campbell. 'Drugs, I suppose? And what else?'

Carmen was again left wondering how much this man knew, how keenly he wanted to lure her into further deceptions which he could expose. 'Only soft drugs. Everyone used those a little. It was part of the beach culture, on the warm nights. And we were charged once with causing an affray. It was only a street fight that got out of hand. Too much rum, I suppose. We were very young then.'

Peach nodded. 'Nineteen, I believe. Not so very young. And I wish I had a pound for every young ruffian who has offered me the excuse that he was drunk when he committed a crime. And causing an affray is a serious charge, especially when people are gravely injured: the magistrate didn't take as light a view of it as you, did he? I gathered that it was only your youth that protected you from a custodial sentence.'

Carmen tried not to show how angry she felt. He had done his homework before he came here, this odious man. At least she had been right in electing not to lie about her past. She looked at the rather more reassuring face of DS Blake, who had encouraged her to come clean about her earlier troubles, and said with a touch of truculence, 'That's all a long time ago. It didn't prevent me getting to Harvard.'

Perhaps the waspish tone of this provoked Peach. He smiled grimly. 'No, it didn't. You were obviously a very bright young lady. But it wasn't the end of your difficulties, was it? The law-abiding citizens of Massachusetts had a little trouble with you while you were attending their ancient university.'

So he knew about that as well. There was nothing for it

but to brazen things out. She said defiantly. 'They're a bit staid, around the American Cambridge. We livened things up a bit. Youthful high spirits.'

'I see. But at the time you were twenty-two, and in the final year of your degree course.'

Carmen's heart seemed to stop for an instant, then start beating again furiously, as if it needed to make up for this omission. It was something she could never remember happening to her before. She found she was breathing unevenly as she tried to make light of the episode. 'We were all bikers together. Only two of us were girls. It seems to do something to you when you put on the leathers: makes it feel as if you can do almost anything. But you wouldn't know anything about that, Detective Inspector Peach.'

She managed to edge the last sentence with contempt, but Peach only gave her a small, confident smile. 'As a matter of fact, I might. I used to ride a Yamaha 350 myself, when I was about that age. One or two of the gang had Harley-Davidsons, but we considered them a bit middle-aged.'

She wanted to fling herself at him, to wipe the smile off that smug face with her fists. Instead, she held herself steady for a full two seconds before she said, 'Then you'll understand the feeling of power you get in a group. That was when I became really interested in social psychology, I think.'

'After you'd smashed up a drug store and seriously injured the owner? Group pressure again, was it?'

'I took no part in that! I didn't even know one of the boys was carrying a gun, until it was too late.'

'But you were charged, along with the others. And found guilty. Miscarriage of justice, was it?'

She knew he was trying to rile her. Worse than that, she knew that he was succeeding. She said roughly, 'They pin whatever they can on you, don't they, the police? You should know that.'

Peach smiled. She was softening up nicely: would be ready for the real questions any time now. 'Not always. Not everywhere. Otherwise we might be talking about a murder charge now, Miss Campbell.'

She glared at him. 'Anyway, the judge must have felt I wasn't guilty. I only got a suspended sentence.' She could see again that hushed courtroom in Massachusetts in 1991, with the electric silence as the white boys were sent down and the single, strikingly beautiful coloured girl was released. Surely this man who seemed to know so much wouldn't have seen the front pages of the local press screaming about political correctness after the verdicts?

Peach watched her for a moment, sensing the turmoil behind the face which gave him so little. Then he said quietly, 'Well, that's ten years and more ago. You've come a long way since then, Miss Campbell. Without any further charges. And landed in the UK, as a respected tutor in the UEL. Tell us about your affair with Dr George Andrew Carter.'

He had come back to it so suddenly that she was caught unawares. The carefully prepared statement she had rehearsed to cover this had fled her mind. She said. 'I'm not sure that "affair" is the right word. It was nothing quite as grand or as ongoing as an affair.'

DS Blake leaned forward and said softly, 'So tell us just what it was, Carmen. How many meetings, and how deep the relationship went.'

It gave her a framework, even it if was not her own framework. She said, 'Four, perhaps five, meetings.'

'Overnight meetings, were they?' Lucy Blake was quiet, even diplomatic, after Peach.

Carmen smiled. 'You don't need to pussyfoot around, DS Blake. I'm a big girl now. The first two weren't what you call "overnight meetings". The other three were. Yes, we went to bed together. In a motel the first two times. In a hotel in Harrogate, on the other three.'

Peach said, 'Thank you for being so precise.' He looked for the first time since he had arrived so abruptly in the room a little uncertain. 'Forgive me, Miss Campbell, but we have to get some clear idea of this relationship, in which one of the partners is no longer alive to give his version. Were you in love with Dr Carter?'

Carmen felt a little easier, a little more in control. But she knew she must go carefully here. 'No. I'm quite clear that I wasn't.'

'Then what was the attraction? You are, if you will allow the description, a vital and attractive young woman of – thirty-three, is it? Without any permanent attachments.' Carmen nodded slowly. 'And Dr Carter was a man of forty-eight, with a wife and two children, no obvious good looks, and a nickname of Claptrap, which implied a certain derision. I'm a stupid and unimaginative policeman, but I can't see any obvious chemistry between the two of you.'

Carmen knew by now that he was neither stupid nor unimaginative: he had played her like a fish on the end of a line when he had raised her past rumbles with the law. She had not expected that the nature of her relationship with George would be raised so directly. She looked at the woman beside Peach and said, with a not unbecoming embarrassment, 'We're not always proud of the things we do. It was power, I suppose – the position George held. We women don't always care to acknowledge it, but for a lot of us power is still the great aphrodisiac.'

Lucy Blake studied her without speaking; it was one of the CID techniques she had learned from Peach, and it often worked. People who were unnerved spoke to fill the silence, often revealing things about themselves they would otherwise have concealed. But this alert girl was a psychologist, an expert in such things.

Lucy wondered about power as an aphrodisiac. Was that what had attracted her in the first place to Peach? She had been aware of being pulled towards him because he was so good at his job, so single-minded in his pursuit of villains. Perhaps that was almost the same thing. But she was sure that the capacity to make her laugh had also been highly important. She said rather woodenly, 'You're saying that it was because Dr Carter was in control of this place that you found him attractive?'

Carmen smiled ruefully. 'I'm trying to be perfectly honest, as you asked me to be. We all know that there is a complex of things involved in any relationship. When George Carter appointed me, it was just before the college got its university status. He was still involved in all the academic appointments, as he no longer was by the time of his death. He seemed to me a very powerful man. And frankly, that power carried a certain glamour. I don't think I'd have considered George as a lover without it.'

Lucy nodded, trying to keep this woman's tongue running whilst she was in confessional mode. 'And how deep did the relationship go?'

Carmen shrugged, allowed herself a regretful smile, and said, 'Not very. We went to bed together a few times, as I've told you. It promised more than it delivered – probably for both of us. There wasn't much more than sex. It wouldn't have lasted much longer.'

There was another silence, but Carmen Campbell was too experienced, too much at home with the picture she had given, to try to fill it. It was Peach who asked her quietly, 'And who would have ended it?'

'I would. But for all I know, George might have found that something of a relief, as well as me.'

'Thank you for being so frank. Where were you last Saturday night, Miss Campbell?'

She had known it would come, but had not been prepared for it to be dropped in as abruptly as this, with no preamble about routine enquiries. She tried not to let the shock show as she smiled at them. 'I was in Cheshire. In Altrincham, to be precise. I was at a Who revival concert in Manchester on Saturday night, with a group of people. I stayed the night at my boyfriend's house afterwards. I had no car with me, on this occasion: I travelled from Brunton by train and came back the same way on Monday evening. I had someone with me, from four o'clock on Saturday evening until the next morning.'

Game, set and match, as far as her own guilt was concerned. Her smiling, untroubled face proclaimed as much to Peach. She gave the details as asked to Lucy Blake, even volunteered her boyfriend's phone number so that her story might be checked out.

'What does Keith Padmore know about your relationship with Dr Carter?' asked DS Blake without looking up, as she recorded the information in her own version of shorthand.

'Very little. As far as Keith's concerned, George Carter was merely the Director of the university I worked in, and I knew him only on those terms, as a rather remote academic figure. And I'd like it left that way.'

Peach regarded her curiously, wondering about the mores that could accommodate a brief fling with the Director along-side an apparently serious, perhaps long-term relationship. They came across the full gamut of sexual liaisons in CID work, but this seemed one of the more curious combinations. Perhaps this lively and attractive woman was one of those sexually voracious modern females who took a variety of sexual partners almost casually. Carmen Campbell would certainly not be short of offers.

He offered her the routine final enquiry, not expecting any very useful response on this occasion. 'You must have gained an impression of the state of George Carter's private life, even from your relatively few meetings with him. Can you think of anyone who might have hated him enough to kill him?'

Carmen felt an immense relief as the questioning turned away from her own part in this. She tried not to show it, to give every impression of treating Peach's enquiry with serious reflection. After a moment, speaking as if the words were drawn unwillingly from her, she said, 'You must be investigating the people who live on the site. Members of staff, I mean, not students.'

'We are in the process of doing that, yes. Why do you think

them particularly worthy of our attention, Miss Campbell?'

Carmen was as wary as Peach was watchful. He was an intelligent man this, a worthy opponent. She mustn't overplay her hand. She smiled. 'The same reasons as you, I suppose. They had the easiest access to the victim, didn't they? And people living on the campus get to know each other, over eighteen months or so.'

They followed that up, tried to get more out of her about what lay behind her statements, but she wouldn't – or couldn't – go any further. Perhaps she shouldn't have said as much, she said. It wasn't fair of her to speculate, in something as serious as murder. Perhaps it was just feminine intuition, and should be treated no more seriously than that.

Carmen Campbell sat motionless for ten minutes after they had gone, reviewing what she had said and how it had been received. They were a pretty good combination, that unlikely pair, she decided: they had caught her off guard, once or twice. But the important sections seemed to have been all right.

As DS Blake drove the Mondeo, DI Peach was speculating also. It was some time before he said quietly, 'A busy girl that. And a dangerous one, I'd say. I wonder if her affair with Carter was as passionless as she claims it was.'

Thirteen

The student bar in the UEL was quite full by nine o'clock on that Wednesday. The visiting football and rugby teams from Liverpool University had been there for some time, and were making the most of the last half hour before boarding their coach for the forty-mile return journey. The songs were vulgar, the merriment was strident, the decibel level was high.

No one took much account of the tall young man with the head of curly black hair as he sat with a book and a pint in the corner by the door. He was perhaps a little older than the average in the bar that night, but it was scarcely noticeable. A postgraduate student, perhaps, or a research assistant; the new university, anxious to build up its status as quickly as possible, had brought in a few of both these exotic species.

People expected students to read books, and the one this fresh-faced young man immersed himself in so deeply would excite no comment in any university in the world: it was a Penguin paperback edition of Niccolò Machiavelli's *The Prince*. He turned the pages at regular intervals, and only the very observant would have realized that his eyes moved sometimes above the pages of the book he held, and took in everything that was happening in that raucous, unevenly lit room.

The merriment was at its height and the bar at its fullest when the moment came for which DC Brendan Murphy had waited.

The man in the greasy navy anorak was perhaps three years

older than him, and unshaven, with a little more stubble than was fashionable, even in a student community. He slid himself behind a rectangular table no more than ten yards from Brendan, on the other side of the entrance door. This man made no attempt to buy a drink, but sat in a pool of shadow, with his hands in his pockets and his neck shrunk within his anorak, silent and watchful as a sewer rat.

He did not have to wait for long. Two youths came from the other end of the bar, where they had been invisible to Brendan behind the waving arms of the soccer and rugby teams. They had obviously been expecting this arrival, though they exchanged no greetings with the newcomer. There was far too much noise for Brendan to hear what was said, but he saw the man spread polythene sachets on the table ahead of him, saw the students nod and pass ten-pound notes across the table. Cannabis, he thought, parcelled in quarter- or half-ounce packets; enough for twenty or forty good spliffs. The drug was now so common in environments like this that its purveyors scarcely troubled to conceal their trafficking.

A third student joined the table, then a fourth. There were swift enquiries, in response to which the man looked round, took in Brendan, apparently engrossed in his book, and motioned with his head to indicate that his customers should follow him outside. Brendan let them get through the door before he slipped the paperback into his pocket and followed them cautiously.

He could not see them at first. Then, as his eyes grew more used to the darkness, he found them. They were very close to the windowless brick wall which formed the back of the bar, where empty steel kegs stood awaiting collection when the brewery van made its delivery the next morning. The man in the anorak had spread out some of his wares on top of one of the big kegs; it was so dark that he was demonstrating the genuine nature of what he offered by the light of a small torch.

Brendan crept to within five yards of them but stayed invisible behind the corner of the building. The man in the anorak was giving the nearest he came to a sales pitch. 'This crack coke is good: none of your adulterated rubbish. Fifty quid for three rocks. The Ecstasy is forty pounds for three big tablets. What you lads want is this: Rohypnol. It's what we use in date-rapes. Completely undetectable. Fifty quid for a good supply. Quick as you can, lads, I can't hang about here. I've bigger fish to fry tonight!'

Brendan Murphy waited until he saw money changing hands under the pale spotlight of the torch before he made his move. When he acted, he moved swiftly, arriving like a black angel of vengeance out of the darkness. He didn't make any attempt to lay hands on the students, knowing that there were others to deal with them. He had the anorak's hand up his back between his shoulder blades before he could attempt resistance, heard the man's oath and yelp of agony even as he hissed the words of doom into his ear: '*I arrest you on suspicion of dealing in Class A drugs. You do not have to say anything, but it may harm your defence if you do not mention when questioned something which you later rely on in court. Anything you do say will be recorded and may be given in evidence.*'

Quite a mouthful to deliver under stress, but he was used to that. Two of the lads had run straight into the arms of the three uniformed men around the corner. Brendan held the arm of his captive until he was able to push him roughly into the back of the van with the youths who had bought from him. Anorak said nothing on the way to the station, beyond the brief advice to his fellow prisoners that they should 'say nothing to these bastards'.

It was, thought DC Murphy, a highly satisfactory evening of overtime.

At ten forty-five on that Wednesday evening, at the very moment when Brendan Murphy's prize was being charged and delivered to his cell, Detective Inspector Percy Peach had other problems.

He wasn't sure he was going to be able to solve them, but the problems themselves were wholly more pleasurable than those posed to Brendan by a greasy anorak with halitosis. For Percy was studying Lucy's winceyette nightie again. And it seemed shorter than even his inflamed memory had pictured it.

He was on his own ground tonight. His 1950s semi was older and more spacious than Lucy Blake's trim little modern flat, but nothing like as neat and tidy. He had done his best to make it look spruce tonight, once he knew he was on a promise, but the house still carried that air of a place which was scarcely lived in and resented it.

Still, Lucy was used to that by now. She had put away his breakfast dishes from the drainer and approved his purchase of the instant coffee she had suggested during her last visit. They had watched the ten o'clock television news, and found that even in the local section there was no mention of the murder of the Director of the University of East Lancashire. Even a sensational murder like this had held its place in the news for no more than two evenings. The two of them were rather pleased about this: CID work was not easy when conducted in the blaze of publicity which stemmed from media attention.

And now they were in the bedroom, and Lucy was voicing her first criticism of his residence. 'It's cold in here!' she said. She ran her hands along the top of Percy's ancient, lukewarm central-heating radiator, then rubbed them vigorously together and flapped her bare arms violently across her chest.

The movement, in that celebrated nightie, excited Percy, and he gave a low moan, part pure pleasure, part agonized anticipation. He did a good moan, full of pent-up emotion on its sustained, plangent note. 'It won't be cold when you get into here!' he promised fervently.

He was lying in his double bed, his head exactly level with the lower fringe of the nightie, his concentration on the artistic appreciation of the scene absolute. He allowed himself a quieter, less agonized moan.

'You make me self-conscious! Every bit of me's cold, while you just lie there whining!' she complained. She turned her back on him, bent automatically to take off her slippers, then hastily changed her position, lest she should reveal enough to cause a cardiac arrest in her excited lover. Percy began to croon his own erotic version of 'Blue Moon'.

'I think I'll put on my bed-socks and get myself a hot water bottle,' said Lucy vindictively.

'Bloody 'ell, Norah!' said Percy. It was a comment he offered for all occasions, sometimes in mock horror, sometimes in awed appreciation. He followed this one with another moan, to show that it was appreciation. 'That were an ejaculation, lass, that about Norah,' he said. 'Does tha like it when I talk dirty?'

Lucy's shiver developed into a giggle. She didn't mind whether he talked dirty or not, but she liked it when he thee'd and thou'd her. She couldn't say why; perhaps it was something connected with being a Lancashire lass who had grown up in the country, where the old accent and even bits of the old dialect were still strong.

DS Blake laid her clean pants and bra for the morning carefully on top of the aged radiator, in the faint hope that they might gather some warmth to receive her then. She took a deep breath, steeling herself for action. Then she whipped the nightie up and her pants down, depositing them in one continuous movement in the darkest corner of the room. This disrobing of the nymph provoked DI Denis Charles Scott Peach into an uninhibited yell of pure pleasure.

'You haven't warmed my half!' complained Lucy, as her teeth chattered and she tried to ward off three indecent assaults at once.

'Then come into mine!' said Percy. He managed to get both

arms round her shapely shoulders and heaved her expertly on top of him.

'Ooh!' said Lucy. It was only proper to show a decent degree of surprise.

'Aaaaaargh!' said Percy. Curious how your moans became so much lower, when you had a weight on top of you, even such a delicious weight as this. Still, you had to show your appreciation.

'This nightie's too short!' said Lucy modestly into the well-formed ear where her lips had landed.

'Just the right length!' Percy differed, with a low, animal growl which said far more than words. He didn't know where the nightie had gone at the moment, and he didn't care. His hands fell on what it should have been covering. There seemed an awful lot of precious flesh here, for a small piece of winceyette like that to cover. It was only right that he should offer a helping hand. Or hands.

Decidedly expert hands, Lucy found. She allowed herself a low moan of her own: womanly, if not exactly ladylike.

Fifteen minutes which seemed like one passed before Percy sank back into his pillow, adjusted his breathing to the slowing palpitations of the form above him, and muttered through the chestnut hair a heartfelt, 'Eeh, lass, that were champion!'

Lucy smiled in the darkness, shifted her head to give a gentle kiss to the man below her, touching his chin lightly with soft lips, running the tip of her tongue lightly across his neck. 'Tha weren't too bad thiself, Percy. Not for an old 'un, like.' She slipped her body from above his and pulled down her nightie. 'Fanny pelmet you called this, and fanny pelmet is just about all it is!' she said. Everything she had hoped it would be when she bought it, she thought happily.

They lay with their arms around each other, pleasurably warm and content, drifting towards sleep and yet with part of them anxious to stay awake, to prolong the intimacy of the post-coital moment. She was breathing regularly, and he thought she must be asleep when he heard her mutter drowsily, 'I hope we didn't disturb the neighbours!'

'Might 'ave,' he murmured, with a touch of pride. 'They're not used to noises like that. They think I'm a sad divorcee who lives in a state of quasi-monastic seclusion. You'd best show yourself at the window in that nightie in the morning. I wouldn't like them to think I was making noises like that playing solo.'

She giggled. She liked the idea that there hadn't been others here before her. She had no right to expect it, but it gave her satisfaction, nonetheless. It was her last thought before she fell into a deep and dreamless sleep.

One of the reasons Percy Peach's bedroom was so cold was that it faced due east. Even on the 21st of November, the grey light of dawn crept under the ill-fitting cotton curtains before seven o'clock. Lucy Blake, rolling on her back and stretching sensuously, thought at first that it was the light which had wakened her. Then she heard the rattle of crockery and found a cup of tea on the small bedside cupboard beside her.

She had been given a cup and saucer, but Percy clutched his favourite mug as he moved round to his side of the bed. He was naked. 'Winceyette doesn't do the same things for me as it does for you,' he explained. He slid between the sheets and gave a theatrical shiver. 'God, but that lino's cold on the kitchen floor, lass.' He contrived somehow to raise a cold foot and place it precisely between her warm buttocks.

She screamed. That would give those neighbours something to think about. 'I'm going to wear flannel pyjamas when I come here next!' she said. 'With a padlock and chain, I should think!'

He removed his foot, sipped his tea, and said, 'That should give the locksmith a few moments of pure pleasure. If I get Horny Harry from Oswaldtwistle, he might pay *me* the call-out fee.'

Lucy had no idea whether Horny Harry existed. He might, because Percy knew some pretty dodgy characters, having worked for so long in the area. She allowed him to warm his hands in more conventional ways. Then she finished her tea and gave the neighbours more grounds for noise speculation.

They had time only for the briefest of breakfasts. They met the man from next door outside, getting into his car as Percy unlocked his. They exchanged good mornings and the man, a friendly looking chap of around fifty, cast an appreciative glance over the girl whom that lonely inspector next door had managed to secure for himself.

He had found Percy a pleasant enough chap, in their limited dealings. He was quite glad for him. And not a little envious.

Fourteen

The anorak's name turned out to be Kevin Allcock. After a night in Brunton nick and a police station breakfast, he was at a low ebb. Even from the most charitable viewpoint, his stubble was now definitely long enough to be scruffy rather than fashionable. Moreover, he had been forced to empty his pockets at the desk before he was charged with the possession and supply of drugs. The very substance which might have helped him to keep up his spirits through a long night had been left behind with the station sergeant.

It was a situation tailor-made for Percy Peach.

The Detective Inspector arrived in the interview room like a bouncing ball. He looked his adversary up and down, approved of the state he was in, and said, 'You remember DC Murphy from last night. I think we'll have the recorder on; I often like to play things back later, when a prisoner and I have had a few laughs together.' He put a cassette in the machine and announced that the interview with Kevin Charles Allcock was beginning at eight forty-two, with DI Peach and DC Murphy present.

Then he pretended to study the notes he had already memorized before he came into the room, while the sallow face opposite him looked unwillingly up from the small square table into the features of his latest tormentor, and Allcock's narrow hips shifted uneasily on the hard chair. Peach shook his head sadly and tut-tutted twice before he allowed his round face to relax into a satisfied smile. 'Lot of trouble you're in, Mr Allcock.'

'Wasn't doing anything.'

Disappointment flooded back into the moonlike face around the black moustache. 'Aw, come on, Kevin, you can do better than that. Make a game of it! We'll be handing you over to the Drugs Squad team, presently, but the least you can do is give us a good game first.'

'Fuck off, Peach. I wasn't doing anything.'

'Just going about your lawful business when this great rough copper grabbed your collar and dragged you in, were you?'

'That's about it, yes.'

'Well, well, well! I thought Kevin was a good name for a man never seen without an anorak. I'm beginning to think Allcock is an even more appropriate handle for a man attempting to sell us tales like this.'

'Fuck off, Peach!' But now there was fear in the grey, slightly bloodshot eyes. Allcock had expected the head-on attack. Being flicked about like a captive mouse was much more unnerving. He was already sorry that he'd refused a brief.

Whereas Percy Peach was pleased about that refusal. Much easier to conduct a proper dialogue with a known villain when there wasn't some poncy young lawyer reminding him of his rights all the time. He said with a sudden harshness. 'Caught in possession of Class A and B drugs with a street value estimated at eight thousand pounds. Caught selling three different Class A drugs to students at the University of East Lancashire.'

'I wasn't pushing. I admit possession. The drugs were for my own use. Private and recreational.'

Peach leaned back and laughed out loud. 'That's all cock, Allcock!' He beamed a simple delight in his wordplay. 'And you know it. You were caught red-handed and banged to rights. Wasn't he, DC Murphy?'

'Certainly was, sir. Never seen anything so blatant. Almost gave himself up, he did, poor sod.' Brendan Murphy was happy to make his contribution. He sat just behind Peach's left shoulder, and in his very different young, fresh face, his smile was an unnerving replica of his leader's.

Kevin Allcock was duly unnerved. His brain wouldn't work properly, just when he most needed it. He fell back on the villain's last resort. 'You just prove that! I wasn't pushing drugs at all. Most of that eight thousand quid's worth was planted on me by this bugger!'

The two grins grew wider, instead of disappearing as he had hoped. Peach said with a weary disdain, 'Tell him, DC Murphy.'

'Yes, sir. We've got signed statements from the lads we brought in with you, Allcock. They handed over money to you in return for class A drugs. Ecstasy, rock cocaine and Rohypnol. After you'd given them a sales pitch for Rohypnol as the ideal tool for date-rape.'

Allcock's sallow face became older and greyer beneath the stubble of beard. His last hope had just died. He said automatically, hopelessly, 'You'll have to prove it.'

Peach was almost sorry for him. 'We just did, sunshine. When you get the brief you so unwisely refused, he'll tell you to plead guilty. You'll go down for this. For eight or ten years, I should think, with your record.'

Allcock had been done for supplying drugs before. He'd known they would throw this at him, but it had still come as a surprise to find his record pitched in like this, just after the body blow that those bloody students had grassed him up. He said dully, 'They can't do that. I'm just a small man, earning . . .' His shoulders dropped hopelessly and his slight figure seemed to shrink even further.

'Earning an honest living, Kevin? I'm glad you stopped in time. That really would have been all cock. You've strained our patience quite enough. I think we'll let you stew in a cell for a while and wait for the Drugs Squad. Tell them everything you know about the people who were providing you with your supplies.'

'Not me! Kevin Allcock ain't no grass.' The stubborn, hopeless attempt at pride, the familiar Pavlovian reaction of the small-time crook.

'Then you'll go down for a long time, Kevin.' Peach, looking as if that would be an entirely satisfactory happening, folded his papers and seemed ready to leave. Then he said, almost as if it were an afterthought, 'Unless, of course, you happen to be implicated in this murder we're investigating at the UEL, in which case it could be life.'

The word 'murder' was inserted at the perfect moment, when the defeated pusher thought that things could not possibly get worse. It was a word which carried a certain glamour, even among lesser criminals. And to Kevin Allcock, the mention of the word brought a new fear. 'What d'you mean, murder? I 'aven't never—'

'On the site at UEL, Kevin. Not more than two hundred yards from the spot you were apprehended trafficking in drugs last night.'

'But murder's nothing to do with me. I never—'

'Often involved in modern murders in some way, the drug industry, isn't it, Kevin? Billions of pounds involved. Well worth the odd murder, some people think.'

'I know nothing about any murder.'

'Have you for an accessory, I shouldn't wonder, with your record.'

'Look, I'm no murderer, Mr Peach. I'm a small-time pusher, that's all.' The defiant obscenities were now long gone, the tone was wheedling.

That whine of supplication, familiar in Peach's ears from his dealings with hundreds of small criminals, showed that this meat was nicely tenderized. 'You'll need to prove that to me, Kevin, by telling me everything you know about the drug scene on the site. Completing the picture for us, as you might say.'

Perhaps Allcock really believed the bluff that the CID already knew a lot about the drug scene at UEL – Peach actually knew nothing, and a call to the Drugs Squad super-intendent before this meeting had revealed that they knew precious little more. Or perhaps the shabby figure in front of them was merely frightened out of his wits by now. He took a long breath and made a last attempt to be crafty, 'Help me, won't it, when it comes to sentence? If I tell you all I know now, I mean?'

'We don't do deals, Kevin. Not with the likes of you. The drugs people will very likely point out to the judge that you've helped them to name some bigger boys, if that's the way it turns out.'

'Anyway, I 'aven't much choice, 'ave I? You've got me banged to rights, as you said.' He was rationalizing the fact that he was about to grass, as small men usually did. He looked desperately from Peach's impassive face to Brendan Murphy, who gave him the briefest of confirmatory nods. 'I don't know where my drugs come from – honest I don't. There's a drop for me. I pick up what I've ordered and leave a list of what I want the next week.'

'Where's the drop, Kevin?'

'Behind an empty warehouse, in Burnley. Small room at the back. Used to be a nightwatchman's place, I think.'

Peach would leave the Drugs Squad to get the details, to see how much more they could squeeze out of this dubious accessory. It was their case, once he had checked there was no connection with the Carter killing. 'What about the university site, Kevin? Fill us in on what you know about that.'

There was the briefest of hesitations: they could see him forcing himself to break the only real code he had, that you didn't grass. Then he said, 'I guess you know most of this. The guy who controls drugs in the university works on the site. McLean. Malcolm McLean.'

Peach concealed his excitement beneath a nod which implied that this was no news to him. 'And how does he control it, Kevin?'

'Tells me where to contact people. How and what to supply.

127

Lets the students and a few of the staff on the site know where
to come for the goods, I suppose.' He had turned sullen,
but he was giving them information, which was all that
mattered. He looked up suddenly. 'But you know all this
already, don't you.'

'Maybe, Kevin. But I'll put in a word for you, whenever
I can. Say you did your best to be helpful. Know where he
lives, do you, this McLean?'

'No. He's a lecturer in the place, though, isn't he?'

They dismissed him then, quickly. Peach could scarcely
conceal his excitement until the wretched figure had been
led from the room. A drug scene at the UEL, and a member
of staff controlling it, apparently. Murder might have a drugs
connection, after all.

On a crisp November morning, Detective Sergeant Lucy
Blake was quite envious of the students of the University of
East Lancashire. There seemed more sun and more bracing
air here on this green campus than in the old cotton town
of Brunton, which was no more than four miles away but
completely invisible from this site in the Ribble valley.
The students ran or walked between the modern, well-
spaced buildings of the different faculties, hailing friends,
exchanging banter. They were privileged, spending three
years in a place like this, whilst the contemporaries of their
school years were discovering the harshness of real working
life in factories or offices. She didn't mind the privilege:
she just hoped they appreciated it. Not yet twenty-seven and
already thinking like a middle-aged woman, Lucy told herself
ruefully.

Give extra attention to all the people who live or work
on the site, Carmen Campbell had said. It remained to be
seen whether that was genuine advice or an attempt to get
the police attention off her own back. The man Lucy was
going to see didn't live on the site. But he held a unique
position there, and occupied his own headquarters. And

cross-referencing on the police computer had thrown up one startling fact about him.

She had parked her bulbous little Vauxhall Corsa in the main car park quite deliberately. It wasn't just that it would be nice to arrive unheralded at her destination; she wanted to absorb as much as she could of the atmosphere of this academic centre where a murderer might be lurking. It took her ten minutes to walk to the extreme edge of the campus which was her destination, but she found the walk in the sunshine instructive as well as enjoyable.

The Reverend Thomas Matthews had been disappointed by the attendance for Holy Communion on this Thursday morning, but the few students who were there had promised to try to drum up a little more support for the three Thursdays which remained before the Christmas vacation. He was wandering round the cold and rather bleak chaplaincy when he saw the red-haired young woman studying the board outside which announced his name and the hours he was here.

His first thought was that this was someone wanting his services as chaplain; he was both disappointed and disturbed when she showed him her identification as a detective sergeant from Brunton CID. They went into the small study cum robing room behind the main room of the chaplaincy where he held his services and talked to his religious action groups.

'This is a routine visit as a result of our investigation into the murder of Dr Carter,' Lucy said. 'We're questioning everyone who has a base on the site. There may be things which don't seem important to you but which become significant to us, as part of the picture of the life of Dr Carter which we are assembling.'

He had seemed nervous when she mentioned the purpose of her visit, which the detective in her said was a good start. She had never had to question a clergyman before, not on her own. She had to conquer a surprisingly deep-seated prejudice which told her that a man in a dog collar could not possibly be involved even peripherally in a murder inquiry. The Reverend

Matthews now said, 'I don't live on the site, you know. I have a base here, but I live at my parish: St Catherine's, in Brunton. They've sold the old Victorian vicarage and build a small modern replacement; it's more than adequate for my needs.'

He was talking quickly, in danger of saying too much: it was another sign that he was uneasy. Lucy said, 'You have a special position here, though, and I imagine that because of your function you move about the campus more than most tutors.'

'Yes. I go wherever it seems I can be of use. I visit a student who has problems on his or her own ground, if that seems appropriate. But only if they invite me, of course.'

'So you know what is going on better than most.'

'I wouldn't say that. Sometimes I think I'm the last to get to know things.'

'But you knew about Dr Carter's death pretty quickly.'

He started visibly, as if this were an accusation. He was probably in his early forties, but he had the fresh complexion and open face on which emotions are quickly visible. He had plentiful dark hair, cut short in an almost military fashion; with the curious combination of a thick-ribbed, V-neck green sweater and a dog collar above it, he looked younger than his years and curiously vulnerable. Or perhaps, thought Lucy Blake with quickening interest, he really had something to hide.

For he now said, as if he were framing an apology. 'It's true that I was aware of what was going on pretty quickly on Monday morning. But it's part of my job to be aware of such things, I'd say, so that I can offer any spiritual help that's called for. And the whole site was seething with the news very early on Monday, you know.'

'Yes, I know that. I was here myself pretty early on Monday.' But according to your board outside, you're normally here on Tuesdays and Thursdays, she thought. And you're embarrassed about something.

'In that case you'll know how people were talking. And the place was alive with police cars and vans.'

Not quite. The only police vehicles on the site had been discreetly parked up against the double garage of the Director's house, where they were invisible from most points on the site. So this man had been round there, or found some vantage point from which he could watch what was going on. Curiouser and curiouser. Lucy said as casually as she could, 'Did you know the Carters well, Mr Matthews?'

An innocent enough question, surely. And one he should have known she was bound to ask. Yet he had twitched a little, again, she was sure of it. He said, 'Do call me Tom, please. Everyone does. Well, I suppose I did know the Carters quite well, yes. That's why I went round there so promptly to offer my condolences when Ruth came home on Wednesday.' He said it almost aggressively, as if he were challenging her to defy his logic.

Lucy looked squarely into his blue, anxious eyes. 'I see. And what about Dr Carter himself, Tom? Would you say that you knew him pretty well?'

'No. He wasn't – well, he wasn't an easy man to get to know.'

It was lame, and she could see he realized that. And it contradicted his first statement that he had known the Carters 'quite well'. There was something here he didn't want to reveal, but Lucy couldn't see what it might be. It was frustrating, because the Reverend Matthews didn't strike her as a very good liar. But he was not under arrest; he was merely helping the police of his own volition, and he could refuse to cooperate at any point. She said gently, 'He's been murdered, Tom, and we're trying to build up a picture of him. You can help me a little more than that, I'm sure. It's not a time for mistaken loyalties: we're trying to establish who might have disliked him enough to kill him.'

Tom Matthews nodded his acceptance of that. 'But it might have been someone who scarcely knew him at all, mightn't it? He might have simply stood between someone and something they desperately wanted.'

'Yes, he might well have done just that. There are all kinds of reasons for murder. But it's your duty to tell us as much as you can about him.'

He seemed to take a decision. 'All right. No one liked him very much. He was a pompous ass, in many respects. But a dangerous one. If anyone stood in the way of his own career, he wouldn't scruple to trample over him. Or her.'

'Do you speak from personal experience?'

'No. Rather the reverse, in fact. He was very anxious that the new university should have a chaplain of some sort; he thought it would be good for its image in the local community. The funds would only run to a part-time appointment, but he was determined to have one. I could afford to take two-fifths of a university lecturer's salary; indeed I was delighted to do so. It's a good supplement to the meagre stipend of a parish whose congregation has been in steady decline for fifty years.' He sounded like a man anxious to do justice to a Director who could no longer defend himself.

Or perhaps, thought Lucy, he was just happy to divert the talk into areas he knew were safe. She brought him gently back to the subject which interested her. 'But Dr Carter had a reputation for ruthlessness.'

'Yes. It's mostly hearsay, as far as I'm concerned, but well established. And, well – he wasn't very well respected as an academic. That matters in a place like this, you know. They used to call him Claptrap Carter.'

'Yes. Everyone seems to say that. What else can you tell us about him, Tom?'

Perhaps he caught her impatience. He looked at her quickly and said, 'His children didn't like him, I'm afraid. Part of it was probably just adolescence, but it went deeper than that.'

There was a little pause before Lucy said, 'Treated his wife badly, did he?'

He glanced at her sharply. 'Yes. That was quick of you. I suppose you get used to seeing these things.'

'Just as you do, I expect.'

'Yes. You see things in other people's lives that you'd never have met in your own, when you're a clergyman. Or a police officer, I suppose. Yes, George treated Ruth badly, over the years. No beatings, or anything like that – as far as I'm aware. More what the courts would call mental cruelty, I think.'

'Anyway, their relationship wasn't good.'

'That would be putting it mildly. As a matter of fact, I know Ruth was planning to divorce him, later this year.'

That was the first they'd heard of that. The enigmatic Ruth Carter hadn't pretended the marriage had been ideal, but had certainly not mentioned a break-up. It made this death very opportune for her. Lucy said as casually as she could, 'And do you know what George Carter's reaction to this would have been?'

Tom Matthews looked at her sharply, in that curious, open-faced way of his, like a child faced with an unexpectedly difficult question. He said roughly, 'He wouldn't have had much choice, would he? Not under the modern divorce laws. Anyway, he's hardly led a blameless life himself.'

With the eminently beddable Carmen Campbell for one, thought Lucy. For a man sixteen years older than the lithe Barbadian, without obvious physical attractions, old Claptrap had done rather well for himself there. She said, 'Other women, you mean. You'd better let me have the details, Tom.'

He shook his head violently. 'I couldn't do that. For one thing, I don't know any details.'

'Then it's just gossip?'

He looked thoroughly uncomfortable. 'No, I wouldn't say that. But I really don't know the details. And I can't give you any source. This has to be confidential.'

'Even in a murder inquiry?'

'Even then. I shouldn't have said so much, I suppose. But I thought you'd be certain to find out anyway, in the course of your investigation.'

'We already do know a certain amount, that's true. But I was hoping you could add to our knowledge. It's—'

'I can't. I'm sorry.'

His lips set in a line of determination, like a child's when it has said too much. More to keep him talking than for any other reason, Lucy Blake said, 'You were an army chaplain at one time, I believe, Tom.'

'Yes. I quite enjoyed it, to tell you the truth. Went into Kosovo in 1999 and 2000. They always like to have the padre with them, on active service, the armed forces. And it's surprising how any prospect of death makes young men interested in religion. It was the time when I did my most valuable work, I think.' His enthusiasm for those days came leaping out of him.

'You were an expert marksman, too, I believe. That must be unusual, for a padre.'

She had tried to throw in this one strange fact lightly, but he became suddenly guarded, as if she had been making an attempt to trip him. 'It is quite unusual, yes. But I'd shown an aptitude, for small arms shooting in particular, at school, and the army likes to foster the idea that all officers are potentially fighting men, so they encouraged me to develop it. They even sent me to shoot at Bisley, in 1997.'

There was something here, she was sure. He had shown a flash of dismay when she raised his shooting prowess, and then tried to divert her back to Bisley in 1997. She said, 'I don't suppose you fired a gun in Kosovo, though, did you?'

'No. I was strictly non-combatant there. That's how it had to be, and how I wanted it. It's far easier to offer spiritual help when soldiers see you as a colleague, but not a fighting one.'

'So you haven't been back in civilian life for very long.'

'Fourteen months. I was lucky to get the post at St

134

Catherine's.' He grinned. 'Well, not so lucky, perhaps, to be honest. The Church of England is chronically short of vicars, as you probably know, and the stipend was quite small. I was delighted to get the job here a month later to supplement it, as I said.'

Lucy nodded, then made a last attempt to drag him back from an area where he was comfortable to the one which had seemed to disturb him. 'Dr Carter was shot through the head with a revolver, you know. A Smith and Wesson, according to the ballistics experts at forensic.'

He looked shaken again, but determined. He said without a smile, 'I was something of an expert with a Smith and Wesson, DS Blake. But I didn't shoot George Carter.'

Lucy permitted herself the smile he had not been able to manage. 'I see. And have you any idea who might have done?'

'No. If I think of anyone, I'll contact you immediately.'

It was as near as a polite man could get to telling her that the interview was over. And indeed, she had nothing else to ask him, for the moment.

But Lucy Blake felt sure as she drove away that this would not be the last she would see of the Reverend Thomas Matthews.

Fifteen

The elderly lady had plainly never been inside a police station before; she looked quite distraught. The station sergeant prepared himself for a lost dog or cat: that combination of anxiety and determination usually stemmed from a missing animal.

He prepared himself to be avuncular and consoling, to offer the usual assurances about pets turning up safe and well in the most unlikely places. Station sergeants are programmed to deal with the mundane daily round of trivia. When the lady said her name was Mrs Gwendolyn Crowthorne it did not immediately ring any bells. She wanted to see Detective Inspector Peach, she said, and the sergeant prepared to deliver his spiel about how busy senior CID officers are and to deal with her himself. It was only when she said that she was the mother-in-law of the murdered Dr George Andrew Carter that she got his full attention. Two minutes later, Mrs Crowthorne was ushered into the office of DI Peach.

It was plain to Percy that she was very upset, that she had needed to screw up all her courage to come here. But that courage gave this determined old lady a surprising dignity. He made her as comfortable as he could on the upright chair before his desk, tried to order tea for her, and found it refused by the lady herself. 'I'd much rather gets this over as quickly as possible, Mr Peach,' she said in a high, quavery voice. 'This isn't easy for me, and if I take too long over it, my nerve may fail.'

Peach recognized her now, despite her distress and the best

136

clothes she had put on to come here. 'I saw you briefly, in your own house, in Kendal, didn't I, Mrs Crowthorne?' She nodded vigorously. 'There was no need for you to come all the way down here, you know.'

She managed a smile at last, reassured by his kindly reception. 'I couldn't have done it on the phone, Mr Peach. Didn't have one until I was past forty, and I've never really felt comfortable with them – not when there's something delicate to say. Besides, I thought if I came down here I'd go and see my daughter first. Explain what I had to do.'

'And did you do that?'

'No. Ruth doesn't know I'm here. I should have told her, but I was afraid she'd talk me out of it. I'm not as strong as I used to be.'

Not physically you aren't, thought Percy. But I'd still back you to carry something through, if you set your mind to it. Gwendolyn Crowthorne reminded him of his own mother as she sat there: she was distressed, confused, lonely, and not very far from tears, but also absolutely conscious of what was the right course of action and determined to carry it through. Perhaps it was something which would die with this generation, that moral certainty about the right thing to do. No one – and least of all the errant modern youth with whom Percy dealt for so much of his time – seemed now to have this clear, unfaltering idea of what was right and what was wrong.

People of Mrs Crowthorne's generation sinned from time to time, as people always have, but they knew sin when they saw it. Percy Peach had been brought up on sin, in a school run by the Catholic clergy; he could have taken a degree in guilt. But sin was an old-fashioned concept, nowadays.

All this flashed through Percy's mind before he said quietly, 'This is about your daughter, isn't it, Mrs Crowthorne? And your dead son-in-law?'

She nodded, tight-lipped with emotion, appreciative that he had introduced the subject for her. Then she blurted out, 'Ruth told you she was with me last weekend, didn't she? Well, she wasn't. Not for the whole of it.'

Peach nodded quietly, indicating that she was only confirming what he had already known, making it easier for her, though this was in fact the first he had heard of this. He said, 'She was there when I came to the house on Monday. How long had she been there, Mrs Crowthorne?'

Mrs Crowthorne's small, taut face had relaxed a little, with the relief of confession. He could imagine how she had agonized for three days before coming here to reveal the truth and be a traitor to her daughter. 'She came on Sunday evening. She hadn't been there for the whole of the weekend at all.'

That left a full two days unaccounted for: Ruth Carter had told him that she had gone to her mother's house when she left the UEL site on Friday morning, and spent the whole of the weekend there. Where had she been during that missing time? Most pertinently of all, where had she been on the Saturday night when her husband had been shot?

Percy saw that the old eyes opposite him were brimming with tears. One of these stole softly down Mrs Crowthorne's wrinkled cheek, cutting a path through the powder she had put on to come here, making her suddenly raddled and old. He said gently, 'You must have been very fond of your son-in-law, Mrs Crowthorne.'

She nodded, and the tear dropped from her chin on to the lapel of her dark blue coat. As if this had made her conscious of her weeping for the first time, she pulled a handkerchief from her pocket and rubbed vigorously at her face. It smudged the powder further, made this woman who had been well groomed when she set out from her house sixty miles away more than ever like one of the ageing, pathetic, drunken females who ended their nights in the Brunton nick. Her voice seemed to come from a long way off when she said, 'He was always very kind to me, was George. Very considerate.'

Peach said conventionally, 'That's good to hear.' Where there were no considerations of career or prestige, Claptrap Carter had obviously had a much better side: it was another facet of the personality they could only study after the man's death, and a surprising one. 'But your daughter didn't feel the same about him, did she?'

'No. That upset me, but there was nothing I could do about it. Ruth was planning to get rid of him.' She realized what she had said and looked up at Peach in alarm, but he gave her nothing more than a reassuring smile. 'I mean that Ruth was planning to get a divorce. She said that now that the children had virtually left home and George was in the job he'd never dreamed he'd get, she could go without doing him any damage.'

That phrasing didn't sound like a woman with murder in mind. But this was a mother speaking, no doubt anxious to put the best gloss she could on the relationship, especially in view of the fact that she was now feeling like a traitor to Ruth. Peach said quietly, 'Mrs Crowthorne, do you know where your daughter was on Friday and Saturday, when she claimed she was with you?'

'No. She didn't say.' The bedraggled, desperately unhappy lady looked unseeingly at the papers on Peach's desk.

He wanted to leave it at that, to tell himself that this elderly woman had been through enough anguish and he should be happy with what she had brought him. But he could see that she knew more than this. He did not even have to harden his heart: he was so much the detective after his years in the job that he knew he must have every scrap of information which the old lady could give him. He said, 'But Ruth asked you to conceal the truth for her, didn't she? She asked you to say that she had been with you for the whole of the weekend.'

'Yes. But I told her I couldn't guarantee that I'd lie for her.' A sad little smile of pride flitted across her smudged face. 'That's why she didn't want you to see me at all, when you came to my house on Monday.'

139

'And you've a good idea where she was on Friday and Saturday, haven't you, Mrs Crowthorne?'

She nodded wearily, her eyes cast down. She moved one small foot against the other, watching the blue leather shoe as if it was a vitally important movement. She was still watching those feet when she said, 'She didn't tell me where she was, and I didn't ask her. But I suspect she was with a man. I don't know his name; I was too upset about the break-up with George even to ask her about it.'

Peach stood up, came round his desk, broke one of the unwritten rules of police practice as he laid a hand upon a female interviewee. He dropped his fingers lightly on the bowed shoulder of the small woman who sat so precisely on the upright chair and said, 'You've done the right thing, Mrs Crowthorne. I know it wasn't easy, but it was right. We'd have found out eventually, you know, but it would have taken us a little longer and probably been a lot messier. Now, before you leave here, you're going to have that tea.'

He went down to the canteen himself and came back with a pot of tea and two cups and saucers, a refinement he did not normally practise. She had pulled a mirror and comb from her handbag and repaired her face while he was away. They sat companionably for ten minutes together, munching ginger biscuits, talking of her house in Kendal, of her dead husband, of the nice girl with the chestnut hair who had gone with him to that house, of anything rather than the thing which had brought her here.

Mrs Crowthorne spoke of how unhappy she was with the very idea of divorce, and Percy Peach told her that it had happened to him, that it wasn't the end of the world. She reminded him irresistibly of his dead mother as she said, 'You should try walking out with that pretty girl who works with you, if she's not spoken for. A man like you needs a good woman.'

She was so much like his mother that he wanted to say that he would call in and see her, when all this was over. But he

140

couldn't say that. Not when it was much more possible than it had been an hour earlier that he would be arresting Mrs Crowthorne's daughter as a murderer.

Superintendent Thomas Bulstrode Tucker was wondering whether he should set up one of his media conferences. He had already popped out during the morning and had his hair trimmed, just in case he should be parading it before the television cameras in the next couple of days.

He was good at public relations, good at smoothing ruffled feathers, at delivering the clichés which had to be used with ringing sincerity – this came easily to him, because he rarely recognized them as clichés. With his trim figure in his tailored uniform, his strong profile, his still plentiful head of groomed, greying hair, he was an excellent police front man, well practised in reassuring the public that no stone was being left unturned, that the Brunton Police Service never slept.

The Chief Constable and the Deputy Chief Constable knew well enough who did the work, who achieved the results. But because it is not easy to get rid of the inefficient, particularly once they have attained a certain rank, they tolerated Tucker, even encouraged him, in those fields where he was moderately effective. The CID unit he headed solved a surprising percentage of the crimes which came its way, so why rock the boat? Tucker might be a balloon of hot air, but he could be a useful one, if he was not pricked in public.

DI Percy Peach pricked him very often, in private. And now, when he was irritated by Tommy Bloody Tucker's pompous fumblings, after the sincerity of the old lady he had just escorted to her car, Peach thought alarming Tucker would give him an agreeable few minutes of light relief.

'I need you to brief me on the latest state of play in the Carter inquiry,' said Tucker. He puffed out his chest. 'I may have to conduct a media conference, before you disappear for the weekend.'

Before you do, you mean, you idle old sod, thought

Percy. He volunteered the most inane of his vast range of grins. 'Nowhere near an arrest yet. Plenty of suspects,' he summarized cheerfully.

Tucker sighed wearily, produced a pencil from the top drawer of his desk, and prepared to make notes as he said, 'I hope you're not causing mayhem among important citizens of the area. You'd better brief me.'

'Yes, sir. Well, the victim's wife, to start with. You said most murders were domestic, and directed me to check whether she might have been lying about her whereabouts at the time of death. With your usual perception, sir, it now emerges, because it seems—'

'I've remembered the lady since I saw you yesterday, Peach. I've met her myself, as a matter of fact, at Masonic Ladies' nights. And a more charming lady you couldn't wish to encounter. So I can save you a bit of time there. I should put her way down on your list of suspects, and devote your energies to some more worthy possibility.'

'Really, sir. An interesting thought, that. Because I've just been told that Ruth Carter wasn't where she says she was at all, at the time when Claptrap Carter bought it.'

'I hate these Americanisms, Peach, as I'm sure I've told you before. And Mrs Carter – Ruth, as you say – struck me as a woman who would certainly never commit homicide. I'm sure whoever has denounced her is quite unsound. Who is it?'

'Her mother, sir. Most respectable elderly lady, she seemed to me, sir. But I haven't your eye for these things, I know. I'd better let the team know Ruth Carter's not to be investigated. But I think I'd better say it's on your orders – the fact that she seems a charming lady may not be enough to convince them, in itself.' He was staring at the wall behind Tucker, on a line two inches above his head, which his chief should have seen as a danger signal.

'Of course you must investigate her, Peach! Why on earth must you take things I say so literally? Who else have you got in the frame?'

'Senior Tutor at the UEL, sir. Walter Culpepper. Told you about him before, sir. His ancestor rogered Queen Catherine Howard, sir, if you remember, and was executed for it. So, you could say he comes from a criminal family, in a way.'

'Isn't he the man you thought was desperate to become the Director of the UEL himself?'

'That's the cove, sir. Right clever bugger, he is.' Percy knew brains always made his chief wary, if not suspicious.

'You'll need to handle him carefully, you know. Treat him with kid gloves.'

'Really, sir?' Peach looked immensely disappointed. 'I'd rather thought we might give him a bit of third degree, if you gave the word for it. Shine a light in his eyes, shout at him a bit, maybe make sure he fell off his chair once or twice in the course of an interview. He's sixty-one and a bit frail-looking, and I think he might blurt out everything he knows if you just give us—'

'*Peach!* You will do nothing of the sort. That is an order. Is that quite clear?' Tucker couldn't believe this awful man was serious, but he was never really certain of him, even after more than seven years.

Percy looked suitably disappointed. 'Very well, sir. I'll remember. Superintendent Tucker says that there is to be no third degree with a pensioner, on this occasion.'

Tucker had been hoping for a quick arrest, preferably of some known low-life criminal, with minimum disturbance to the new university, which he saw as raising the tone of the area. 'Who else have you got to offer? No more university dons, I trust.'

Peach pretended to think for a moment, then beamed delightedly. 'All of 'em, sir. All the main ones that we've come up with so far, that is.' He didn't know if a chaplain was a don, but he was prepared to stretch a point, to appal Tommy Bloody Tucker.

Tucker was duly appalled. 'Are you sure of that? All members of the university staff?'

'You and I know that it's usually someone who knows a man pretty well who kills him, sir. And a man who lives on a university campus is bound to have lots of people around him who know him pretty well, I suppose.' Peach beamed complacently at his supposition.

Tucker's gloom was at the other end of the facial continuum. 'Well. You'll have to go very carefully. I don't want any complaints about police insensitivity.'

'Right, sir. Not easy for us coppers at the crime-face to be as sensitive as you, sir, but we'll do our best.'

Tucker peered at him suspiciously, but found the DI's glance on that point above his head again. 'Well, as you've come up here, you'd better give me everything you've got on these other people.' He seemed to have forgotten that it was he who had summoned Peach to his office.

'Yes, sir. Well there's another woman, sir. Youngish. Lecturer in social psychology.'

'Ah! Sounds a possibility.' By which, Peach knew, he meant that she was female, young, and a psychologist; three of Tommy Bloody Tucker's greatest bigotries. Tucker leaned forward a little, spoke confidentially. 'You could lean on *her* a little, I should think.' He gave Peach his version of a confidential smile, which appeared in Percy's vision like a paedophile's leer.

Percy brightened. 'Third degree, sir?' he said innocently.

Tucker recoiled. 'No! Nothing like that. I just thought you might be a little more harsh in your questioning techniques than with more – well, more respectable people. Of course, I won't interfere, but—'

'Say no more, sir! Understood. Just as well you said, because I was planning to treat Carmen Campbell with kid gloves, sir. Her being black, and a citizen of Barbados, and—'

'Black, Peach?' Consternation flooded into the Tucker visage.

'More coffee-coloured, I'd say, to be strictly accurate.

144

Very attractive, actually. And she's a bright woman. Feisty, I think they call it nowadays. She'll give us a good run for our money, but I'm glad you think we can rough things up a bit. Don't think I'd have had the guts to do it myself, without the authority from above, but—'

'And a foreign citizen?' Tucker was aghast.

Peach beamed. 'From Barbados, sir. May have dual nationality, but I didn't ask her. It will probably come out, once she begins to fight back, so—'

'You will handle this with great care, Peach! With diplomacy, if you know the meaning of the word.'

'"Skill in negotiation", sir, I believe. You wouldn't like to go to see Carmen Campbell yourself, sir? Feisty lady, as I say. You'd probably enjoy the challenge, with your diplomatic skills.'

'Handle the situation with care, Peach. If in doubt, back off. With all these guidelines about racialism, we can't be too careful.'

'Yes, sir. We need to be careful about whom we allot to delicate tasks. That's why I sent DS Blake out to see the clergyman.'

'The clergyman.' It hardly seemed possible, but Tucker's apprehension actually increased.

'Chaplain at the UEL, sir. Quite a learned chap, apparently. Doctor of Divinity. Doubles the job with being the vicar at St Catherine's.'

A local vicar, a pillar of the established Church, and chaplain at the university as well? And Percy Peach trampling all over delicate clerical sensibilities? Tucker said faintly, 'Why on earth are you questioning him? He surely can't be involved in anything like murder.'

'Possibly not, sir. But the Reverend Matthews is an ex-army padre, and apparently an expert in small arms. And Claptrap Carter was killed with a Smith and Wesson .357 revolver.'

'I do wish you'd stop calling him that, Peach. Show some

respect for the dead. And surely the fact that this clergyman is a bit of a dab hand with a revolver doesn't make him a murderer?'

'Certainly not, sir. But he has his chaplaincy on the site of the UEL. And he knew the Carters. And he's been sniffing around Ruth Carter, ever since old Claptrap— since she became a widow.' Percy thought he might chance his arm so far, on the strength of the brief report on Tom Matthews he had received from Lucy Blake at lunchtime.

'Well, for God's sake go carefully with him.'

'Am doing so, sir. That's why I sent DS Blake up there on her own this morning.'

'You sent a woman to interview him?' Tucker gasped as if Peach had said he'd dispatched Crippen to do the job.

'Yes, sir. No hard stuff, as you said. But he's not married, the Reverend Matthews. I thought she could show him a bit of thigh, maybe cross and uncross her legs a few times, flash him a bit of this, that and the other, and then—'

'Peach! I trust you gave her no such orders!'

'Oh no, sir! Nothing as crude as that.' Peach leant forward confidentially, a mirror image of Tucker's effort on the same lines a few minutes earlier. 'I just told her to get up there and use her initiative. And to go in there on her own.' He tapped the side of his nose and gave his chief a grotesque wink.

This time Tucker's groan was audible. This odious man was surely pulling his leg. But once again, he felt he could not be absolutely sure of that. And he certainly wasn't going to take over the direct control of the case himself. He said faintly, 'For God's sake, be careful! Sometimes I wish I'd never assigned that woman to you as your detective sergeant.'

'DS Blake, sir? Very competent officer. Very pleased with her, I am.' Percy noted delightedly that the man still wasn't on to their special relationship.

Tucker felt as if he'd been interrogated himself, when he had merely wanted a report from Peach to prepare him for a media conference. He said, 'Look you'll need to sort this lot out. Come here with something more definite than all this speculative nonsense and—'

'There's another one, sir.'

'Another what?'

'Another leading suspect, sir. You said you wanted to know about all the main ones.'

'Well? Who is this one. Some other minority figure we'll be accused of harassing? A one-legged Asian homosexual, is it?'

'Oh, very good, sir, I must remember that!' It *was* quite good, except that Percy knew it had been lifted directly from a speech of the Chief Constable's about the difficulties of modern police work. 'No, sir, nothing like that.' He leaned forward again and spoke confidentially. 'But between you and me, sir, I've got hopes that this might be the one.'

'The one? You think this is a prime suspect?'

'Statistically, sir, he has to be a strong bet.'

Tucker was suspicious by now, but he could not resist the possibility that Peach had saved the prime suspect until last: he had done that sort of thing before. 'I'm a believer in statistical trends. They can be very helpful.'

'Yes, sir. And the pleasing thing about this is that it's my own research that has thrown it up. I can't resist a little personal pleasure in that: I'm only human.' Peach put on his modest choirboy's smile and looked at the ceiling.

You couldn't glare with any effect at a man who focused on the ceiling; Tucker had tried it before. He said irritably, 'Stop being so smug about it and give me the facts. Don't tell me this man is another lecturer at the UEL.'

'Yes he is, sir. But the really interesting thing is that a few discreet preliminary enquiries have revealed to me that this man is a Freemason. And as I said to you yesterday, my own private piece of research has shown that last year a Mason was four times as likely to commit a Brunton crime as your ordinary citizen. So it seems that there is four times the possibility of Malcolm McLean being our man than there would be if the same fellow was not a Mason. It's interesting how research can have practical implications which we might otherwise—'

'McLean, did you say? Malcolm McLean?'

'That's the cove, sir. I must say I never—'

'He's a member of my Lodge,' said Tucker dully. He looked like a man who had been hit over the head with a sock full of wet sand.

'Really, sir?' Peach concealed his delight. 'Well, as I was saying, he looks a most promising candidate for—'

'He can't possibly be a criminal. He'll be candidate for Master of the Lodge, in a year or two.'

'I see, sir. Does that mean I don't see him?'

'What on earth makes you think he could have killed Dr Carter?'

'He's involved in drugs, sir. In controlling and manipulating the supply of drugs on the campus of the UEL.'

'Malcolm McLean is?'

'Yes, sir.'

Tucker buried his face in his hands. Just when he had thought the afternoon could not get any worse, it had gone completely dark. He said hoarsely through his fingers, 'I introduced him to the Lodge.'

'Oh dear, sir.'

Tucker groaned. He said between his fingers, 'Even if you can prove the drugs connection, what makes you think Malcolm McLean might have killed Dr Carter?'

'Well, there's often a connection between hard drugs and murder, sir. Another statistic, that. National, not local, that one.'

'But you haven't got a connection between Malcolm McLean and Dr Carter.'

'Not yet, sir.' Peach watched the Superintendent's face emerge slowly from behind his fingers and then said, 'But I haven't seen him yet, you see.'

Tucker twitched. 'There is probably no connection whatsoever.'

Peach appeared not to hear this. He said excitedly, 'Old Claptrap might have been on to him. Might have been about to expose him. McLean would have found it easy to get a Smith and Wesson, from his drugs hierarchy. Might have gone in there on Saturday night and blown the Director's head apart, to preserve his empire.'

Peach seemed as excited as a schoolboy as Thomas Bulstrode Tucker sent him on his way. The Superintendent sat looking miserably out of the window when he had gone. Eventually, he buzzed his secretary.

There would be no media conference, after all.

Sixteen

M alcolm McLean was a lecturer in organic chemistry at the University of East Lancashire.

That didn't convey very much to Percy Peach, but he was determined to see him on his own patch and without prior warning. This was Drugs Squad business really, but a murder investigation took precedence over even that dark industry. McLean would be interrogated and investigated by the Drugs Squad officers in due course, but Percy had persuaded them that he needed to be certain first that there was no connection between the drugs traffic on the UEL campus and the murder of its Director.

A call to the faculty office elicited the information that Mr McLean had a laboratory session with second-year students which would finish at 4 p.m. Peach arrived with Lucy Blake at 3.55 and watched the students coming out of the chemistry laboratory in ones and twos. Catch him off guard at the end of a busy working day, thought Percy: you didn't give any consideration to a man who might be distributing enough drugs to ruin the life of untold numbers of young people.

They went through the laboratory and found McLean in the small room behind it. He tried to dismiss them brusquely. 'If you're reps, you're wasting your time. We buy all our laboratory equipment and supplies on official requisition forms through the faculty office.'

Peach flashed his identification, introduced himself and Lucy Blake, and said, 'We'd like to have an informal exchange with you, Mr McLean. Here or at the station.'

McLean did not seem either threatened or irritated by Peach's uncompromising opening. He was a man in his late thirties, with deep-set, watchful brown eyes. He had a square face which was lengthened a little by a luxuriant but neatly trimmed beard, silvered with the first touches of grey. He looked from one to the other of his visitors, then said, 'I don't see how I can possibly help you, but I suppose you'd better sit down.'

There was a semicircle of six chairs, tightly crammed into the small room, which looked as though they were arranged to accommodate a small tutorial group. McLean pulled two of these forward towards his desk, then sat down in his own chair on the other side of it. He said, 'Is this in connection with the murder of our respected Director?'

Peach noticed the edge of contempt in the last phrase, noting again how that traditionally hostile figure, the mother-in-law, was still the only person they had encountered who had shown any real affection for Dr George Andrew Carter. More importantly, he noted how McLean had immediately gone boldly for the murder as the reason for their presence. A diversionary tactic, to deflect them from the drugs connection he wanted to hide? The safe raising of a crime of which he knew he was wholly innocent? Or a bluff, hoping that his very boldness would diminish any suspicions they held about his connection with the death of the Director?

Peach smiled grimly. 'We may wish to question you about the murder of Dr Carter. Eventually.'

'Eventually?' McLean's eyebrows arched theatrically. A cool customer, this. Peach thought he held a reasonable hand, but recognized that he would need to play his cards skilfully against such an opponent.

He said evenly, 'Mr McLean, we are here to question you about the possession and the supply of illegal drugs.'

Beyond a raising of the eyebrows again, McLean did not react facially. He said, 'I've no idea what you're talking about. And I hope you have some reason for making such wild statements. I'm sure some of my colleagues in our Faculty of Law would be most interested in the legal implications.'

Flannel, thought Percy. This bugger's playing for time while he thinks. But he doesn't know how much information we've got, and he won't, until I tell him. He said, 'I should get yourself a practising lawyer, if I were you. One well versed in criminal law. I've no doubt the other, non-university, organization which employs you will come up with one.'

'I've told you. I've no idea what you're talking about.' McLean gave them a mirthless smile, but Lucy Blake was sure as she made a note of his denial that the brain behind those deep-set brown eyes was racing.

Peach did not smile. He said carefully, 'On Monday evening, a nineteen-year-old UEL student from the Faculty of Humanities, Peter Tiler, was arrested in central Brunton. He was carrying quantities of cannabis and Ecstasy.'

'Silly young fool. Deserves all he gets, if you ask me.'

'I don't, Mr McLean. Tiler was unable to identify his supplier, but he gave us details of the time and the place where this man regularly sold drugs to UEL students.'

'Very interesting, I'm sure. But I don't know why you should think—'

'As a result of this information, an arrest was subsequently made. The man was eventually identified as a Kevin Allcock.'

This time there was a reaction to the name, a tiny start of alarm which McLean controlled but could not quite eliminate. The tip of his tongue moved over the lips within the beard, like the beak of a fledgling bird seeking nourishment. He said, 'As I said, this is all very interesting. What on earth it has to do with me is quite—'

'Kevin Allcock remains in custody, and will do so after he has been charged whilst awaiting trial. That way he will be safe from anyone higher up the chain who would like to prevent him giving evidence.'

'Very efficient. But not—'

'As a result of this and other information gathered through our enquiries, we are quite sure that a certain Malcolm McLean is controlling and developing a lucrative, evil and highly illegal business on the residential campus of this university.'

McLean had been leaning back in his chair whilst he affected a disdain for Peach's earlier revelations. Now he dropped any pretence of disinterest in the matter. He leaned forward on his chair, put his hands on the edge of his desk, looked from the Inspector's intense face to the softer oval of the female one beside it, and rasped, 'Prove it! If you can!'

'Oh, I think we can, Mr McLean. Fortunately, that won't be my concern. I'm here to discuss the link between the drug-dealing on the campus and the death of its Director.'

Perhaps it was the sudden switch which made this seemingly most impassive man gasp; or perhaps it was the sudden mention of murder, with the charnel-house allure and fear that word still held, even in an increasingly violent world. But they had seen the first sudden flash of fear on the pale, bearded face before there came the ritual denial, 'I can't think that you're now trying to connect me with the unfortunate death of Dr Carter.'

Peach grinned, exulting in the first real sign of alarm he had seen in his quarry. 'Oh, I'd be delighted to do that, Mr McLean, if it's possible: I don't like people who make money out of the misery hard drugs bring. Where were you last Saturday night?'

The suddenness of the question cracked like an accusation across the table at Malcolm McLean. He was almost equal to it, however. There was a tiny, electric pause before he said, 'I was at home, Inspector Peach. Not that it's any concern of yours.'

'Oh, I think you'll find that it is, Mr McLean. With the wife and family, were you?'

'I don't have a wife and family, Inspector. I did have a wife, but we're now divorced.'

'All alone, were you?'

'No. I had someone with me, for most of the evening. And before you ask, I'm not prepared to reveal his or her identity.' He looked straight into Peach's dark eyes and allowed himself the first smile he had ventured for several minutes.

He's trying to imply he had a woman with him, thought Percy. He wants me to think he's too gallant to give away the identity of some married woman. But I don't buy that: this man is far too ruthless to keep her name concealed if he thought he could save his skin by revealing it. If he did have someone with him on Saturday, it was more likely someone from higher up in this drugs empire which is operating so lucratively for him.

What was interesting was that this cool opponent had clearly been shaken when he mentioned Carter's death. Perhaps there was a connection, after all. Peach said, 'It would be in your interest to provide us with a witness to your whereabouts on Saturday night and in the early hours of Sunday. Mr McLean, how well did you know George Andrew Carter?'

Again that tongue-tip appeared briefly amidst the nest of beard. 'Scarcely at all.'

'But you had worked under his direction for some years. You were on the staff of the old college of higher education, before the foundation of this university.'

'Yes. All right: I knew old Claptrap Carter, and he knew me. But we weren't on first-name terms. And I didn't kill him.'

'I didn't really think you would have. If someone gets in the way of the drug industry, the barons usually employ a contract killer.'

They both knew that was true, and McLean didn't bother with any denials. There was fear in those deep-set brown eyes for a moment before he said, 'I didn't kill Dr Carter. And I've no idea who did.'

Peach's departure was as abrupt and unexpected to Malcolm

McLean as his arrival and the conduct of the interview itself. He stood up and said, 'That's it, Mr McLean. For the moment, that is.' He glanced at his watch. 'My colleagues in the Drugs Squad will be along to question you within the next few minutes. Here or at the station, as you prefer. We like to offer our clients a choice of venue, whenever possible. Come on, DS Blake, let's go and continue our enquiries into the death of Mr McLean's Director.'

They walked out from the chemistry laboratory and back onto the main drive, looking up towards the old mansion, ignoring Malcolm McLean's anxious face at the window behind them. Peach almost wished the man could still hear him as he said, 'I think we'll check Mr McLean in the staff files in the Bursar's office. We know he hasn't a criminal record, but there may be things in his previous career which could interest us.'

The files were kept under lock and key and were highly confidential, but all security gives way to a murder inquiry. The Bursar himself unlocked the cabinet and flicked through the files, which were in alphabetical order and clearly labelled. He came to the 'M's', then frowned and extracted a short typewritten note.

Malcolm McLean's file was missing. It had been sent downstairs to the Director, three days before Dr Carter's death.

There was a cold north-east wind blowing through the darkness of the November evening. Walter Culpepper zipped up his coat, went to the door, then turned back and put on a woollen bobble hat to protect the balding dome of his cranium. 'I shan't be more than half an hour,' he called back to his wife as he emerged. Poking his red nose tentatively through the wide yellow doorway of the steeply roofed Senior Tutor's cottage, he looked more than ever like a weather-house figure or a garden gnome.

He walked rapidly through the familiar trees towards the

centre of the campus, wishing he had a little more flesh on his thin limbs to protect him against the cold. Suddenly he stopped dead, waiting until the figures moving towards the old mansion passed under one of the lights beside the drive to confirm his suspicion. He was right: it was that crafty, unexpectedly well-read Inspector Peach and his voluptuous female side-kick.

They were still about the place, then, still turning over stones. He had thought they would come back to him before now; they surely would, in due course. He stood quite still until they disappeared into the old house. Then he looked at his watch and hurried on. The man hadn't really wanted to meet him at all; he had been able to detect his reluctance from his tone on the phone. If he was late, the fellow might very well be gone.

The chaplaincy was a miserable building. It was dimly lit. Its fluorescent light was at once harsh and inadequate, with a constant, irritating flicker. A symbol of the uncertain and diminishing place of religion in the modern world, thought Walter Culpepper with satisfaction as he approached. He could smell the fumes from the ageing oil heater, which provided a little warmth for the interior, before he even opened the entrance door.

The Reverend Thomas Matthews seemed to be as nervous as he felt himself. Walter said, 'They didn't give you much of a place here, did they? Cold wooden building, without proper heat and light.' He grinned his elfish grin as the clergyman looked embarrassed, then said, 'It's the best I can do as a conversational opening, young man. Like Henry Higgins, I'm not too bad at the large talk, but I have no small talk at all.' The words died into his involuntary high-pitched giggle.

The Reverend Matthews didn't pick up his allusion. He said, 'Forgive me, but it's time I was getting back to my church in Brunton. It would be better if you came straight to the point, Mr Culpepper.'

'I shall do that, young man. I approve of plain speaking.'

Yet he couldn't quite bring himself to broach the matter, not directly. He rubbed his thin hands together. 'Been bothering you, have they, these CID people?'

'Not really. I had a female detective sergeant in to see me this morning.' Tom Matthews certainly wasn't going to reveal his misgivings about that exchange to this puckish figure.

'Dark red hair? Very attractive, in a Rubenesque sort of way?'

'Yes, I suppose she was.'

'DS Blake, that would be. Very nubile. Wouldn't mind her taking down my particulars!' Again that high-pitched cackle rang round the ceiling of the big, empty room.

'Don't you think you'd better talk about the reason you wanted to see me? You said it was urgent when you rang.'

'You're quite right. I shouldn't be wasting your time and mine with futile fleshly imaginings! It's about the death of old Claptrap Carter.'

'I see. I don't mean to be rude, but wasn't Dr Carter younger than you, Mr Culpepper?'

'Touché, Reverend Matthews!' A theatrical giggle. 'Indeed he was, considerably younger than I am – but not in spirit! I intend to maintain a Falstaffian zest for the good things of life for another twenty years, if I'm spared. Whereas old Claptrap had been fifty-eight from the day he reached eighteen, I should think!'

Tom Matthews smiled in spite of himself. There was something infectious about the older man's mischief, about learning which carried itself so lightly. He knew Culpepper was a considerable scholar, had himself read and enjoyed the Senior Tutor's excellent little book on the poets of the First World War. He said, 'I know what you mean. But perhaps we shouldn't speak ill of the dead.'

'A very pious sentiment. Appropriate in a man of the cloth! But it's that death I want to talk about. It's causing some of us a bit of embarrassment, isn't it?'

Tom wasn't going to comment on that. He said rather

stiffly, 'What was it you wanted to see me about, Dr Culpepper?'

'Walter, please, my dear fellow! We can surely dispense with the formalities, between friends. Well, look here. The CID people are still ferreting about. And it could be quite awkward for some of us if they start prying too deeply into our private lives. It's no secret that I had no time at all for old Claptrap—'

'Hated him enough to kill him, I heard!' Tom grinned: the old boy's waspish humour must be infectious.

Culpepper looked at him with his head on one side like a startled bird, then cackled heartily. 'Indeed I did, I don't deny it! When he got the directorship of the place and I didn't, I could have cheerfully shot him!' He straightened his face with an effort. 'I didn't, of course.'

'Of course not.'

Culpepper looked at him quizzically again. For a sky pilot, this man seemed to have a highly developed sense of irony. 'No. But it seems Claptrap was killed last Saturday night. Either late Saturday night or early Sunday morning, from what I can gather from the questions being asked about the site. So we all need an alibi for those hours.'

'Some of us might. Those who feel they are under police suspicion.' Tom gave him a small, not unfriendly smile.

Enigmatic as well as ironic, now. You couldn't even rely on the established church of the realm for respectable dullness now. Walter gave up the pretence of lightness and ploughed on resolutely, 'I thought I was in the clear. I told this miniature Oliver Hardy who's strutting about the place – DI Peach, I think he called himself – that I was up at Lancaster at my son's place on Saturday. They made us a bit of a party for the wife's birthday. I gave the details of all that to this Peach fellow. But we were back about eleven thirty. And it now seems we need to be able to account for ourselves for several hours after that.'

'But your wife can alibi you for those hours, surely?'

Culpepper looked uncharacteristically embarrassed. 'Well no, actually. She went to bed, you see, as soon as we got home. And I – well, I went for a bit of a wander round the campus, to clear my head. Perhaps I'd drunk rather too much – I'm rather fond of the port, but it doesn't seem to agree with me any more.' He stopped, perhaps aware that he was talking too much, to cover his discomfiture.

Tom Matthews looked at him hard. 'This is all very interesting, Walter. But I don't see how I can be of any help.'

'Well, I thought that if we said I'd come round for a chat with you at the vicarage, it might help both of us.'

Tom felt himself flushing as he said, 'I can see how it might help you. I don't see how my telling such a lie could possibly help me.'

The red, old-young face was suffused with a crafty smile. 'Don't you? It would surely help you to be able to provide an account of where you were in those hours, with a witness to it. In view of your relationship with Ruth Carter, I mean. The lover in the eternal triangle is always a suspect. Even someone as unworldly as me knows that.' He grinned his gnomic grin, looking as happy as an awful child in his attempt at blackmail.

The Reverend Tom Matthews was outraged. He didn't often stand on the dignity of his cloth, but it seemed an insult to his Church, to all clergymen, that he should be asked to take part in a sordid pact of dishonesty like this. Yet he found it difficult not to smile, to giggle with his sprightly tempter, as he said, 'I can't lie for you, Walter. But it would in any case be impossible. I was away at the weekend. I came back early on Sunday morning, in time for the ten o'clock service at St Catherine's. My housekeeper knows that. So I couldn't possibly tell anyone that you came to the vicarage late on that Saturday night, even if I was willing to do it.'

Walter Culpepper looked like a disconsolate Mr Punch. He said sadly, 'I was counting on you, Tom. I can't think of anyone else who might do it.'

There was a pause, whilst Tom Matthews wondered just

why it should be so important for the Senior Tutor to have his alibi. Eventually he said, 'Did you see anything significant? When you were wandering about the campus on Saturday night, I mean.'

'No, it was pretty quiet, really. It usually is on a Saturday night. There were the usual student drivers and motorcyclists, coming in late. I had to dodge about a bit. But there's nothing unusual in that.' He intoned:

> '"Every one-horsepower mind has bought
> Its ninety-horsepower juggernaut;
> And rideth handsome, high and wide,
> In registered, licensed homicide."'

He cackled delightedly. 'Not a great poet, perhaps, Ogden Nash, but he has wit and perspective, both qualities increasingly rare in the modern America.'

The Reverend Matthews smiled, stood up, looked down on his roguish visitor as affectionately as on a mischievous small boy. 'I really must be going, Walter. I'm sorry I wasn't able to help you.'

He saw the Senior Tutor off the premises, then went and turned off the big oil heater, which gave out such consistent fumes. As he switched off the lights and made the chaplaincy as secure as an ageing wooden building could be, he wondered what on earth Walter Culpepper had been up to on Saturday night, that he should ask a man he scarcely knew to lie for him.

Outside, the wind was colder and keener than ever, gusting around the tall new buildings which had been erected for the expanding university. Walter Culpepper, thrusting his frozen hands deep into the pockets of his coat, was already regretting his trip to the chaplaincy. For his part, he wondered just what the Reverend Thomas Matthews had been up to on that fatal Saturday night, when he had admitted being away from the vicarage at St Catherine's.

Seventeen

O n the next morning, the Friday after her husband's death, Ruth Carter looked out nervously through the big modern window of the Director's house onto a scene which held not a single human figure.

It had always been one of the advantages of the house that it was secluded and relatively private, even on a campus which accommodated two thousand students by day and a residential community of six hundred overnight. She had been happy that the tall trees from the more gracious age of the mansion and the three-hundred-acre private estate had been preserved when this new house was built. They had provided a welcome curtain from the curious attention of the academic world around them, had secured the family against the goldfish-bowl effect which a starker position for the house would have afforded.

Now what had usually felt pleasantly secluded felt isolated from the rest of the campus; the trees which had stood like friendly sentinels against a curious world seemed ominous, even brooding. She was almost glad when the dark blue Mondeo eased into view round the tall cedars, exactly at the time arranged, the note of its engine totally inaudible behind the double glazing. At least the tension of waiting was over.

She was wary of Peach: she did not take her eyes off him as he came strutting aggressively into the drawing room where she had the coffee and biscuits waiting on the long, low table. He still managed to surprise her, simply by letting his sergeant fire the opening salvo. Lucy Blake opened her notebook and said unhurriedly, 'You said you spent the whole of last weekend at your mother's house, Mrs Carter. We now know that isn't true.'

Ruth Carter tried hard to take her time. She had known it would be this, but she had expected questions and the opportunity to revise her position with some dignity. When it was boldly and calmly stated to her like this, it seemed more difficult to argue. Yet she knew she must: she couldn't just collapse into abject apologies and beg for mercy, if she was to convince them of other things. She said, 'May I ask what grounds you have for calling me a liar?'

Her resistance brought in Peach, in full battle order. 'No, you may not, Mrs Carter. Do you wish to stand by your original account of where you were on Saturday night and Sunday morning? I should warn you that we shall have it presented to you for signature as an official statement, if you do so.'

Ruth Carter was not prepared for this bristling aggression. For the last eight years, she had been the wife of first a college Principal and latterly a university Director, and people had accorded her the status and respect due to those roles. Few people outside the family had even ventured to argue with her, in the last few years, and Peach's confrontational stance shook her far more than she would have expected. She said quietly, 'No. What I told you on Monday about my whereabouts at the weekend isn't true. I'm sorry, but I had good reason for the deception.'

'No! Let's be clear about this, Mrs Carter. There are no good reasons for lying. Not when a man has been murdered and we are trying to conduct a proper investigation into that death. Especially when that man is your husband.'

Ruth Carter sat very erect. She wore a rich blue sweater above a pale grey skirt, lighter than the one she had worn when they had interviewed her at her mother's house four days earlier. She was a woman who had run many committees in her time; a person who was used to controlling the pattern of events rather than being at their mercy. Being confronted, questioned, accused, like this, was a situation she had not had to meet in her forty-five years. It gave her an unfamiliar feeling of vulnerability. But she still had certain advantages. The biggest one was that she found her shrewd brain was still working clearly, even in this situation of extreme stress.

She said calmly, 'I'm sorry. I hadn't appreciated that private feelings and relationships cannot be protected, in a situation like this. My mind was still trying to absorb the shock of George's death, when you spoke to me on Monday. I concealed things I realize now that I should have revealed.'

Lucy Blake spoke equally calmly, equally quietly. 'I spoke to you when you returned to this house on Wednesday morning, Mrs Carter. You could have told me the truth about your whereabouts at the time of your husband's death then, but you chose to go on concealing it.'

Good girl, Lucy! thought Percy Peach. Once you've got a batsman on the back foot, keep him there and dodging about – even when it's an elegant woman who may never have touched a cricket bat. It was time for the fast yorker. He said, 'So the only conclusion we can draw is that you would have gone on deceiving us indefinitely, if I had not been able to confront you with your lies this morning.'

He saw the hostility in the blue eyes beneath the ash-blonde hair. But Ruth Carter sounded calm enough as she said, 'That is entirely possible. I am not used to parading my private life before strangers.'

She made it sound as if she were defending her integrity, instead of a series of lies, thought Peach. He said, 'You had better tell us now exactly where you were last Saturday night and the early hours of Sunday. Preferably with the name and address of someone who can confirm the details. I'm afraid you can no longer expect us to accept your word at face value, Mrs Carter. You have forfeited that by your earlier deceptions.'

'Very well. I was with a man, Inspector Peach. As you may or may not have suspected.' A slight, acerbic smile edged the lips in the oval face.

DS Blake had her small gold ball-pen at the ready. 'We need to know exactly when, Mrs Carter.'

'For Friday night and Saturday night. Until about eight a.m. on Sunday, in fact.'

A strange time to leave a lover; or for the lover to leave you. If she appreciated that, she gave no sign of it. She sat very still and erect on the edge of her armchair, awaiting the obvious and inevitable question. It came not from Peach, as she had expected, but from DS Blake, who did not even look up from what she was writing as she said, 'And what is this man's name, Mrs Carter?'

For the first time, she hesitated. Then she said. 'I do not wish to tell you that. I realize that when you are investigating a murder, ordinary decencies and confidentiality go by the board. But the circumstances are unusual. I know he had nothing to do with the murder, and I must respect his privacy against the intrusions of the tabloid press.'

Peach said, 'I'm afraid you do not have a choice about that, Mrs Carter. You still do not seem to recognize either the reality of the situation or the seriousness of what you have already done. You could be facing a charge of obstructing the police in the performance of their duties unless you now cooperate with us as fully as you possibly can.'

He was coldly polite rather than vehement, watchful as he spoke, considering this cool woman for the first time seriously as a major suspect in this strange killing. She didn't give much away, behaving as if she knew that he was observing her, was weighing her qualities as a murderer. There was anger in her dark blue eyes, and a hint of strain as she brushed away a non-existent strand of hair from her forehead. But her voice was level enough as she said, 'Do I have your assurance that whatever I tell you will be confidential?'

'No! I cannot give any such assurance, and nor could

any investigating officer. All I can say is that if, at the conclusion of the investigation, whatever you tell us has no part in any subsequent court case, we shall not release it. That is something I say to everyone involved in questioning, but there can be no guarantees. Now, it is high time you told us exactly where you were last Saturday night.'

'I was in a guest house in the Yorkshire Dales. In Kettlewell.'

Lucy Blake noted the landlady's name and the phone number, whilst Ruth Carter poured coffee with a steady hand and the tension built in the quiet, elegantly furnished room. Peach and the Director's widow eyed each other, not without a certain respect on both sides. Then Peach asked the inevitable question. 'And who was the man who was with you on those nights?'

She looked him full in the face. Her resentment was contained in the cold, measured way in which she articulated the information she had known all along she would have to give him. 'The Reverend Thomas Matthews. Vicar of St Catherine's Church in Brunton, Chaplain to the University of East Lancashire.' She intoned the titles carefully, syllable by syllable, and her eyes blazed with challenge as she concluded them.

Peach wasn't going to rise to that challenge: any moral condemnation was both beyond his remit and outside his personal code. He said quietly, 'Thank you. We shall confirm these facts with the gentleman concerned, of course. If they prove to have nothing to do with the murder of your husband, they will not be released by us. I have no control over the actions of non-police personnel.'

'Journalists, you mean, don't you? Oh, they'll have a fine time, won't they, with this situation? You can see the head-lines now. "Brunton Vicar Forms an Adulterous Relationship with the Wife of the Director of the New University of East Lancashire!" "Randy Wife of Dead Director was Dropping her Drawers with Local Vicar!" "University Chaplain Gets his End Away on Dirty Weekends with the Wife of the Boss who Appointed Him!" The gutter press will have a field day. And Tom Matthews will be destroyed overnight.'

Peach sipped his coffee, nibbled his shortbread, took his time over the opportunity with which she had presented him. 'Not necessarily. Not unless you are involved in murder. I said we would only release the information if it was strictly necessary to do so, that is, if it proved that either or both of you were in some way involved in the murder of George Andrew Carter.'

Her breasts rose and fell under the fine wool of the dark blue jumper as she glared at him, realizing the implications of what he said, furious with herself for affording him the opportunity to say it. She did not answer him directly. Instead, she said, 'Tom Matthews is a fine man, Inspector Peach. A lonely man, perhaps. But he has no wife and no close attachments. If anyone is at fault, it is I.' She kept the grammar correct, he noticed, selecting her words as carefully as the head girl she had once been, even when she spoke of adultery. 'I was the bored housewife, if you like. I was the woman whose marriage was at an end, who was waiting until the children should have left home and the husband should have made his final career move before she finished with her husband. My marriage was at an end, Inspector Peach! I was at fault only in not waiting until the formal ties had been severed.'

She was speaking with real passion, for the first time in either of the interviews he had conducted with her. Peach said quietly, 'Mrs Carter, I have neither the right to make moral judgements nor any interest in doing so. Your conduct is of interest to me only in so far as it has any bearing on the death of your husband.'

She looked at him, breathing hard, as if she suspected he was lying. Then she nodded her head curtly. 'Thank you. I suppose what I'm saying is simply that it's important to me that people don't see my relationship with Tom as some sordid tale of a bored, pampered woman seeking a bit of casual sex on the side. I shall marry Tom Matthews, in due course. I should have done that even if nothing had happened to my husband.'

Peach nodded politely: such questions, as he had indicated, were not his concern. 'So you were at this guest house in Kettlewell on Friday night and Saturday night.'

'Yes. We spent the daylight hours of Saturday walking in the Grassington area. We returned to the guest house for the evening meal, and we didn't go out again that night.'

So they were alibis for each other in the important hours when Carter had been shot through the head. Peach said gently, 'Is there any independent witness who can confirm this?'

She looked outraged for a second that her word should be doubted. It was probably a long time since either she or the Reverend Matthews had had their probity questioned. But she saw the logic of his question, even underlined for him the grounds for his persistence. For she said with a wry smile, 'I suppose I should have expected whatever I said to be questioned, once I had lied to you on Sunday about where I was at the weekend. And no, I don't think I can provide you with an independent witness. You can ask Mrs Jackson, who keeps the guest house, when you are confirming that we spent the two nights there. But she has her own quarters, at the back of the house, and I doubt whether she would have been aware of whether we went out or not that night, after about eight thirty.'

'Were there any other people staying there?'

'No. She only has two double rooms for visitors, which is one of the advantages for Tom and me. We were the only people there last Friday and Saturday. By the way, you'll find that she knows Tom and me as Mr and Mrs Clark.' She smiled bitterly at the admission, and they caught a glimpse of how abhorrent this hole-in-the-corner conduct was to her. And probably also to the Reverend Tom Matthews, thought

Lucy Blake, recalling her exchanges with him in the morning. He had seemed an attractive, open personality, but with some of the stiffness of army rectitude about him, which recalled his days as a service padre.

It was Lucy Blake who asked, 'And what time did the Reverend Matthews leave in the morning? You say he left before you.'

She nodded. 'Tom was up at seven and away by half past. He had to be back at St Catherine's in Brunton for his morning service. I had a leisurely breakfast and set off to drive across country to Kendal at about ten thirty.'

'And Mrs Jackson didn't see anything unusual in this?'

Ruth Carter smiled. 'It had happened before. She must have wondered about us arriving in separate cars, but she never mentioned it. This was the third time we'd stayed there.'

DS Blake gave her an answering smile, then switched her questioning with all the aplomb of her mentor, Percy Peach. 'Do you possess a firearm, Mrs Carter?'

Ruth Carter's experienced but attractive features froze for a moment. Then she forced the smile back onto them and said determinedly, 'Not only do I not possess one, but I don't think I have handled one in my entire life. I have certainly never fired one.'

Lucy nodded. 'But Tom Matthews is something of a small arms expert, isn't he?'

'He is a fine shot with both rifle and revolver, I believe. That has never been demonstrated to me, though. I have never even seen Tom with a gun. We have never discussed the matter, but I fancy he knows that I would not like to have such weapons anywhere in my house.' Ruth Carter knew perfectly well what she was saying, that this was a firm denial of any involvement in her husband's death. Yet she smiled a little as she spoke, exulting in the thought that her lover would know such things about her without the need for them to be put into words.

Peach studied her for a moment, then said quietly, 'It is

168

now over five days since your husband was murdered in this house. And at least four days since you knew about it.' His eyes never left her, and he was sure that she realized that the words 'at least' meant that she was still in the frame for the murder of her spouse. But she was not visibly ruffled by it. 'You must have been thinking about who might have pulled the trigger on that revolver.'

'I have thought of little else, Inspector Peach, in the last few days.'

'So you must by now have some opinion on who might have killed your husband. In this case, Mrs Carter, I can assure you that your thoughts will not go further than this room.'

As if to emphasize the fact, DS Blake shut her notebook and put away her ball-pen, an action registered with a wan smile by Ruth Carter. She raised a forefinger to push away that non-existent stray tress from her forehead again, then said with a sigh, 'I wasn't the only one to have relationships outside our marriage, you know. George picked up what he could, where he could. Without damaging his career, of course.' The contempt which seared these phrases gave them at last a glimpse of her sour disillusionment with a marriage which had run its course.

This was difficult ground, but an area which might well prove fruitful. Peach said gently, 'Can you give us the details of any recent liaisons your husband was conducting?'

She thought for a moment, sipping coffee which was almost cold, wrinkling her lips in disgust at the taste of it. 'Not going to be much use as a vicar's wife, am I, if I can't serve decent coffee?' It was an assertion of the seriousness of her relationship with Tom Matthews, a notification that whatever the CID thought about her or Tom's guilt in this, they would have a life together in the future. 'I haven't paid much heed to these things recently. Not since Tom and I got together so unexpectedly. George didn't know about us, incidentally. He was far too preoccupied with his own concerns.'

Peach brought her gently back to his question. 'But do

you know of any recent relationships, casual or serious, which Dr Carter might have been involved in at the time of his death?'

'There was that black girl, of course. I think George was having a go at her. I couldn't see what she could possibly see in him, but I suppose she had different eyes from mine. Very attractive eyes, as a matter of fact. Very attractive girl. Intelligent, too, but I can't remember what her subject was. She's taught in the States, but I can't recall her name – she's from Barbados, I think.'

'Carmen Campbell?'

'That's the one. You know about her, then.'

'Yes. Can you think of any reason why she should have wanted Dr Carter dead?'

'None whatsoever. I should think our Senior Tutor is a better bet than any woman. He's never made any bones about his dislike for George. I share a lot of what he feels, of course: George was a charlatan and a hypocrite. But for Walter Culpepper it was verging on paranoia. He's a genuine scholar, which is why he saw more clearly than most, and earlier than most, what a poser George was. And the fact that George got away with it made Walter really furious: I'd say it turned his contempt into a real hatred. And an unbalanced hatred, I'd guess. Don't be deceived by his learning and his jokey exterior: our Senior Tutor can be a dangerous enemy.'

'Dangerous enough to kill? To shoot someone through the head in cold blood?'

'That's for you to decide, Inspector Peach. You asked me to speculate, and I've done so. I've watched Walter Culpepper's frustration growing over the years – they were in a college of higher education together before this university was even thought of, don't forget. When it was, Walter was passed over for the post which will next year become a vice-chancellorship, in favour of a man he detested. I think he's unbalanced – how seriously, and whether he's unhinged enough to have killed George, is up to you to decide.'

Peach nodded. 'We try to decide on the basis of the facts available, of course. People have to have the opportunity for crime, as well as the motive and inclination. But thank you for those thoughts. Is there anyone else you can think of who had reason to wish your husband dead?'

She thought for a moment. 'No. I saw only a very limited part of his professional life, of course.'

'Have you any knowledge of a drugs traffic on the site?'

She shook her head. 'I know that it is a danger in all student communities. I suppose in a new and rapidly expanding university like this, there might be rich pickings for drug dealers. But I have no knowledge at all of anything happening on this campus.'

Peach was disappointed, but not surprised. He believed her: it was what he would have expected. He wondered just what the Drugs Squad officers had been able to get out of Malcolm McLean, whether there was in fact any connection with the death of Claptrap Carter.

He stood up. 'Thank you for the coffee, and for being frank with your thoughts about this death. No doubt you will be in touch with the Reverend Thomas Matthews.' He allowed himself the ghost of a smile. 'If when you talk you can recall any fact or any person who will confirm where either of you were on Saturday night, please get in touch with us immediately. If we can eliminate anyone from our enquiries, it will speed up the processes of detection.'

Ruth Carter stood beside them as they got into the car, watched the rear of the Mondeo until it disappeared beneath the cedars. That was a formal way of telling her that they were both still under suspicion, she decided.

Eighteen

The police machine is thorough, but sometimes it seems to be using a lot of manpower for very little result. Eventually, however, this thoroughness often throws up unexpected and welcome results. Percy Peach received two such pointers when he returned to the Brunton CID section on the morning of Friday the 22nd of November.

The first came from a routine trawl of army records. It appeared that the Reverend Thomas Matthews had retained a Smith and Wesson revolver when he finished his service and moved back into civilian life. There was nothing sinister in this: the weapon was private property; Thomas Matthews, like most expert shots, owned his own weapon. During his army service he had only ever used the revolver in shooting contests.

Examination of the Firearms Licence Register showed that the Reverend T. R. Matthews was a member of a shooting club, but did not hold an individual licence to keep any weapon at home.

The second windfall for DI Peach concerned Malcolm McLean, the chemistry lecturer who had virtually admitted his involvement in the supply of illegal drugs on the UEL site, but strenuously denied any connection with the murder of its Director. The Drugs Squad, pursuing McLean hard about his control of the drugs traffic on the campus, had turned up a witness who had seen him on the site, within two hundred yards of the Director's house, at ten o'clock on the Saturday night when Dr Carter had been murdered.

Percy Peach sat with his hands on his temples for two minutes in his office, deciding how he was going to use these two precious snippets of information. Then he was summoned by his superintendent, and he went upstairs to report the latest information to the man officially in charge of the investigation. Might as well give Tommy Bloody Tucker every chance to make a fool of himself.

Carmen Campbell was stretching her long legs languorously on her desk and looking out of the window when the phone rang. It was Keith's voice from Cheshire, sounding as clear as if he was in the next room. Carmen was immediately erect and alert on her chair.

Keith's voice had that familiar hint of uncertainty which she found sometimes attractive, sometimes irritating. She did not like men who were too sure of themselves, especially in the matter of her affections. But she sensed that this was one of the occasions on which she might find his lack of confidence annoying rather than consoling.

'The police are coming round to see me. You said they might.'

'I said they *would*, Keith. But it's nothing to worry about. They'll probably want to confirm that I was with you for all of last Saturday night, that's all.'

'What if they ask about the nature of our relationship?'

'Then you may tell them whatever you think fit, Keith. I might be interested to hear it myself.' She grinned into the mouthpiece, picturing his anxious, innocent white face at the other end of the line. 'But I would be surprised if they asked you much about that. It's only routine. Just tell the truth and shame the devil, as my mother used to tell me.'

'Mine, too. The truth about Saturday night, you mean. That's easy enough. We went to the Who concert, and then we came back here. You spent the night with me. We made love some time during the night, but I'm not certain when.'

She laughed. 'I'm sure you don't need to tell them the last

173

bit. It might enliven their dull lives, if you gave them action replays.'

'Do I tell them we were stoned out of our minds?'

'No, I wouldn't do that. None of their business, is it? We might have had a few spliffs too many, but lots of people do that, during and after a concert. It's part of the unwinding, isn't it? But you'll only embarrass them if you tell them. The police know it goes on, but they don't want to do anything about it. Not pot. Not nowadays. Not unless you're dealing, which you aren't.'

'No. There isn't any in the flat at present, if they start looking around.'

She could hear the doubt in his voice again, and this time it really was irritating. 'I'm sure they won't want to search the place. Look, Keith, this is no big deal. Don't get yourself worked up about it. It's just routine, when there's a murder. The police have to eliminate me from their enquiries, along with a lot of other people. Just tell them the truth: that's all you need to do.'

'You're sure they won't want to know about the pot?'

'Don't mention it. All they want to know is that we were together from four o'clock on that day onwards. So you just tell them the truth and that will be the end of it.'

'All right. When shall I see you again, Carmen?'

'I've a hell of a lot on for the next couple of weeks. Student assignments to mark and return. I like to discuss each one with the student concerned.'

'You're too conscientious, you know. I've told you before.'

'Maybe. Anyway, I'll give you a ring on Sunday evening.'

Carmen Campbell put the phone down and stared at it hard for a moment. She couldn't see the two of them going on beyond Christmas.

'I can only give you ten minutes, Peach.' Superintendent Tucker stared at Percy over his gold-rimmed half-moon glasses, as if the report he had called for was an intrusion in a hectic day.

'That's enough, sir. Brief report on the progress of the case.' Percy spoke in clipped tones, through a face rigid with discipline, like a soldier at attention on parade.

'Well?'

'You were right about the murder victim's wife, sir. Mrs Claptrap Carter. She appears to have an alibi.'

'Didn't I tell you it would be so? Nice lady, Mrs Carter. Pillar of rectitude.'

'Yes, sir. Except that her alibi is that she was being adulterously shagged out of her mind at the time, sir. By a clergyman.'

Tucker thought this could not possibly be right. But he looked at Peach's rigid face, with his eyes trained above his superior's head, and as usual he was not sure. He had heard of people standing to attention, had even demanded it himself, on the occasional police parade. But Peach was the only man he had known who could sit to attention. He was doing it now, with his short legs thrust out in front of him, his back ramrod straight, his neck seemingly made of iron, his features frozen. Tucker said incredulously, 'This surely can't be so.'

'Told me it herself, sir, not an hour ago.'

'With a clergyman, you say?'

'Reverend Thomas Matthews, sir. Doctor of Divinity. Vicar of St Catherine's. University Chaplain.' Percy piled on the details in his clipped, neutral voice, each one more shockingly sensational than the last.

Tucker sought for some kind of relief from this lurid picture. 'Well, at least it means that neither of them is guilty of the murder of Dr Carter.'

'Unless they were in it together, sir. At it like knives one minute, blowing the husband's head off the next. It's not unknown.'

'But a lady like Mrs Carter. And a local clergyman, who

seems to be highly regarded by his parishioners. It's hardly likely, is it?'

'Doesn't seem so, sir. Except that they've no witness to support their story of where they were on Saturday night. And we've just had word that our vicar seems to be holding a Smith and Wesson .357, without licence.'

Tucker's jaw dropped, most appealingly for the man staring rigidly over his head. 'Remind me again, Peach, about the weapon which killed Dr Carter.'

'Smith and Wesson .357, sir.' Percy had the greatest difficulty in preventing a smile, but succeeded.

'And – and have you questioned the Reverend Matthews about this firearm?'

'About to do so, sir, when you called me up here. News only in this morning.'

'Well, complete your report to me and get about your business, then.' Tucker did his best to make any delay seem his inspector's fault.

'Yessir. Checking up on the West Indian bint's – sorry, lecturer's – alibi. Carmen Campbell. Planning to give her a bit of the third degree, sir, as you suggested. No marks left on her, of course, just firm questioning and bright lights in the face.' Peach kept his gaze upon the wall, but permitted himself the ghost of a conspiratorial smile.

'I never authorized any such thing! I don't want any accusations of institutional racialism cast at this force, Peach. Is that crystal clear?'

'Yes, sir.' Peach, who had never conducted a racist inter-view in his life, managed to imbue the two syllables with disappointment. 'Might be able to frighten the Senior Tutor, sir, with your permission.'

'Senior Tutor? At the UEL?'

'Walter Culpepper, sir. One of his ancestors rogered Queen Catherine Howard, sir, if you—'

'Yes, yes, I remember, Peach! What a squalid mind you have! What sort of man is this Culpepper?'

'In his sixties, sir. Lively mind, but quite frail physically. No experience of police brutality. Even waving a truncheon at him might loosen his tongue, make him smile the other side of his clever little face.'

'Peach! You will go very carefully. This man might become the first Vice-Chancellor of the University of East Lancashire.' Tucker rolled out the titles sonorously, as if he hoped to milk some vicarious intellectual dignity himself from them.

'Yes, sir. That might give him a motive for bumping off Claptrap Carter, you see. That and the fact that he'd hated him to the point of paranoia for many years. Your Mrs Carter told me that.'

'Not *my* Mrs Carter, Peach!' The horror of being dubbed the friend of a murderess suddenly reared itself before Tucker's fearful imagination. 'Do you think this Culpepper might have done it?'

'Might have, sir. He's a genuine intellectual, I think. Kept quoting *Hamlet* at me.' Percy knew how Tucker feared intellectuals. 'And he's no alibi for late Saturday night and early Sunday morning.'

'Well, then. Follow it up, get the evidence, and bring him in. Is that all?'

'Almost, sir. Except for the man who seems to be statistically the strongest bet of all.'

'Statistically?' Tommy Bloody Tucker took on the look of a suspicious goldfish, an expression which Percy would have loved to catch and fix for posterity. But we live in an imperfect world.

'Involved with drugs, sir. In a big way, it seems. Plenty of money and guns floating about in the drugs world, sir. And lots of murders.'

'Yes. I don't need you to tell me that, Peach. This seems much the likeliest area for an arrest.'

'Yes, sir. And the man in question was seen on the campus on Saturday night, sir. Drugs Squad have come up with that.'

'Pity you couldn't be so efficient yourself, Peach. Anything else against the fellow?'

'Yes, sir. Malcolm McLean, sir, that's the chap. And my own research supports the view that he's our man.'

Tucker peered darkly at the man still sitting so rigidly upright on the chair in front of him. 'Your own research? You're not referring to that ridiculous—'

'Masonic Prominence in Crime in the Brunton Area, sir.' Percy enunciated the words as if they were already a title for the monograph he had threatened. 'That's it. Four times more likely to be guilty of serious crime round here if you're a Freemason. Malcolm McLean's a Mason, sir!'

Peach produced his last sentence like a schoolboy triumphantly concluding a geometrical proof. For the first time, he relaxed his pose, and gave Tommy Bloody Tucker the most seraphic of his smiles.

It was but a short journey to the vicarage of St Catherine's parish church. The church itself rose high in smoke-blackened stone. The forty chimneys King Cotton and its associated industries had brought to Brunton had gone now, and there was a fund raising money for the cleaning of the stone, but the declining number of parishioners made it doubtful if the tall spire would ever rise in pristine glory above the houses which surrounded it.

The Victorian vicarage had been pulled down and six modern detached houses built in its grounds. The Church Commissioners had used some of the profits to build a practical, boxy, modern vicarage, a hundred yards from the church itself. 'Designed for a small family, really. Plenty big enough for a single man and his housekeeper,' Tom Matthews explained, as he led DI Peach and DS Blake into the square, rather clinical drawing room where he received church visitors.

He was dressed in a black clerical suit with a dog collar. He said to Lucy Blake, who had seen him in a green sweater and jeans on the UEL campus, 'I always wear formal clothes here. It's what most of my parishioners seem to expect.' He was patently nervous, and Peach saw it and delayed his first question accordingly. Not many people got less nervous if you kept them guessing about the purpose of your visit.

He waited until they were all sitting rather awkwardly in the heavy, worn leather armchairs which had come from the former vicarage before he said, 'We need to ask you a few important questions, Reverend Matthews.'

'Please call me Tom. Everybody does. I told DS Blake that when we met yesterday.' He grinned affably, looking younger than his forty-three years.

Lucy Blake countered with, 'There was quite a lot that you didn't tell me, though, wasn't there?'

Peach was ready to attack now. 'Quite a lot of vital information that you chose to conceal, in fact,' he said. 'Facts, or your version of facts, which you knew were quite vital to police officers investigating a brutal murder. I'd say to withhold information quite deliberately in these circumstances amounts to lying, wouldn't you, DS Blake?'

'Yes, sir, I think I would.'

Tom found the two pairs of eyes which studied his face and his every reaction, steadily and without embarrassment, more disconcerting than he could ever have imagined they would be. He said, 'I could hardly be expected to know what was going to be—'

'Definitely amounts to lying, I should say. Not very nice, in a clergyman. Not the sort of thing to inspire confidence in a congregation, young or old.' Peach shook his head sadly.

'Look, perhaps I should tell you that I've spoken to Ruth Carter this morning and I now feel that I can—'

'Thought you would have. Need to put your heads together, when you're compiling a new alibi for a murder.'

'Not compiling, Inspector Peach. The facts Ruth gave you earlier today were entirely accurate. We were at Mrs

179

Jackson's guest house in Kettlewell for the whole of Saturday night.'

'That remains to be seen, Tom. When someone lies to us as Mrs Carter did, we regard everything she subsequently tells us with a healthy scepticism. When a clergyman chooses to withhold information he knows to be central to a murder investigation, we do the same with him. Not that I can remember that happening before.'

Tom Matthews was rattled and discomfited, but he did not make the mistake of losing his temper. 'I can see what it looks like, from the police standpoint. Ruth wanted to protect me from exposure to the media: she knew what they'd make of her relationship with a clergyman. People may have stopped going to church, may even have ceased believing in God, but they're more prurient than ever when a clergyman is caught out, whatever his Church.' There was a flash of genuine resentment in the last sentence.

Peach said evenly, 'I can see all that. But let us be quite clear about what has happened. This isn't a matter of the *News of the World* catching a vicar with his trousers down. It's a murder inquiry, in which the wife of the victim chose to lie to the police about her whereabouts at the time of the killing, and her lover chose to collude in that deception.'

Tom Matthews listened carefully to each phrase, as if trying to find a flaw in the logic and failing to do so. He could see no room for bluster here, and bluster was in any case not his style. He said, 'All right. I'm sorry. Ruth was trying to protect me, and I didn't feel I could let her down, once she'd told you her original story about being at her mother's. For what it's worth, I can confirm that the facts she gave you earlier this morning about our two nights in the Yorkshire Dales are accurate.'

Peach's eyes had never left his face, observing his distress as well as his sturdy support for Ruth Carter. He said, 'That would be worth considerably more if there was an independent witness to support it, Mr Matthews.'

'I'm sorry. Both Ruth and I have thought hard about that,

as you might imagine, but we have no suggestions. We went to the Dales not just because it was near enough for me to get back here early on a Sunday morning, but because there are vast open areas where you can walk and get away from people. We chose Mrs Jackson's guest house because it was small and very quiet, reducing the chances of anyone seeing us together. That very quietness seems now to be a factor against us.'

Peach nodded. If the man was telling the truth, he was right. If he was lying, the absence of witnesses was in his favour. 'How long has your affair with Mrs Carter been going on?'

Matthews gave them a wan smile. 'If you mean how long have we been lovers, five months. We've known each other for just over a year. Ruth came across to help me set up the University Chaplaincy, once I'd been allotted that wooden terrapin building. She was kind and helpful with furnishings and so on, and I suppose we were both lonely. In my case, I was free of any encumbrances, but both of us knew that Ruth's position as wife of the Director could land us in a public scandal. As Ruth said, a lot of people in the UEL would have delighted in seeing Claptrap Carter cuckolded, and we've already spoken of the tabloid reaction.'

'But nevertheless you chose to become involved with each other.'

'Yes. We agonized for a few awful weeks, but it was obvious that Ruth's marriage was over. She was very clear that she was going to institute proceedings for a divorce, whether I was around or not.'

'Did Dr Carter know what was going on?'

'No. Ruth was sure he didn't, and she'd have known. George was more concerned with what he could get for himself than with watching his wife.' He allowed himself an acerbic and uncharitable smile.

'Do you know any names? I should emphasize that we should regard it very seriously if you again chose to withhold information from us.'

'No. Ruth had given up bothering, and I didn't want to know. As a matter of fact, his philanderings were useful to us. It was when he announced that he was going to be away – usually at some non-existent higher educational conference – that we had our weekends together. I didn't need much notice, you see: unless I have a wedding on, my Saturdays are normally fairly quiet. But of course, I had to make sure I was back here early on Sunday morning for the services.'

'And you've no idea who George Carter was with on any of these occasions?'

He looked troubled. 'There is one woman. But it's hearsay rather than any definite knowledge. West Indian girl I think, with an American accent. Tutor in the Psychology Department, I think. Very striking, very confident.'

'Carmen Campbell.'

'That's her! She came over to the chaplaincy a couple of times in the early days, with students. We had a lively discussion on one occasion, but she said eventually that formal religion wasn't for her, and I haven't seen her for months.'

'So how did you know about her meetings with Dr Carter?'

'I didn't, at the time. She discussed George Carter with me once, when there were just the two of us in the chaplaincy, after the students had gone. But only as a Director. What we made of him from the little we'd seen, that sort of thing. It must have been Ruth who mentioned that George was spending the night with her, much later on.' He grinned, a male grin which overrode the clerical garb. 'I remember thinking he was doing rather well for himself with Carmen Campbell!'

Peach grinned back; that had been his very sentiment, when he had first heard of the liaison. Power was definitely a better aphrodisiac than a dog collar. Tom Matthews had had to settle for Ruth Carter, an attractive enough woman, but one who brought with her dangerous baggage for a clergyman, as events were now demonstrating.

182

Peach said, 'We've interviewed Miss Campbell. It seems that she was forty miles away from the UEL at the time of Carter's death.'

'I'm pleased about that.'

He looked as though he genuinely was pleased, but perhaps that was the professional clergyman coming out, thought Percy. He said, 'Mr Matthews, you withheld information from us at the beginning of our investigation. I hardly need to say that you must now keep absolutely nothing back from us if you wish to be treated with any sympathy. Have you any information which you think might be significant in relation to the murder of George Andrew Carter?'

The Reverend Matthews looked very troubled: like a man struggling with his conscience, thought Peach as he waited. Very appropriate, for a clergyman – so long as conscience won the struggle. It did. Tom Matthews said, 'Walter Culpepper came round to the University Chaplaincy to see me last night. He's the Senior Tutor, lives on the—'

'We know Dr Culpepper.'

'Yes. Well, he came to ask me to help him.'

'To lie for him, no doubt.'

Tom Matthews looked thoroughly uncomfortable. 'Yes, I suppose so. He wanted me to say that we'd been together late last Saturday night, that he'd come to the vicarage here to talk to me about something.'

'But, being a pillar of rectitude, you told him you couldn't do it.'

'I wasn't here at that time, as I've told you. So I couldn't help him.'

Peach frowned. 'What time did he want to cover?'

'He said he'd been up to his son's house at Settle for the day. But he was back on the campus by about eleven thirty. He wanted me to say we were together for the hours after that. I never found out for precisely how long, because I wasn't able to help Walter, and I told him so.'

'Do you know precisely what he was doing at the time when he tried to arrange an alibi with you?'

Matthews hesitated, seemingly having to persuade himself again to let down the older man. 'He said that his wife went straight to bed when they got back to their house on the campus. He went out for a walk round the site. He didn't say how long he was out for, but it was that time that he wanted to cover.'

So that highly strung little intellectual gnome might yet be their man. Culpepper, who was not a churchgoer, must be frightened or desperate, to see the Reverend Thomas Matthews as a possible salvation. Peach looked forward to hearing what that entertaining and unpredictable man would have to say for himself.

But there was still work to be done here first. It was time to play his ace of trumps. He said, in the same calm tones he had used for the last few minutes, 'I believe you have a Smith and Wesson .357 revolver.'

Tom Matthews's open, fresh face paled visibly. 'How on earth do you know about my—'

'But no licence for that devastating instrument.' Peach carried on as if the clergyman had never spoken.

'I – I always meant to get a licence for it. No one has ever asked me about it. I kept it when I left the army, because it was my own weapon. Most of the army officers were rather tickled by the idea that a padre could be an expert shot. I only owned it because I was interested in firearms, and I had a certain expertise. The Smith and Wesson is a wonderful revolver, as you say, and—'

'Why no licence, Mr Matthews?'

'I always meant to get one. But then I found the licensing laws had changed and all the firearms I was interested in had to be kept at gun clubs. I belong to a gun club, but I've scarcely been there: it's not quite the image expected of a clergyman, in a conservative parish.'

'So where do you keep the Smith and Wesson?'

'In the chaplaincy at the university. I've nowhere here where I could keep it hidden, nowhere I could lock it away.' He glanced at the wall to their right, and they knew immediately that he was thinking of his resident housekeeper. 'At least I could lock it away in my desk in the chaplaincy.'

Peach nodded. 'You'll have to hand it over, Mr Matthews. And we shall have to check it against the bullet which killed George Carter.'

Tom Matthews's eyes widened with alarm. 'I can't. It went missing. A month and more ago. I can't be precise, because there was no sign of a break-in. The desk drawer had been opened with a key, as far as I could see. I don't suppose those locks are very individual.'

Peach regarded him steadily. 'Let's be clear about this. You've admitted that a weapon of exactly the type which killed George Carter was held illegally by you. You're now claiming that the revolver was stolen from your desk in the University Chaplaincy, at least a month ago, and that the theft was not reported.'

'I know. It doesn't sound convincing. But it's the truth.'

Peach stared at him for a moment. 'It might sound more convincing if you'd reported the theft at the time.'

'I couldn't. I hadn't got a licence for the Smith and Wesson, had I?'

'So you let a dangerous weapon disappear without any report of it.'

'I know. But I didn't want to confess I'd even held a revolver without a licence. It doesn't look good, for the vicar of a church like this. I thought it was probably a harmless student theft, that someone wanted it as a sort of trophy. And there are a hell of a lot of unlicensed firearms in the country. You know that.'

That was true enough: it was easy enough to get your hands on revolvers and guns, if you moved in certain circles. But Peach wasn't going to admit that. 'I'll tell you what I know, Mr Matthews. I know that Dr Carter was killed by a Smith and Wesson .357. I know that you held such a weapon. I know that you concealed a connection with the wife of the deceased, and supported her in a lie about her whereabouts at the time of his death. All now established facts. And now you tell me that the weapon was stolen from your University Chaplaincy, some weeks ago. Not an established fact; on the contrary, something I only have your word for. All in all, it doesn't look too good for you, Mr Matthews, does it?'

Tom Matthews ran a finger round the inside of his dog collar. 'I should have reported the disappearance of that revolver. I see that now, of course. But as far as you were concerned, it didn't exist, did it? I would have been opening a whole can of worms for myself if I'd come in and told you it had gone missing.'

'You seem to have opened an even bigger can by concealing its disappearance. If that is what you did, of course. We weren't expecting to find the murder weapon. It's a fair bet that it's safely at the bottom of some river by now.'

Peach never took his eyes off his man, looking for some disturbance in the vicar's troubled face which would tell him that this had struck home. But all Matthews did was to lift and drop his shoulders hopelessly and say, 'I've told you the truth. I'm not proud of it, but you now have everything I know about the murder of George Carter.'

Peach and Lucy Blake agreed as they got into their car beneath the towering black spire of the church that clergymen were in some respects exactly the same as ordinary mortals. You didn't know whether to believe them or not when they came up with something which was possible, but preposterous.

Nineteen

Malcolm McLean was in custody at Brunton police station. The Drugs Squad was holding him for twenty-four hours, whilst they followed up information he had given them in interview and framed the charges he would eventually face.

On Friday afternoon, when he should have been teaching chemistry at the UEL, McLean was languishing in a police cell. The morning interviews with the Drugs Squad superintendent and sergeant had been harrowing for him. They had played their man expertly, never revealing to him just how much they knew about the grim world of drugs which lay behind his burgeoning profits on the UEL campus, contriving to convince him that they knew more of his own activities than they actually did.

In the end, McLean was glad to remain in custody, after what he had told them. The barons of the vicious drugs industry, the top men whom he had never even met, did not take kindly to the release of any sort of information to the police. Swift and anonymous retribution to those who grassed on them was one of the pillars of their trade. Malcolm McLean knew well enough that these men would eliminate him with no more thought than they gave to a troublesome wasp if they discovered what he had said to the persistent police questioners that morning.

At least you were safe here, within these stark walls, beneath the single, small, high window with its black iron bars. The police lunch had been basic, but better cooked than

187

he had expected. It was a grim prospect he faced, all the same. There would be imprisonment for what he had done: the only thing at issue was the length of the sentence. He felt desolate and alone. For almost the first time since she had left him four years ago, Malcolm McLean yearned for the company and support of his wife.

Then, just when it seemed that things could not get any worse, he was taken up to the interview room again, to be questioned by Percy Peach.

Percy and Lucy Blake observed him closely as he was led into the small, square room by the uniformed PC. Malcolm McLean looked older and considerably less suave than when they had visited him twenty-four hours earlier in his chemistry laboratory. His face appeared thinner, almost gaunt; his deep-set eyes, which had then been so watchful, now looked hunted. After his hours of interviews and confinement in a cell, even his beard seemed ragged, rather than the well-trimmed addition to his features they remembered.

Percy Peach believed that the most rewarding time to hit a man like this was when he was down. 'Been doing some research on you, Mr McLean,' he said.

McLean raised his haggard face to confront this latest tormentor. 'There's nothing left to tell,' he said wearily. 'Those buggers had everything I know out of me this morning.'

Peach smiled. 'I heard you were unexpectedly forthcoming. Spilled quite a lot of appetizing beans, I believe. Some of which I might come back to.' He glanced down at the sheets in front of him and ruffled them threateningly. 'But I don't mean what you told the Drugs Squad lads, richly interesting as it was. We've been doing a little research at the University of East Lancashire.'

The deep brown eyes looked suspiciously into Peach's even darker ones. 'What do you mean by research?'

'Oh, nothing as grand as you university chaps would mean. It's not material for a doctoral thesis. Or even a dissertation. But it gave DS Blake and me a modest satisfaction. It might even put someone not a million miles from me behind bars for life.'

To Malcolm McLean, this man with the immaculate finger-nails, the muscular torso, and shining bald head above the jet-black fringe of hair, looked like a medieval torturer. He wanted to throw in the towel, to tell the police to do what they pleased with him. Yet he could not take his eyes off Peach's face. He said wearily, 'I don't know what the hell you're on about. I'm not going down for life; not when I've been cooperative; not for drugs.'

Peach regarded hem unblinkingly, then leaned forward so that his eyes were even closer to the prisoner's. 'For murder, you might.'

Fear started into the eyes which lay so deep within the head. It made Percy think he was on to something, even as McLean said roughly, 'Fuck off, Peach! I haven't murdered anyone! You can't fit me up for that!'

He switched his eyes away from the torturer to the softer face of his assistant, to the unusual ultramarine eyes and rich red hair of the woman who observed him so closely. But there was no relief here, just the beginnings of an explanation. Lucy Blake said, 'We've been talking to Miss Burns, the Director's secretary at the UEL. She helped us interpret some entries in the late Dr Carter's appoint-ments diary.'

Malcolm McLean wasn't even sure whether he was still thinking straight, but he knew this was important. He tried desperately to muster his few remaining resources. 'So what? I expect the old dragon told you I had appointments to see old Claptrap from time to time. So did lots of other people.'

Lucy smiled, 'Not so many people, Malcolm. Not many of your rank in the place ever saw the Director. As the university grew rapidly, he was much too remote a figure for ordinary lecturers to have many dealings with him. There are exceptions, of course. You are one of them.'

'And we were right! They are interesting, these exceptions,' said Peach, with immense satisfaction. 'You are the living proof of that, Mr McLean.'

'What do you want me to do?' said the man on the other side of the small, square table. He knew now he should not have refused the offer to bring in his brief. But he had not wanted to call in the lawyer whose name had been given to him for emergencies by those further up the ranks in the drugs racket: that would have told his superiors that he was in trouble, that he had slipped up and been taken in for questioning. He had not wanted that.

But he had quickly been out of his depth, and now he was floundering ever deeper. He felt an immense desire to confess everything he knew, to end this cat and mouse game once and for all. He said wearily, 'What have you dreamed up now?'

'Not dreamed up, Mr McLean. Filling in the picture, I prefer to call it. And I think the picture in which you figure is now very nearly complete. You had seen Dr Carter twice in the fortnight before he was killed. He had your file in his office at the time when he died. You were due to see him again, on Wednesday, had he lived. His elimination was very convenient for you, wasn't it?'

Malcolm McLean felt an appalling weariness, a wish to be finished with all this, a wish to be back in that bleak cell, which suddenly seemed a haven from this dark-eyed, round-faced, impossibly clean torturer. He muttered, 'It may have been convenient, but I didn't kill Claptrap Carter.'

Lucy Blake's quiet voice seemed to McLean to come from a long way away as she said softly, 'Tell us why it was convenient, Malcolm.'

'You know that, don't you? He was on to me. He knew what was going on.'

Lucy felt Peach tensing beside her as she said, 'He knew about the drugs, didn't he, Malcolm? Knew that you were the man organizing the distribution on the UEL campus.'

'Yes. Someone on the campus had told him. He'd never

190

have found out for himself.' It was the last vestige of defiance in him, the last faint trace of the perverted pride which had made him think he would never be exposed.

'Who told Dr Carter?'

He shrugged hopelessly. He didn't know and he no longer cared. 'Students, possibly. A tutor, after students had been to him or to her. Maybe someone who lived on the campus, one of the residents. Someone might have seen my dealers, got something out of them, like you did with Kevin Allcock. That crafty little sod Culpepper seems to know everything that goes on in that place. Anyway, Claptrap Carter knew, and he was going to make me resign. He wanted me to do that rather than expose a drugs scandal in his new university, he said. But he'd see I didn't get another job. Sanctimonious sod!' But McLean couldn't summon much energy, even to denounce the man who would have ruined him.

There was a lengthy pause, until he looked up from the table and into the relentless eyes of Peach. The DI's voice came at him in a passionless monotone as he said, 'What did you do with the weapon after you'd shot him, Malcolm?'

It was so quiet, so matter-of-fact, that it took the exhausted man a moment to assimilate it. 'I didn't kill Claptrap Carter!' he gasped after a second. 'I was exultant when I heard he was dead, ready to give three private cheers, but it wasn't me who shot him.'

'You're going to have to convince me of that, Malcolm. In view of what we now know about you.' Peach waited patiently for the logic of this to sink in. He wouldn't reveal the final, damning fact which the Drugs Squad had given him until he found whether McLean would lie about that, too.

Malcolm McLean would have compelled sympathy, even in Peach, in other circumstances. But this was a man who had cynically exploited the young people he was paid to teach and guide, who had probably killed the director of the institution in a ruthless attempt to protect himself. At this moment, Percy was merely glad the man hadn't given himself the protection of a lawyer. He waited through seconds which must have seemed like minutes to the man struggling to organize his thoughts, until McLean eventually muttered, 'I was nowhere near Claptrap Carter when he died.'

'Know just when he died, do you, Malcolm? Interesting, that. Because even we aren't sure of the exact time. Perhaps you could enlighten us.'

'I – I didn't mean that. I meant I wasn't around on Saturday night, when he died.'

'I see. Where were you at that time?'

'I don't know. At home, I expect.'

'With witnesses?'

'I live on my own, Peach. You know that.'

'Interesting. As is the information my colleagues have collected about your whereabouts late last Saturday night. You said you were at home at the time. But you were seen, Malcolm. By more than one person.'

'Seen where?'

They watched the hope draining from his face. 'On the campus of the University of East Lancashire. To be precise, in a storeroom adjacent to the chemistry laboratory, to which you no doubt had a key. Within two hundred yards of the Director's Residence where Dr Carter was shot.'

A blanket of despair fell over the shoulders of the defeated man. McLean said dully, 'I was there. There's no use denying it, if you know. If you have witnesses.'

Lucy Blake felt the thrill which surges through all CID officers when they scent a confession to a serious crime. It was still relatively new to her, and she felt her pulses racing in the silence which stretched as they waited to see whether McLean would go on. Eventually, taking her cue from Peach without needing to look at him, she said, 'What were you doing there, Malcolm?'

He didn't look up now. 'You know, don't you? I was meeting Kevin Allcock and my other distributor on the site. Seeing what supplies they needed. Keeping an overview of the situation.' That phrase was from a time of prosperity for him in his grim but lucrative trade, a time which had vanished without trace in less than twenty-four hours; he smiled mirthlessly at the quaintness of his words.

Lucy's voice was light but insistent, a stiletto after Peach's bludgeoning blade. 'And when you'd finished your review and your juniors had gone, you went and shot Dr Carter, didn't you, Malcolm?'

'No. I didn't kill Carter. I don't know who did.' He looked up eventually, when they did not speak. 'Are you going to charge me with murder?'

Peach grinned at him, back in torturer mode, stretching the moment of suspense. 'Not at present, Malcolm. No need to, have we? You're safely in custody. You'll be charged with serious drugs offences by tomorrow morning, and kept under lock and key. Gives us plenty of time to ferret about at the UEL campus and other places and come up with the evidence for a murder charge.' He stood up, nodding to the uniformed constable at the back of the room that he could take his man back to the cells. 'It also gives you time to review your situation. To come up with a confession that puts murder in the most favourable terms possible. I should get myself a brief, if I were you, Mr McLean.'

It was advice Percy Peach never gave until he was sure there was nothing more to be wrung from an opponent.

Brendan Murphy was waiting to report to Peach in the CID section. The detective constable had just got back from a journey down the motorways to Cheshire. 'That bloody M62's hell on a Friday afternoon!' he said with feeling.

'Nice day out for you. Expect you've been swanning about filling in the time and chatting up the girls at the motorway services. Any joy in Altrincham?'

'No. Unless you think a negative result is helpful. Carmen Campbell's boyfriend is a Keith Padmore. Very smitten with her, he seems.'

'Nothing surprising in that. The dusky Miss Campbell is both bedworthy and bright, a fatal combination for susceptible young lads like you. Dangerous as well, perhaps, but racing hormones never did notice danger.'

Brendan grinned. 'Keith Padmore's not a susceptible young lad like me. He's over thirty, I should think.'

'Ancient, then. What did he have to say for himself?'

'Not a lot. I should think Carmen Campbell runs their relationship, most of the time. But he convinced me he was telling the truth.'

'Which is?'

'Carmen Campbell was with him from four o'clock on Saturday evening until the next day. With others too, apart from the time when the two of them were in bed together. Party of six of them went to a pop concert, then back to Padmore's place. Two of them left before eleven, two others as well as Carmen stayed the night.'

Peach nodded. Every person you eliminated from the hunt enabled you to concentrate more fiercely upon the others. 'You're convinced this is a genuine account of what happened?'

Murphy nodded, glad of the chance to display his thoroughness. 'I pressed Keith Padmore a bit about the evening, and he eventually admitted they were all stoned on pot. Out of their minds, he said. Carmen Campbell was as high as anyone and handing round the joints. Doesn't sound as if she'd have been capable of killing anyone, even if she'd been in the right place to do it. She'd no vehicle in Altrincham, by the way, she went there and back by train. Anyway, there's no way she could have been anywhere but at Padmore's house in Altrincham at the time of the murder. Not unless we assume an elaborate conspiracy. I took the details of the other two men who were there overnight, in case we wanted to check the story with them, but I'm sure Keith Padmore was genuine.'

Miss Angela Burns, lately Director's secretary and this week unofficial aide to DI Peach, took them to the room. 'He's in the Bursar's office,' she said to Peach and DS Blake. 'Sit down and make yourselves comfortable and I'll make sure he's down immediately.'

The Senior Tutor's room was the most pleasant in the whole university. It was on the ground floor of the old mansion. Its big bow window came almost down to the floor and gave a view over a small walled garden. A few brave roses still flowered in the shelter here, and late dwarf Michaelmas daisies were making the last defiant colour burst of the year. Beyond the walls, the leaves of mature maples glowed vivid orange and crimson in the early autumn twilight.

Walter Culpepper looked even smaller and thinner than they remembered him as he came in and went to sit behind the huge curved desk. 'I used to see students in here, when we were just a college of education,' he said sadly. 'Now I'm mainly an administrator, overseeing the numbers in the different faculties. I think I told you last time we met that I'm supposed to maintain standards; what I do most of the time is to tell various people to lower their standards of entry, if they aren't getting enough students. I shall change my title next year.'

But would it be to Director or to murderer, thought Peach. Would this appealing little man be in the Director's Residence or in one of Her Majesty's prisons for life? He broke one of his rules of objectivity, allowing himself to hope that he wouldn't end this case by arresting Walter Culpepper.

He looked from the desk and the man behind it to the wall beside him, which was lined from floor to ceiling with books. Peach had studied them whilst waiting for the Senior Tutor's arrival. Most of them were books of English poetry or prose, but there were history and philosophy, too, and a host of other ephemera, including two volumes of Wisden. Culpepper caught his glance and intoned:

'"And still they gazed, and still the wonder grew,
That one small head could carry all he knew." '

He cackled, that mirthful, high-pitched peal they had heard before, but which still startled them. 'I do occasionally find the time to dip into my books, which is more than I can say for some of my colleagues.'

Peach smiled. 'Goldsmith has something for everyone, even detectives,' he said. 'Wasn't it he who said, "The true use of speech is not so much to express our wants as to conceal them"? I often find that's true, when I'm interviewing people.'

Culpepper was delighted. 'You're wasted in the police force, Percy Peach.' Both the CID officers wondered how he had got Percy's nickname, unheard of outside police circles. As Malcolm McLean had told them earlier that afternoon, this man seemed to know about everything that was going on around him. 'Should be more read than he is nowadays, old Oliver Goldsmith. "No man was more foolish when he had not a pen in his hand, or more wise when he had." Samuel Johnson said that of him: pompous old fart at times, the Doctor, but rarely wrong about people. What can I do for you, Inspector Peach and glorious comrade?'

The sudden switch from learned levity to the serious issue might have disconcerted some people, but Peach was used to this hopping, bright-eyed magpie. 'You can tell us what you were doing last Saturday night,' he said with a smile.

Culpepper's face changed as rapidly as a schoolboy's from mirth to concern. 'I wasn't here. I was up in Settle at my—'

'Until eleven thirty you were, yes. What about the next three hours?'

'Is that when Claptrap Carter was killed?'

'Yes. Almost certainly.'

'Ah! And you have intelligence that I was abroad at that time. The clergyman has peached on me to Peach!' He cackled at his wordplay. 'I should have known better than to confide in an Anglican priest. Swift said you couldn't trust them, and he should have known, he was one of them!'

There was something febrile about him now, and they

realized he was diverting his nervousness into a spatter of words. Peach said, 'The Reverend Matthews had no choice, Dr Culpepper: we had him against the wall at the time – metaphorically speaking, of course.' They grinned at each other across the big desk. 'Where were you after ten thirty on Saturday, please?'

'Wandering round the campus. I'm sorry, but there it is.'

'Until what time?'

'I can't be precise. We got back from Settle about half-past eleven. My wife said she was going straight up to bed, but I couldn't settle. I tried reading, but my head was splitting. My own fault: I'd drunk too much red wine at my son's house, then topped it off with a couple of glasses of port – I knew Patricia was going to drive us home, you see. But while the booze goes down very nicely at the time, I suffer later, these days. I took a couple of aspirins, then went out for a walk, at about half-past midnight, I suppose. I did a full circuit of the campus, as I used to do when our old dog was alive.' The red, humorous face of Mr Punch was suddenly melancholic with the thought of mortality.

'Did you meet anyone who can confirm this for us?'

He smiled sadly. 'Come on, Percy Peach, you know the answer to that. I wouldn't have asked the clergy to help me out if I'd had anything better available, would I?'

Percy forced himself to remain grave and unsmiling. This might be a murderer who was playing word games with him. 'How long does a circuit of the campus take?'

'I wasn't hurrying, so the best part of an hour. It was certainly well after one when I got back.'

'So on your own admission, there is no one to account for what you were doing between, say, midnight and half-past one last Saturday night. You were out on the campus on your own, very probably at the very time when Dr Carter was killed.'

'And I hated old Claptrap, didn't I? And I might, just might, become the Director in his place.' He thrust two bony wrists

197

forward at Peach, so that they projected like white sticks from his cuffs. 'It's a fair cop, guv'nor! Put the bracelets on me, I won't give you no trouble.'

Peach looked at the wrists and held his face impassive until they were slowly withdrawn. 'Did you see anything on your walk which might help us?'

The thin red face looked crafty. 'I saw that bearded chemistry teacher, McLean. Talking to some bloke I didn't recognize, in the shadows, near his chemistry lab. I remember wondering what he was doing on the campus, at that time on a Saturday night, when he wasn't even resident. I might have asked McLean to confirm my presence, but I doubt whether he saw me, and then I found you'd taken him in anyway – it was me who had to cancel his lectures.'

'Anything else?'

'No. I was nearly hit by some student roaring up the main drive on a motorcycle, so I kept to the smaller paths after that. It was dark, but I've lived on this site for years – long before we became a university!' He pronounced the last word with bitter irony, as his comment on modern academic standards.

Lucy Blake shut her notebook. 'Carry on thinking, please, Dr Culpepper. Anything else you recall from that time may be helpful to you as well as to us.'

'For you, my luscious one, I shall cudgel my brain without mercy!' He looked her up and down with what she could only afterwards recall as an affectionate leer. 'I expect that is politically very incorrect.'

She smiled back as she and Peach stood up. 'Extremely incorrect, I'm sure. I shall forgive you, if you can provide us with useful information.'

As they drove away from the old mansion at the centre of the UEL, Lucy said with a touch of irritation, 'He doesn't seem terribly worried. But I'm sure that man would go down to hell with a smile on his face!'

Twenty

'Sorry to bother you on a Saturday morning, but it's necessary, I'm afraid.'

He sounded apologetic, and he gave her one of his smiles. The flawless coffee-coloured skin and huge brown eyes of Carmen Campbell made even Percy Peach polite, thought Lucy Blake, as she followed him into the flat. Or was it the long, athletic legs and the shimmer of her hips beneath the plaid skirt as she led them into the neat living room? Coffee in a large blue pot was already on the table, though at Peach's suggestion she had given Carmen only twenty minutes' notice of this visit. At half-past nine on a Saturday morning, the flat was neat and tidy, smelling as fresh and wholesome as its occupant.

The modern room was also as elegant and startling as Carmen Campbell. It had a dark blue wall and three very pale yellow ones, whose austerity was broken by David Hockney prints. There was a sideboard of rich dark rosewood, on which stood colour photographs of a smiling, white-haired West Indian couple on a surf-fringed beach.

'Your parents?' asked Lucy Blake.

'That's right. They're both dead now.' She picked up the half-plate picture in its silver frame, looked for a moment at those smiling faces frozen in time, and then set it down carefully and precisely in the spot from which she had lifted it. She poured the coffee from the pot. 'You'll have to have it in mugs, I'm afraid, it's all I deal in! And don't let the coffee pot fool you: it's instant.'

Neither of them would have known that. The coffee was hot and strong, with the aroma of newly ground beans. When you were used to Brunton police station coffee, you lost any pretensions to being a connoisseur. Peach said, 'I thought we should come and have a word. Clear up one or two things.' He was watching her closely as he took sips of his coffee and piled up the clichés. She had given them the two armchairs and curled her knees beneath her on the sofa. Even in a skirt, she managed to do that gracefully, without flashing too much satiny thigh at them. She did not seem nervous.

Carmen said politely, 'How's the investigation going? Are you near to an arrest yet?'

He wondered how carefully that was calculated. It was innocent enough, but it subtly distanced her from any central part in the case. He said with a smile, 'You wouldn't expect me to tell you if we were.'

She wrinkled her forehead for an instant, then smiled back. 'No, I don't expect I would. I'd forgotten that you knew I had experience of policemen in my past, Inspector Peach. They were not British policemen, though. Barbadian police and American police are more excitable. More – confrontational, I think we psychologists would call it.'

Peach smiled. Confrontation was very much his style in normal circumstances. He remembered being distinctly confrontational with this woman, at their last meeting, when he had raised those very criminal acts to which she had just referred. But this morning's were not normal circumstances.

Peach took another appreciative pull at his coffee, crunched a mouthful of shortbread without hurry, and said, 'Your name keeps coming up in this case, Miss Campbell. Sometimes in unexpected contexts. You'd be surprised how many people have mentioned you.'

If she was dismayed or irritated by this, she did not show it. She picked up a biscuit and nibbled it in turn, almost in a mocking parody of Peach's action. Her eyes never left his face throughout the action. Then she said, 'Is that supposed to alarm me, Inspector Peach?'

'Not at all. I thought you might find it interesting, I suppose. It interests me, from a professional point of view. I find that people who figure in everyone's thoughts usually have some part in a crime.' He doubted even as he said it whether that was true, but he kept his features bland, his slight smile constant.

'Interesting. But in this case, perhaps you'd expect most people to be aware of me. I'm fairly noticeable, it seems to me. Most people remember me. I expect it's my colour, you see.' She grinned at them both, switching her eyes from Peach to Blake, enjoying her tease. 'I'd expect the wife to be aware of her husband's sins, and Ruth Carter is no fool. And Walter Culpepper, though I like him, lives on the site and makes it his business to know everything that's going on around the place. And as he hated George Carter, he was probably well aware of any small conquests like me which the man enjoyed.'

She'd mentioned two of his suspects, so she was taking a lively interest in his investigation. But you'd expect that, when the victim was a man she'd slept with. She'd want to know who had shot her lover, even if as she claimed the affair would not have lasted much longer. She hadn't mentioned Malcolm McLean, so perhaps she hadn't heard of this recent development. Nor had she raised the name of the Reverend Tom Matthews. But perhaps she didn't know of his relationship with Ruth Carter: the pair seemed to have concealed it pretty well, even if that twenty-first century John Aubrey who was Walter Culpepper had found out about it.

As if she read his thoughts, Lucy Blake said quietly, 'Have you been to the University Chaplaincy recently, Miss Campbell?'

The huge brown eyes, which had been studying Peach for any clue about his thoughts, transferred themselves calmly to Lucy Blake's young, earnest face beneath the aureole of red-brown hair. 'Not for many months now, no. Presumably there's a reason for that question?'

The blue-green eyes were as unblinking as Carmen Campbell's as Lucy said, 'He was another man we have been talking to about this death. Another man who mentioned you.'

Carmen smiled. 'I can't think why. I went there once or twice, when a couple of my students were using the place. I was curious, that's all. When one is working in a new place, one tries to find out as much as one can about the environment. He was a nice man, Tom Matthews, but we don't believe in the same things.' She smiled, presumably at the thought of how different their creeds were. 'Do you think he killed George Carter?'

Peach smiled back at her, acknowledging the fact that he had no monopoly of the abrupt question. 'Tom Matthews is an expert shot.'

She frowned. 'I seem to remember that, now that you remind me of it. But the press releases say George was shot through the head at point-blank range. That doesn't need any great skill, does it?'

'No. But the Reverend Matthews happens to own a Smith and Wesson .357 revolver. Dr Carter was killed with one of those.'

She nodded thoughtfully. 'But you can test it, can't you? Check whether his was actually the weapon which killed George?'

Peach was reminded again that this woman had been involved in a shooting incident when she was at Harvard, even though she had never been accused of handling the gun herself. He smiled grimly. 'We could, if we had the gun. The Reverend Matthews claims it was stolen from a locked drawer in the University Chaplaincy some time ago.'

She looked astonished. 'And do you believe him?'

Peach had no idea whether he believed Matthews or not, though he had puzzled about the question ever since he had heard the story. But he said blandly, 'I think I do, yes.'

She looked at him quizzically for a moment, then said, 'That's good to hear. I didn't think the police believed anyone. But perhaps it still helps to be a clergyman, in Britain.'

Peach did not rise to the bait. Instead, he said, 'Your boyfriend in Altrincham has confirmed that you were with him at the time of the murder.'

Carmen Campbell nodded. 'I told you he would. I was with him from four o'clock last Saturday, right the way through the night. There were other people with us, at the concert and afterwards. Do you want details of the Who concert? I can give you the order of their songs, if you like. More than there was in the programme, which anyone could buy.' She gave him a confident smile, mocking him, knowing that her story could not be shaken.

He smiled back. 'As I say, Keith Padmore confirmed that you were with him at that time. Unfortunately, DC Murphy, who went to see him, is a bit of a stickler for detail, and he pressed him about the circumstances. Mr Padmore was unwise enough to tell him that there were drugs around that night.'

This time she was surprised. They could see her thinking quickly, wondering what the implications of the statement were for her. She said carefully, 'As I remember it, there was a certain amount of pot smoked. Nothing else. And no one was selling the stuff.'

'Possession is still against the law, in this country.' Peach's voice was at its steadiest, his face at its most inscrutable. 'And we have only your word for it that nothing stronger was involved.'

'So what do you propose to do about it?'

Peach leant forward a little. 'Nothing, if it's left to me. I have more than enough on my hands with a murder investigation. But you must understand, I have a young, enthusiastic detective constable, anxious for results to put on his curriculum sheet, suspicious of any old sweat of an inspector who seems to be standing in the way of his keenness.' Percy offered up a mental apology to Brendan Murphy for the picture he was presenting.

Carmen Campbell studied Peach's earnest countenance. She didn't trust him, but she was still relatively new in the country, with convictions for drugs and an assault in her past. She said stiffly, 'There was nothing more than pot involved. I thought you ignored that, when it was just recreational use.'

Lucy Blake took her cue. 'Would you mind if I had a look round the place, while we're here? It would help if we could report back that your flat was clear of drugs.'

The Barbadian looked hard at her. 'Do I have a choice?'

'I think you know you do. We haven't a search warrant. We might not get one, even if we applied.'

They could see Carmen Campbell trying to decide what lay behind the request. A few seconds elapsed before she said, 'It's a long time since I had anything to do with serious drugs. But if I refuse, you'll conclude the place is stuffed full of drugs, with my record.'

Lucy smiled at her. 'And if it is, you'd have the place cleared and smelling as clean as a mountain stream, by the time we got back with a warrant!'

Carmen swept her feet from beneath her to the floor in a lithe movement. 'Search to your heart's content, DS Blake, you won't find anything.'

Lucy was on her feet immediately. 'Thank you. You may accompany me, if you wish.'

Carmen shook her head. 'If you're going to plant anything, I won't be able to prevent it. Not with two of you on the job. Leave the doors open and I'll listen! And don't pinch my shampoo!'

She and Peach watched each other like terrier and lithe black cat for a few moments, whilst they listed to the sounds of Lucy Blake opening and shutting drawers in the bedroom.

Peach said, 'You said you were going to finish your affair with George Carter, even if he hadn't been killed.'

'Yes. I'm not sure it was anything as grand as an affair.'

'It seems an unlikely liaison, for a girl like you.'

'A woman like me, Inspector. I ceased to be a girl a long time ago now, and modern women don't find the term very flattering.'

It was an unreal conversation, with both their minds on the sounds off-stage. Lucy Blake had left the room doors open as she entered, and they heard the door of the bathroom cabinet been eased back, the moving of bottles and packets inside it. Peach noticed that the flat's occupier did not seem at all worried by the sounds as he said, 'Nevertheless, from what we now know of Dr Carter, he seems an unlikely choice for you.'

'Ah, but how little you know of me, Inspector! Wasn't it a British composer who said you should try everything once, except folk-dancing and incest? It may well be the only chance I get to sleep with the head man of a university! I told you, power is a great aphrodisiac, for most women. I'm sure your colleague would confirm that.'

'Why didn't you go to Altrincham in your car last weekend?'

The sudden switch startled, but did not disconcert her. There was scarcely a pause before she said with a smile, 'I didn't fancy leaving my car outside Keith's house for the weekend. And if I'm honest, I suppose I thought there might be a little pot-smoking on the Saturday. I didn't want to be talked into driving the others about, if I'd had the odd spliff.'

'So how did you get back from the concert in Manchester to Keith Padmore's house?'

'One of Keith's friends drove us. Six in the car and lots of hilarity. The driver was perfectly OK, but even if he'd been a little high, you can hardly pinch him for it now, Peach!'

It was her first sign of impatience, but the slightly surreal conversation came to an end with Lucy Blake's return to the room. She gave a slight shake of her head to Peach behind Carmen Campbell's back before the dark woman whirled and said, 'Well, what news, DS Blake? Am I to be charged with possession of the heroin you have planted?'

Lucy smiled at both of them. 'Can't even find a fag, sir. No sign of pot, let alone anything more serious. No sign that anything illegal has ever crossed the threshold.'

Peach beamed. 'I shall tell DC Murphy to turn his keenness elsewhere. Thank you for being so cooperative, Miss Campbell.'

He stood up, moved behind Blake towards the door, then turned. 'I should just ask you, before we leave, whether you have any further thoughts on the murder of George Carter.'

It was a favourite ploy of his, the insertion of a final question when the meeting seemed to be over and the opponent might be caught relaxing and off guard. It did not work with this woman. Carmen Campbell smiled at him. 'I've thought about it, ever since I heard the news – you'd expect that. But I haven't come up with any ideas on who killed George, beyond what we've already discussed.'

Lucy Blake could not work out quite why her companion seemed so pleased on the way back to Brunton CID. The morning seemed to her to have produced nothing very new or useful.

Back in the neat, colourful flat, Carmen Campbell was wondering why they had wanted to search the place for pot. He wasn't straightforward, that Peach. It worried her that she couldn't quite determine what he was about.

Superintendent Tucker had endured an embarrassing Saturday morning on the golf course. He was a twenty-two handicapper, a poor golfer at the best of times. And this had not been his best of times.

He had sliced out of bounds on the second, found the water hazard at the seventh, missed several crucial short putts, and

provided a welter of specious excuses which had only amused
the opposing pair and added to his partner's suffering. Finally,
he produced an air shot on the seventeenth. Arriving at
the green a moment later, he met his partner's silent but
smouldering resentment with the notion that he was 'unable
to concentrate because of this murder of the Director at the
University of East Lancashire'.

Tucker normally used his job as his excuse of last resort.
His frequently proclaimed post as head of Brunton's CID
section gave him a status which he felt extended above and
beyond his fragile golfing prowess. To emphasize how preoccupied he had been with more important things throughout the
morning's trials, he made a great and public show in the bar
of having to ring in to headquarters to check on the progress
of the investigation.

But there is often a downside to things which seem a good
idea at the time. The downside to this one was DI Peach. Percy
divined immediately from the sounds of laughter and glasses
in the background that his chief was at the golf club. 'Good
round, sir?' he asked politely.

'No. Bloody awful. But never mind that, tell me—'

'Cares of office, I expect, sir. Worrying about what was
going on here in your absence. We've been working quite
hard, as a matter of fact, those of us still here. Muddy
underfoot for you this morning, I expect.'

'Yes. Slipping and sliding about. Lost my stance a few
times. Now—'

'Hope to get a game in myself, tomorrow, at the North
Lancs. Drains well up there, you know.' It was a perpetual
cause for the gnashing of the Tucker teeth that Peach, a
much better golfer, had been admitted to the prestigious
North Lancs Golf Club, while Tucker had been turned down
because of his hacker status in the game.

'Think you'll have the case tied up by then, do you?'
Tucker's attempt at sarcasm fell rather flat, in view of the
place he was speaking from.

'Oh, I should think so, sir. I expect you realized we were getting near, when you decided to give yourself the morning on the golf course. We've been out frightening the Barbadian girl this morning, sir, as you suggested. Got what we wanted from her. Searched the place as a matter of fact. Didn't find any drugs.'

'Searched the place? Without a warrant? Peach, you certainly had no authority from me to—'

'We can have the Reverend Matthews if you want him, sir. Keeping a Smith and Wesson .357 revolver without a licence. Expect we could arrest him at the end of his Sunday morning service, if you want a high-profile job—'

'PEACH!' The members of Brunton Golf Club looked at each other in alarm as Tucker's scream of anguish reached them from the phone cubicle. 'You will do no such thing. Is that—'

'He might have passed the Smith and Wesson on to the fragrant Mrs Carter, of course. Quite possible she might have blown old Claptrap away to play girls on top with the clergyman, I suppose.'

Tucker was already regretting his decision to ring in from the golf club. 'All I'm asking you is whether there is any—'

'You'll be happy to hear the Senior Tutor broke down when we used a bit of third degree as you suggested, sir. Roaming about the campus when old Claptrap bought it, he was, on his own admission. Shouldn't be at all surprised if Walter Culpepper—'

'Third degree? I never—'

'Mind you, sir, I must admit I'd really like it to be your Malcolm McLean. Him being a Mason and all that. My research about it being four times as likely to be a Mason involved in serious crime in Brunton supports the view – and of course it would really strengthen my monograph if I could add a murderer to the figures before it's published. And McLean being a member of your Lodge and a friend of yours, it would—'

'Peach! For God's sake, shut up! He isn't a friend of mine, not a particular friend, anyway. And I'm quite sure you're barking up the wrong—'

'Drugs Squad have got more out of him this morning, I believe,' Peach confided sunnily. 'He's been organizing drug distribution in a big way. Heroin, cocaine, Ecstasy, Rohypnol: you name it, your friend Malcolm has been providing it. He hasn't been offering Class A drugs around the Lodge, has he, sir? Because that would really—'

'NO HE HASN'T!' Tucker saw heads turning towards the booth again and modulated his voice to a strangulated whisper. 'And get it out of your thick head that he's in any way a friend of mine. I scarcely know—'

'He's coughed on some of the big boys higher up the chain, sir. Being kept in custody for his own protection, now. Of course, the big men in drugs are heavy employers of contract killers, so it might well be that McLean—'

'It sounds as if this Malcolm McLean might really be your murder suspect. It's a good thing we already have him under lock and key. In view of that, I think I can safely leave things in your hands until Monday morning, when I shall expect a full report.' Tucker articulated the last phrases carefully, in a belated attempt to convince any golf club listeners of his authority in these matters.

'Yes, sir. I see, sir. Of course, we must keep an open mind, as you often tell us. It's entirely possible that Malcolm McLean may have had nothing at all to do with the murder of old Claptrap Carter.'

Peach rang off smartly. Never give a superintendent sucker an even break.

Twenty-One

The phone call Peach had been waiting for came at two fifteen. It confirmed what he had suspected. Twenty minutes later, in the quaint steep-roofed cottage on the UEL campus, Walter Culpepper relived a vivid moment from the night of the murder for Peach and Blake.

By three fifteen on a gloomy November afternoon, the pair were back again at the flat of Carmen Campbell. This time they refused the offer of any refreshment before they sat down opposite the lithe black figure on the colourful sofa.

'You covered your tracks pretty well. It's taken us a while to piece together what happened last Saturday night,' said Peach. His voice was so quiet, his tone so matter-of-fact, that his adversary did not realize for a moment that she was being accused.

The almond-shaped brown eyes rounded a little in surprise. Carmen kept her voice steady as she said, 'You intrigue me. But perhaps that is exactly what you intend to do. Are you accusing me of something?'

'Of murder, Miss Campbell. We shall charge you, presently. But there is no hurry about that. I don't think you are going to deny it, when we've finished here.'

The Barbadian thought quickly: they hadn't cautioned her, so whatever she said now could not be used against her in any court case. Perhaps this odious little man with the bald head and the jet-black fringe of hair was bluffing; she couldn't see how he could possibly know enough to justify the confidence he was exuding. She felt the blood pounding in her head, but

210

she was proud of the level of indignation she achieved as she said, 'Of course I'm going to deny it. The idea that I should kill George Carter is so preposterous that I refuse even to get excited about it.'

Lucy Blake smiled into the smooth, unlined brown face, taking her cue from Peach. 'Do you deny that you stole a Smith and Wesson revolver from a locked drawer in the desk of the Reverend Thomas Matthews, chaplain to this university? A desk which is standard university issue, like the one in your office, with either the same keys or a lock which a child could pick.'

Carmen tried not to show how unnerved she was, not just by this dual attack but by the younger woman's production of this first detail. 'How formal we are this afternoon! Tom Matthews sounds quite impressive, when you give him his full title. Found the weapon, did you, when – at my invitation remember – you searched the place this morning?'

She had flashed the question at Blake, but it was Peach who replied. 'Of course not. I don't expect to see the murder weapon again, unless you later choose to tell us exactly which water it lies beneath. We didn't expect to find the Smith and Wesson this morning. We didn't find the faintest trace of pot, either, or anything to suggest that you were a user.'

Carmen forced a smile. 'I told you, I gave the habit up years ago.'

'I believe you. It was because I thought you were a non-user that DS Blake searched your flat this morning, to confirm that fact.'

'So I'm now accused of being a non-user of cannabis! Charged with what I considered a virtue! Abstention makes me a murderer, does it?'

'It helps. It makes it more remarkable that you should be distributing pot among the company so liberally last Saturday night.'

'I told you, we were all on it. I don't know where it came from.'

'From you, largely, according to the other people present at Keith Padmore's house in Altrincham. Strange that you should have such copious supplies, when you've been a non-user for years.'

'It was a pop concert. A Who revival. The kind where you smoke a bit of nostalgic pot, for old times' sake.'

'I see. Except that I don't think you were smoking anything.'

She shrugged her lissom shoulders. 'Ask around among those who were there. I thought you already had.'

'I'm sure you gave them the impression that you were as far gone as anyone. Easy enough to do, once you've handed around enough spliffs to make sure no one's judgement is what it was.'

She knew where he was going now. Peach was sure of that. But she was good: he conceded that even as he watched her so closely. Perhaps her experience in social psychology, her study of people's reactions in social situations, helped her. She took her time, gave no hint of distress in the bright, open face as she said, 'I should find it flattering that you think I was the only one not indulging, as everyone else got high on pot. But no doubt you have some mysterious agenda for me.'

Peach was equally unhurried. He paused for a couple of agonizing seconds before he said, 'Try this one. You waited until you had engineered the situation you wanted: everyone except you out of their minds on cannabis. Then, when everyone thought you were safely in bed, you went outside and borrowed Keith Padmore's Honda CBR Fireblade.'

She laughed. He had to concede that even in these circumstances it sounded like a genuine laugh. Then she said, '900cc, that Fireblade. One of the fastest machines on the road, Keith tells me. So how do you think a woman like me is going to handle that?'

'With considerable ease and skill, I imagine. You told me the first time we met that you were a biker. Quite a wild one, on your own admission.'

212

'That was a long time ago, Inspector Peach.'

'Old biking skills never leave you, do they? I told you, I used to have a Yamaha 350 myself. I wouldn't mind a burn on a CBR Fireblade myself. I'm confident I could handle it. Especially at the speeds a discreet woman like you would be using. I'm sure you didn't risk drawing attention to yourself. Probably didn't go much above eighty on the forty miles to the UEL campus.'

His chin jutted the challenge to her on the last sentence. For the first time, she was visibly shaken by the accuracy of this absurd, determined little man. She couldn't face the continuation of his uncannily accurate account of the night she had planned so carefully. She said roughly, 'And then I went into the Director's house and shot Claptrap Carter, I suppose. And was back at Keith's house and in bed by one thirty, with no one there any the wiser?'

She tried to give a ringing irony to her phrases, to underline the absurdity of the story he had framed, but Peach just smiled grimly and said, 'Exactly so.'

Carmen paused, thought furiously. He couldn't have witnesses, however well he'd worked this out. She kept her voice level as she said, 'I'm a psychologist by training, as you know. I'm interested to know what set you thinking on such ridiculous lines.'

Peach smiled, aware she was feeling things out, knowing that he had the boss trump still to play later in the game. 'You went out of your way to tell me at our first meeting that you had gone to Altrincham by train on this occasion, instead of taking your car as usual. You didn't strike me as a cannabis user at that time, a fact which DS Blake confirmed by the search of your flat this morning. When I heard that spliffs had been passed around like fags last Saturday night, I wondered if there might have been a reason for that. And I believe that Dr Culpepper, the Senior Tutor at UEL, observed the arrival of your Fireblade on the campus last Saturday night. We confirmed that with him half an hour ago.' He tried to make that appealing gnome's complaint about the big motorcycle in the Saturday night darkness sound more like an identification than it ever could be.

She muttered, 'That sod knows everything that goes on in the place.' It sounded even in her own ears dangerously near to an admission. She said harshly, 'So what's behind this fairy-tale? What reason can I possibly have for blowing away a man who was my lover? For killing the Director who had appointed me to his staff and might well have promoted me, in the years to come?'

'I don't believe you were conducting a normal relationship with Dr George Carter. I believe that in effect he forced you to sleep with him.'

For the first time, she looked in two minds. The woman in her no doubt wanted to admit that she could never have fancied that odious man, but she said, 'I don't know what you're on about. I told you when you first asked me about this: it was the fact that he had power which made me go to bed with George.'

'No. He forced you to sleep with him. He knew something about you which could ruin you, and he took advantage of it to force his attentions on you.'

Peach was icily calm, perfectly confident, and she almost acknowledged what she had known for some time, that the game was up. The arrogance had gone from her own voice now as she said, 'And what have you dreamed up for this? What dreadful crime had I committed that he was able to use in this fashion?'

Peach shook his head. 'It's no good, Carmen. We had the phone call from Harvard this afternoon to confirm that you had never graduated there. Your course was terminated after your conviction in that drug-store raid, wasn't it?'

'And you're assuming that I—'

'We're assuming nothing. We checked your application form for your present post at the University of East Lancashire yesterday. We know you claimed a Harvard degree in social psychology which you don't possess.'

For the first time, that loose-limbed body slumped before them. Her shoulders drooped and she seemed to sink into the big cushions of the sofa as she said dully, 'That bastard Carter knew about it months ago. He used it to blackmail his way into bed with me last July. It was going to be one weekend and nothing more, he said. But he came back for more.'

'Blackmailers always do,' said Lucy Blake softly.

Carmen Campbell glanced at the younger woman, who had been quiet for so long. 'Carter did, anyway. He was exulting in the power over me which he thought this knowledge gave him. It was an arrangement which could go on indefinitely, he said. I couldn't stand his slimy paws upon me any longer.' She looked from one to the other of the two attentive faces. 'I may have done some things you wouldn't approve of in my time, but I've never sold myself before. I couldn't stand it.'

Peach nodded curtly. 'So you committed murder. A murder you planned very carefully.'

She seemed to take that as a compliment. 'Tom Matthews and I chatted about our backgrounds, as new members of the university, and he told me he had a revolver in the chaplaincy. I didn't know that he hadn't a licence for it. I hope he won't get into trouble.' She looked up at them, but received no acknowledgement of this belated stab of conscience. 'I went round to the chaplaincy one day when I knew he was out seeing a student of mine. The desk was exactly the same as mine. I took my own keys and a colleague's and opened the lock without difficulty. I took the Smith and Wesson and just waited for my opportunity.'

'Which came last Saturday.'

'Yes. I was already committed to the concert in Manchester when Carter rang me four days earlier and said his wife was going to be away at the weekend. I explained that I had to go to the concert, or people would be suspicious – he was as anxious as I was to keep our liaison quiet – but I'd join him somewhere around midnight for the rest of the weekend.'

She seemed anxious to talk now, to need only the occasional prompt to display the cleverness of her planning and execution. Lucy Blake said, 'So you made your preparations with the cannabis.'

'Yes. I knew Keith and his friends weren't averse to a little pot. They smoked it like children given sweets.' She grinned that broad, exciting smile they remembered from their previous meetings, and they believed her. 'The only skill was to convince them I was smoking as much or more than they were, and that wasn't difficult – not after their judgement had gone with the first joints.'

'And no doubt you'd ridden pillion on Keith Padmore's Honda Fireblade before.'

'Frequently. I'd even ridden the machine myself, with Keith on the back. I knew he kept his leathers in the utility room of his house. I pretended to go to bed with him, then left him spark out in the bed. The other two were just as far gone in the other bedroom.'

'So they told us. Keith wasn't even aware that you hadn't been in bed with him for the entire night.'

This time she looked at Peach almost as though she resented his interruption. She said defiantly, 'The roads were quiet, at that time of night. I quite enjoyed the ride. And George Carter was waiting patiently for me, just as I'd told him to be.' Contempt flashed into her face and her voice at the recollection of that moment. 'He thought he was going to bed with me. I told him to turn his back whilst I took my leathers off. He liked games like that.'

'And you shot him through the head, in cold blood.'

'Carter asked for it! He wasn't keeping his side of the bargain.' She nodded, as though she had convinced herself that this was an execution, not a murder. 'I'd forgotten how powerful a Smith and Wesson .357 is. It seemed to make a hell of a bang in that confined space. But no one came near.

I was back on the bike within five minutes. I enjoyed the ride back even more than the one to Brunton.'

At a nod from Peach, DS Blake stepped forward and quietly charged Carmen Campbell with the murder of George Andrew Carter. Peach radioed the arrest car which he had waiting outside and two uniformed officers came inside and took away the athletic Barbadian. She stood as tall and moved as gracefully as if she was going out for an afternoon stroll. Their last view of those wonderful brown eyes was through the glass of the police car.

Peach watched until the car disappeared, then shook his head sadly. 'She'll do more damage in the world, before she's finished, that lady.'

Lucy Blake glanced at him sharply; Percy did not often sound troubled in the triumph of an arrest. 'But she'll be convicted for this, surely? She'll get a life sentence.'

Peach sighed. 'She'll be convicted, all right. But she'll get a clever lawyer, and she'll play up the fact that Carter was forcing her into bed. And she'll be a brilliant witness: blackmail will be almost rape before she's finished. With those eyes and that face and figure, she'll make the jury forget that everything stemmed from her own lies on an application form in the first place, that she planned and executed one of the most cold-blooded murders we've come across. There'll be a recommendation for mercy and she'll be out in a few years.'

Lucy considered this. 'Her sex certainly won't do her any harm. But a few years in prison might have a salutary effect. There's no reason why she should harm anyone else, when she comes out.'

Peach shrugged. 'Perhaps you're right. I hope you are. But the trouble with people like Carmen Campbell is that they are incapable of clear distinctions between right and wrong. If they think they can get away with something, they simply do it.'

He was contrasting the woman they had just arrested with

that frail, distressed, but dignified old lady, Mrs Carolyn Crowthorne. Carmen Campbell would not have understood the code which had driven Mrs Crowthorne to come to him with the agonized account of her own daughter's dishonesty. The dead man's mother-in-law, that music-hall figure of fun, had been the only person in this case who had not sought to deceive them at some point.

There had always been a few people around with no clear moral code. But it had been a simpler world for policemen when people like Mrs Crowthorne and Percy's old mother had operated their clear ideas of right and wrong.